Grave secr

Louisa Mary Potter, the century's most notorious child killer, has been granted parole after twenty-five years. A convert to Catholicism and considered to be a reformed character, this living argument for the retention of the death penalty is in urgent need of protection. Someone wants to kill Potter when she's released, someone who knows that she is about to leave prison.

In charge of her safety is Detective Superintendent Mark Pemberton. A widower workaholic revolted by his new assignment, he is nevertheless determined both to protect Potter and also to return her to gaol by re-opening the case of three missing girls she supposedly murdered, but whose bodies have never been found.

During enquiries into the past activities of Britain's most evil woman, Pemberton discovers that Potter's Irish boyfriend, Joseph Patrick Balleen, has vanished and that a hidden fortune awaits her release. So where is Balleen now? Is he waiting to gain revenge and at the same time acquire that fortune? And what is the secret held by a quiet nun, the only survivor of a schoolgirl society called the Secret Seven? The other six were all murdered by Louisa Mary Potter.

Peter N. Walker, who as Nicholas Rhea is author of the 'Constable' series televised as 'Heartbeat', has written a police thriller of extraordinary compulsion on a subject not so deeply buried in the public's consciousness.

Books by Peter N. Walker

CRIME FICTION

The 'Carnaby' series (1967–84)
Carnaby and the hijackers
Carnaby and the gaolbreakers
Carnaby and the assassins
Carnaby and the conspirators
Carnaby and the saboteurs
Carnaby and the eliminators
Carnaby and the demonstrators
Carnaby and the infiltrators
Carnaby and the kidnappers
Carnaby and the counterfeiters
Carnaby and the campaigners
Fatal accident (1970)
Panda One on duty (1971)
Special duty (1971)
Identification Parade (1972)
Panda One investigates (1973)
Major incident (1974)
The Dovingsby death (1975)
Missing from home (1977)
The MacIntyre plot (1977)
Witchcraft for Panda One (1978)
Target criminal (1978)
The Carlton plot (1980)
Siege for Panda One (1981)
Teenage cop (1982)
Robber in a mole trap (1985)
False alibi (1991)

Written as Christopher Coram
A call to danger (1968)
A call to die (1969)
Death in Ptarmigan Forest (1970)
Death on the motorway (1973)
Murder by the lake (1975)
Murder beneath the trees (1979)
Prisoner on the dam (1982)
Prisoner on the run (1985)

Written as Tom Ferris
Espionage for a lady (1969)

Written as Andrew Arncliffe
Murder after the holiday (1985)

NON-FICTION

The courts of law (1971)
Punishment (1972)
Murders and mysteries from the North York Moors (1988)
Murders and mysteries from the Yorkshire Dales (1991)
Folk tales from the North York Moors (1990)
Folk stories from the Yorkshire Dales (1991)
Portrait of the North York Moors (1985) *as Nicholas Rhea*
Folk tales from York and the Wolds (1992)

THE 'CONSTABLE' SERIES

Written as Nicholas Rhea
Constable on the hill (1979)
Constable on the prowl (1980)
Constable around the village (1981)
Constable across the moors (1982)
Constable in the dale (1983)
Constable by the sea (1985)
Constable along the lane (1986)
Constable through the meadow (1988)
Constable at the double (1988)
Constable in disguise (1989)
Constable through the heather (1990)
Constable beside the stream (in preparation)

EMMERDALE TITLES

Written as James Ferguson
A friend in need (1987)
Divided loyalties (1988)
Wives and lovers (1989)
Book of country lore (1988)
Official companion (1988)
Emmerdale's Yorkshire (1990)

GRAVE SECRETS

Peter N. Walker

Constable London

First published in Great Britain 1992
by Constable & Company Ltd
3 The Lanchesters, 162 Fulham Palace Road
London W6 9ER
Copyright © 1992 by Peter N. Walker
The right of Peter N. Walker to be
identified as the author of this work
has been asserted by him in accordance
with the Copyright, Designs and Patents Act 1988
ISBN 0 09 471710 9

Set in Palatino 10pt
and printed in Great Britain by
Redwood Press, Melksham, Wiltshire

*A CIP catalogue record for this book
is available from the British Library*

1

'The Chairman of the Parole Board has presented us with a problem.' The Chief Constable steepled his hands as he faced Detective Superintendent Mark Pemberton across his large polished desk. 'I think you are the man to deal with it.'

'Sir?' Mark had no idea what lay ahead but tried to show polite interest.

'It's not a criminal enquiry,' the Chief explained. 'It's more of a watching brief laced with elements of personal security.'

'Protection, you mean, sir?'

'Yes, that's exactly what I do mean, Mark. Protection.'

'That shouldn't present us with too many problems, sir.' Mark sounded confident. 'We're accustomed to coping with that sort of thing. Most protection jobs are fairly routine, Salman Rushdie excepted.'

'I respect your confidence. Now, the woman is called Kathleen Hicks . . .' Charles Moore paused to await Mark's reaction to the name, but there was none.

'A woman, sir?' In view of Moore's pause, Mark felt he had to make some sensible response even though the name meant nothing to him. Was a local member of the Parole Board being blackmailed? Threatened perhaps? Some released villain causing distress to a lady member?

'Yes, a woman,' Moore went on. 'Kathleen Hicks is not her real name, however.'

'And her real name, sir? Am I allowed to know that?'

'Louisa Mary Potter.' Moore spoke very slowly, pronouncing each syllable with deliberation and clarity.

'God almighty, sir!' Mark leapt to his feet with his eyes blazing and his face suddenly red with anger. 'Not that blood-thirsty bitch!'

'Yes, that blood-thirsty bitch, as you so aptly put it, it's her. I want you to protect her.'

'Protect her? But she's in prison, she's doing life for murder, a series of murders of young children, sadistic and bloody murders they were too. Horrific crimes!'

'She's been granted parole, Mark, she's coming out on licence. It's on the recommendation of the Chairman of the Parole Board and with the Home Secretary's personal approval. She comes out a week today under the name of Kathleen Hicks. She'll live in lodgings on our patch, at one of our safe houses, probably until she establishes herself. It'll take something like six months. A job has been found for her in that name so we must all forget about her past, you especially. You will become her guardian. She's starting a new life and to all intents and purposes, she's a new person.'

'Forget? How can anybody forget what she did!' Mark, still on his feet, gripped the edge of the desk and glared in disbelief at his Chief.

'We must, Mark, it's our job.'

'Job, sir? So you're telling me that I've got to protect the most notorious child killer of this century?'

'Yes, I am. That's exactly what I'm telling you.'

Mark, deflated, settled back on the chair, shaking his head in astonishment. 'But every man, woman and child in this country who knows what she did, wants to see that woman dead . . . She's a living argument for retention of the death penalty, she's evil . . . utterly evil . . .'

'You've met her, Mark?'

'No, of course not, sir, but I do read the papers. I know what she did. And every time she's considered for parole, she's turned down. That says everything! Then every time she's rejected, the papers remind us what she did and the great British public gets angry all over again. The tabloids will have a great time with this, whipping up hatred and animosity.'

'You shouldn't believe everything you read in the papers, Mark, you know that.'

'I don't believe I'm being asked to do this, sir. Who am I supposed to be protecting her against?'

'You've already said it. Everybody, anybody. If her true identity becomes known, there'll be hundreds who'd love to treat her the way she treated those children.'

'But will the authorities announce that she's been paroled? Surely, that will merely encourage unsavoury interest?'

'Yes, they can't keep this one secret. When the time's right, they'll announce that she has been released on licence and that she's living under an assumed name in the south of England. Her new name will not be revealed. But in fact she'll be here in the north, so that's one red herring. As you realize, Mark, the announcement will excite interest, it's bound to. Some members of the public are likely to try and take the law into their own hands and on top of that, the press will surely try to find her.'

'I completely fail to see why she's been let out, sir; of all the villains in our gaols, she's the one who should stay locked up for ever and a day. Even a visiting priest said she was wholly evil; he said wickedness oozed from her, he claimed he could sense it . . .'

'Not any more, Mark. She's a reformed character now. She's become a Catholic, she's changed, she's a different person, pleasant, affable, well-balanced, helpful to fellow inmates, liked by all. She's done very well in prison and now she's anxious to be rehabilitated. She wants to play her part in society, to make full retribution for her past . . .'

'You sound as if you believe all this, sir!'

'I am capable of accepting advice from experts, Mark. In this case, the entire Parole Board, fifty or so members, have considered her most recent request for parole. That's fifty experienced and expert people. From the group of four who studied her particular case, two said she must never be released. They were quite determined about that. But the other two, a magistrate and a psychologist, were of the firm view that she had reformed and that she deserved the opportunities which came with release, albeit on licence.

'As you are probably aware, a two-two split results in further consideration by another group of four and that group was three to one in favour of her parole. Don't forget, they had studied reports from the prison governor and those who had worked with her inside, including prison visitors.

'It all persuaded the Chairman that Potter had reformed; she had fulfilled all the necessary criteria in prison, indeed, the prison staff are full of praise. Expert opinion is that there is no risk of her committing similar murders again and therefore little reason to detain her. Remember, these people are tough nuts, Mark; there are even police officers on the Parole Board and they are not easily fooled, they know all the tricks. Anyway, the outcome is that the Home Secretary, upon the recommendation of the Chairman of the Parole Board, has decided to give her a chance – after all, other killers get these opportunities. But because of the risk to her life if her identity becomes known, she does need our protection.'

'This is bloody ridiculous, sir! The police protecting released lifers, we don't normally do this, do we? We don't protect all released killers, so why do so for a woman who's slaughtered six children . . . ?'

'Three, Mark. She murdered three.'

'She was convicted of three, sir. If the stories are right, she was known to have tortured and killed three more. I know it happened a long time ago – when I was still at school in fact – but I've read the gory details time and time again. Six bairns missing, thought to have been buried on the moors. Three bodies found in separate graves. Three bairns never found to this day. And she'd tape-recorded their voices as she was torturing them . . . there's no bloody wonder folks want her dead. But if she is at such a grave risk, why release her? Surely she'd be safer if she was kept in prison?'

'You can't keep convicts in prison just because some unstable people want to have a go at them. If the authorities took notice of all the threats of revenge, precious few criminals would ever be freed, Mark. Both the Home Secretary and the Chairman of the Parole Board appreciate the risks to this woman and understand the deep public feeling that will be generated upon her release. They do understand the enormity of her past crimes, but, after very careful consideration, they believe that Potter, as Hicks, can readjust to society. It's very common, you know, releasing lifers under false names to start afresh. They're never totally free either, they're always on licence and subjected to constant and close supervision. In Potter's case, the Home Secretary feels she is in need of that challenge and opportunity. So that's it. Orders are orders, especially orders from on high.'

The Chief went on, 'Now, the protection duty is a covert operation, Mark, although Potter/Hicks does know that she is being protected. The public will not know, but you can't do this job alone, you'll need support. A female police presence is necessary, of course, so I want you to select your own team. Allow for twenty-four-hour cover for the next six months. The case will be reviewed towards the end of that period if not before. Select enough officers for that period, allowing for contingencies. I suggest you'll need at least one officer trained in the use of firearms and the capability for providing a full complement of armed officers in any emergency.'

'Firearms? Am I right in thinking we've got some positive intelligence about this, sir?' was Mark's next question. 'It's not just speculation because of who she is?'

'Yes, that's true. I was leading up to this bit. We've heard, on what's known as very good authority, that someone from Rainesbury is intent on killing her. It could be a relation of one of her victims, but that's by no means certain. Whoever he is, he'll be looking for her. There'll be other revenge seekers too, ones we don't know about, and there'll be the inevitable gathering of ghouls if her whereabouts and identity become known. People will turn up at the house wanting to catch sight of the mass killer – and the press will descend. Anyway, all the details are in the file. But if her true identity is kept a total secret, there should be no risk, should there?'

Mark glared at the Chief. 'Sir, anyone who recalls that case will never respect the confidentiality of her circumstances. There's too much hatred. I'm not sure I could trust every one of my own officers to keep this one secret . . .'

'Then don't tell them who she is,' said Moore. 'Be careful who you trust. Her life is in your hands now, Mark.'

Mark released a huge sigh of resignation, then went on, 'All it needs is one clerk in the Home Office or one civil servant working for the Prison Service to realize who she is, or even one of our own staff, and they'll be ringing up the *News of the World* or the *Sun* or some such paper. Once it's known who she is, all the world will want to see her . . . or get at her. She'll not be safe in her bed . . . and quite honestly, I can't say I blame those who want her dead.'

'You're letting your emotions dictate your reactions, Mark. Remember, you are a senior police officer and your duty is to protect her. That's what you swore when you took your oath of office as a constable – you swore to protect life and property. In spite of her past, she is a human being and whatever your own personal views, she is to become our responsibility, your responsibility, for the next few months. That means I want no cock-ups and I want her kept alive. Now, the file is here . . .' The Chief unlocked a drawer in the right-hand pedestal of his desk and withdrew a thick grey file marked 'Top Secret.' He passed it to Mark.

'Read that carefully, take a day or two if necessary, but don't let it out of your hands. Take it home if you think it's safer there. Bring it back to me when you've read it and draw up a plan of action for my approval. Select your team, list their names and then come to see me with your proposals. I'll make one further suggestion, Mark, which you might care to consider.'

'Sir?'

'Why not reopen investigations into the three missing children?'

'After all this time, sir? Twenty-five years? Is there really any merit in that? We'd never find enough evidence to convict her all over again, surely? Besides, it would stir up a lot of unnecessary anguish by reviving old memories, memories best left hidden. And it would increase the hatred of Potter.'

'I still think the proposal is worthy of consideration, Mark. Regard it as part of this operation – think it over and let me know your views when you've thought it through.'

'Yes, sir,' and Mark accepted the thick file, bade the Chief Constable farewell and walked out of the office.

2

Mark put a match to the fire. He'd laid it that morning before going to work and it flickered into life to cast a warm glow across the darkened room. As the blaze spread among the kindling and licked the coals, brightening the inglenook and highlighting the ancient oak beams, he closed the curtains against the dark chill of night, switched on the wall lights and went into the kitchen to prepare his evening meal.

It wouldn't take long. Mark had cooked the occasional meal for himself and June before she'd died, but since her death he'd seldom bothered with the unsatisfying business of cooking for himself. A light breakfast followed by a snack either in the canteen or at a pub enabled him to cope with most days, but he found little pleasure in cooking for himself after work. Instead, he often bought frozen and pre-prepared meals-for-one from places like Marks and Spencer, Tesco or Sainsbury's. Thanks to someone else's anonymous skills, he was able to produce a tasty and even wholesome meal within a very short time. Tonight's offering was Chicken Wings Clamitano with cooked green beans. Sometimes, he didn't bother looking at detailed information such as the sauces which flavoured a packet meal because he liked to surprise himself albeit trying to remain conscious of his cholesterol level.

After studying the instructions, he popped the plastic bag of unappetizing raw food into the microwave oven, pressed the timing buttons and set the process in motion. In the few minutes it would require to transform itself into an acceptable or even tasty meal, he removed his working suit and put on some light, comfortable slacks and a warm sweater.

Feeling more relaxed, he returned to the kitchen to continue the preparation of his dinner. A glass of dry white wine to accompany the main course, with fresh fruit salad for afters followed by a mug of black coffee would complete his menu. June would have grumbled about the mug – she'd always insisted on cups and saucers at mealtimes . . .

He'd eat his dinner from a tray while watching the six o'clock news and, in the absence of any other commitments, would afterwards settle down, perhaps with a glass of brandy, to study the file on Louisa Mary Potter alias Kathleen Hicks.

Without June, his evenings and nights had become empty and at times agonizing. There were times he could weep out of sheer loneliness, times he wanted her there so he could embrace and talk to her, times he yearned for a long-running major investigation or an enthralling murder enquiry just to occupy him and provide him with the companionship of colleagues during the desolation of every boring evening. He'd thought about taking up a hobby, learning to play the piano perhaps or to make wine or to throw pottery or even attempt woodcarving. Evening classes might be an alternative to loneliness.

The moment he'd planned something which required a regular evening commitment, he'd had to work overtime that very same evening on one important investigation or another. He'd never been able to complete a course of any kind; it was just as difficult to follow a television series from beginning to end without interruption. Similar working commitments had arisen when June was alive and eager for his companionship during the evenings . . . now he knew why she had grumbled so much whenever he'd been compelled to work late. She must have been very lonely at times . . .

But, unless the telephone rang, tonight belonged to him and that thick and sombre-looking grey file would have his undivided attention. With the crockery stacked neatly away, Mark poured a generous brandy, put a log on the fire and settled down in his armchair to read this condensed dossier on Kathleen Hicks. The first sheet contained her brief biographical details. Beneath the heading 'Kathleen Hicks' was the reminder, 'born Louisa Mary Potter, 18 October 1943 at Bristol'. From the wording of the biography, Mark knew it had been abstracted from her antecedents which would have been read out to the judge upon her conviction.

As a child of six, Louisa Potter had moved with her parents to live in Derby; her father, Samuel, had been a labourer on the railways, working on the line maintenance side, while her mother, Mildred, was a factory worker who had assembled refrigerators. Both were now dead.

Louisa was one of six children, two boys and four girls, she being the eldest girl; her two brothers were each older than she. The family had always been poor, her parents' joint income being barely sufficient for all the children's needs, but it had been a loving and honest family. There were no details of her brothers and sisters, other than a note to say they had only very occasionally been in touch with her in prison, the last recorded visit being more than fourteen yours ago. Apart from prison visitors, it seemed she was now alone.

The young Louisa had attended an infants' school in Derby and had left her secondary education at sixteen without any academic successes to her credit. She had obtained a job in a factory, spending her days packing motor-car spare parts. After some three years of this mundane work, she'd wanted to explore other parts of Britain and so, when she was nineteen, she had secured seasonal employment at Rainesbury on the north-east coast. This was a busy holiday resort, popular with young people from a wide area due to its beach, lights, dance halls, amusement arcades and range of seasonal entertainment. Louisa had found work in a large boarding house, ostensibly for just one season, but she'd stayed on. There, she'd been all sorts – chambermaid, waitress, cleaner, cook's assistant – and she had then been described as a reliable and very capable young woman who was not afraid of hard work or long hours. She'd stayed in Rainesbury for a few years in the same boarding house, getting winter work in factories and offices.

That employment had usually been in unskilled roles as a cleaner or assistant of some kind – she'd even gutted North Sea fish at one stage. Then prior to each summer season, she would resume her boarding house job, a task which engaged her from Easter until the end of October.

Mark was surprised that the notes contained no details of a romance or involvement with men. No husband or serious male friend was mentioned but neither was there any indication that she was inclined towards lesbianism. Mark felt sure she must have had friends of either sex. If so, who were they? And where were they now?

Another interesting fact was that she had never come to the notice of the police prior to the murders. There were no earlier convictions recorded against her and he got the impression she had led a very uneventful and somewhat lustreless teenage life.

Then for some unaccountable reason she had become Britain's most evil and notorious woman. It was during her time in Rainesbury that the six small girls had disappeared, the bodies of three being buried on the moors above the town. After a long and highly emotive trial, Louisa Mary Potter had been found guilty of murdering all three, but no trace of the others had been found. Although she'd been questioned very closely, Potter had never admitted killing the missing three and repeated searches had failed to find their remains.

The officer in charge of the case had been Detective Chief Superintendent Adrian Kenworthy who'd retired in 1982 at the age of sixty. Potter's trial had been at York Assizes in the autumn of 1967, the Assize Courts having been replaced by the Crown Courts in 1971.

Although Potter had pleaded not guilty on all counts, the jury had listened to the meticulously assembled evidence and had found each case proven. At that time, the death penalty for murder had not been abolished, but it had not been used since August 1964 when two Lancastrian men were hanged for murdering a van driver. The last woman to hang had been Ruth Ellis in July 1955 but the scale, cruelty and sadism of Potter's crimes had brought loud calls for her to suffer the ultimate penalty in spite of being a woman. A selection of press cuttings showed something of the furore, with ordinary members of the public voicing their open hatred and disgust. The judge had imposed a life sentence for each of the murders, the sentences to run concurrently with a recommendation that she serve at least twenty years.

Pemberton then studied an account of her time in prison which was included in the grey file. It showed that she had served in a succession of women's gaols, initially being subjected to physical attacks by her fellow prisoners due to the nature of her crimes. She'd also had psychiatric treatment in the early months of her imprisonment. Latterly, however, the assaults upon her had ceased, her mental state was regarded as normal, and she had shown remarkable progress towards total rehabilitation.

For the last two years, she had served in Askham Grange Open Prison near York, working in the library and showing a high degree of commitment to her new-found Catholic faith and to her academic studies. Reports by prison visitors and by the governor and her staff during Potter's time in that prison were all extremely favourable. Today, therefore, as she approached fifty years of age, Potter had become a voracious reader of non-fiction, particularly historical works and biographies, and during these latter years had been regarded as a model prisoner. Some of the loveless young inmates had come to regard her as a mother-figure.

Although the mandatory period of her sentence had expired some time ago, her repeated requests for parole had all been rejected in spite of her good behaviour. Mark wondered if one reason was the enormity and sadistic cruelty of her crimes or whether it was because of the public revulsion which would manifest itself if and when she was released. There was no such suggestion in this file, however, but attitudes had changed now and this time, her request had been approved.

Her freedom would bring into focus yet again the merits or otherwise of the death penalty; it would revive all the hoary old arguments for and against the release of multiple killers, particularly those who had murdered children, and it would make the public afraid that dangerous people were free to live among them. There would be many who remembered Potter's crimes even though committed quarter of a century ago.

The publicity would produce a whole new generation of haters and the new Kathleen Hicks would not find it easy to live down her past when confronted with press reports and television debate. She might experience difficulty in adjusting to and maintaining her new identity.

Mark paused as he reached this point. Twenty-five years ago he was still at school, a fifteen-year-old lad not at all certain of his own future. Later, with five O levels, three A levels and a lack of direction, he'd become a clerk in an insurance office dealing with motorists' claims until, at twenty-one, he'd wanted more excitement and a job with more challenge. So he'd joined the police service. But even at fifteen, he'd known of the Potter case – everybody had known. The newspapers, radio and television had headlined the news across the nation and the people around Rainesbury especially had known because she had lived there and killed there. Whenever the case had been reported or re-examined, the papers claimed that members and relations of the families of those little girls had vowed revenge. No one had found it possible to forgive Louisa Mary Potter and Mark himself had long nurtured a curious feeling of hatred for her. As he studied the file, he realized that his youthful but deep-rooted opinions had been formed by the adverse publicity to which he'd been subjected as a child. How could he hate someone he did not know? And what of the woman herself? What was she really like? He wanted to know more about this woman before he began his strange duty.

Mark skimmed through the news cuttings in the file, and came across a note which said that a complete transcript of Potter's trial and copies of the committal proceedings at Rainesbury Magistrates' Court were available. The case papers themselves had not been destroyed and were still filed at Force Headquarters. Mark made a mental note to examine the original file in depth; it would take a long time, he knew.

In the relatively modest file before him, however, there were two photographs of Potter/Hicks. Both depicted only her face, one having been taken by the police upon her conviction when she was twenty-five, and the other taken in prison only a week ago. At twenty-five, she had been a beautiful woman with long jet-black hair reaching below her shoulders. She'd been described as being of slim build, five feet five inches tall with an elegant appearance. At fifty, her face was more rounded without being plump; she wore rimless spectacles and had greying, neck-length hair neatly cut into a bob which curled inwards slightly at the ends. A brief note said she was five feet five inches tall with brown eyes and a pale complexion. Her figure was heavier than it had been in her youth, but she was not described as being either stout or heavily built. Mature might be the right word. As Mark studied her picture, he realized that she was still an attractive woman.

Nonetheless, few, if any, would now recognize her and Mark's initial feeling was that, with a name change, it would not be difficult for her to resume her new, secret life.

The file also contained her new lodging address which was 22 Rosebay Avenue, Swandale, a market town some twenty miles from Force Headquarters. The safe house was owned by Mrs Agnes Dawson, a lady in her early seventies who was a retired prison matron. She had been told of Potter's true identity but had agreed to receive the ex-prisoner as a lodger in the knowledge that the local police would be mounting a protection exercise. Mrs Dawson had welcomed other former inmates to her modest home and had been a tower of strength to many, helping them to overcome the trauma of a long custodial sentence as they struggled to survive in a changed world. She was very well acquainted with the procedures surrounding prison release.

When she was free, Potter would take up a job in York's National Museum of Roman Culture, cataloguing exhibits, maintaining the inventory of relics with special attention to the collection of coloured bowls and beakers. Among her responsibilities would be the museum's unique collection of kitchen utensils and the world's largest collection of Roman recipes. She would also be expected to undertake various other unspecified tasks associated with her duties. None of the museum staff, not even the directors or the curator, would know her true name nor details of the crimes she had committed. If pressed about her background, she would say she had served a medium term sentence, ten years perhaps, for manslaughter of a cruel and cheating lover. That might excite compassion for her, not fear or hatred.

As he read the file, Mark began to realize that complete protection of Potter/Hicks was impossible. At work, she would be free to take her lunch break in town and he could not position a detective in the museum all day, every day. That was just not practicable. Then there was the question of her travelling to work. The distance between the museum and her home was about twelve miles; she'd probably get the bus to and from York so how would she be safeguarded during the journey? He could imagine her having problems with the coinage which had been decimalized since her imprisonment, although he guessed she had been permitted day-release sessions in town to familiarize her with a quarter of a century of social progress. But when she was at home in the lodgings her time would be her own. She might make friends, she might join evening classes, she might get involved with the social life of the museum or the small town in which she was to live. Or, at her age, she might stay at home and watch television!

With all those factors to consider, it was nigh impossible to completely safeguard this woman. It seemed that one solution was to learn something about those who were supposedly threatening her. Maybe, instead of concentrating upon Hicks and her movements, he should supervise those who were suspected of endeavouring to kill her? If the intelligence was correct, that might include her young victims' families.

He turned to the relevant section of the file.

3

The list of victims was complemented by family snapshots of the little girls who had died and those who were still listed as missing. Alongside were the names of their parents and some brief details of their domicile.

Mark read the list with suppressed anger, the horror of their cruel and futile deaths adding sadness to his mood which grew darker and more angry as he absorbed the terrible detail. Such precious young lives had been abruptly, senselessly and prematurely terminated at the hands of that evil woman. How could anyone, especially a woman supposedly with caring, maternal instincts, deliberately kill or harm just one small child, let alone six? As he struggled to close his mind to the gross immorality of her actions, he tried to convince himself that she had paid the penalty, then took a deep breath followed by a long sip of brandy and began to read the names. Even after all this time, and after himself hearing the names so long ago, they were still familiar. Rachel, Tracy and Michele, names which had featured in the daily news of the time as a triple tragedy; the three names had become synonymous with infantile murder, with evil and with unspeakable horror. Mention of those three names alone continued to produce feelings of deep anguish and sympathy for the families.

At the time, some sections of the press had called them the Three Little Graces. But these Little Graces, beautiful as they had been, had suffered intolerably. Mark steeled himself to read on. The report listed the victims, who were:

1. Rachel Waterhouse, aged eight. Parents: Tom and Elaine. Home address: 22 Langley Road, Rainesbury at the time of the murders. Now living in Scotland. Potter was found guilty of murdering Rachel.

2. Tracy Halliday, aged eight. Parents: Eric and Una Halliday, still living at Ashdale Cottage, Beehive Lane, Rainesbury. Tracy's bedroom had not been changed since her death. Potter was found guilty of murdering Tracy.

3. Michele Brown, aged seven. Parents: John and Margaret who then lived at 46 Penfield Close, Rainesbury; John had since died. Mrs Brown had remarried and was now Mrs Margaret Harper, living in Middlesbrough, address not known. Potter was convicted of murdering Michele.

4. Suzanne Hayes, aged eight. Her parents, Brian and Jean, then lived in Flat 5, 126a Sandpiper Road, Rainesbury. They now

lived near Darling Harbour in Sydney, Australia. Suzanne's body had never been found.

5. Helen Stabler, aged eight. Parents: Hugh and Eileen, still living in Rainesbury in the same house over their shop at 19 Stewart Drive, Rainesbury. They had always thought that Helen would be traced, and her room remained unchanged. Her body had never been found.

6. Clare Wiles, aged seven. Parents: William and Jean, living in Rainesbury at 42 Crompton Road. William, an electrician, was made redundant in 1991. Jean was a receptionist at Barlow's, the estate agents. Clare's body had never been found.

Mark wanted to meet and talk with each of these relatives but this presented an immediate difficulty. To interview any member of the victims' families would reveal the twist in the development of the old case and it might even cause peaceful families to renew their suppressed antagonism. To obliquely hint that one of them was suspected of intending to murder Potter would never put the police in a favourable light and could even create an unbridgeable gulf. Any investigation of the families' current moods would have to be very discreet indeed.

The more Mark deliberated that problem, the more he realized that the Chief's proposal might provide the opening which was necessary to talk to them. In particular, he was keen to learn the families' reaction to the fact that Potter might soon be walking the streets as a free and ostensibly forgiven murderess. As he struggled to devise his strategy, he realized that the file contained no details of the victims' other relations, not even any of their brothers and sisters. It merely provided their parents' names.

Today, of course, any brothers and sisters of those little girls would be adults, probably well into their thirties. Might they be the ones who were seeking revenge?

To answer many of his queries, there was one source of information which he could use – the officer who'd been in charge of the original enquiry, Detective Chief Superintendent Adrian Kenworthy. He'd retired a few years after Mark had joined the force, but was still alive – a note at the foot of the page simply said, 'Officer in case – D/C/Supt A. Kenworthy, ret.' Mark could obtain his address from Personal Records.

The file went on to itemize a range of moorland locations where searches had been made in the vain hope of recovering the bodies of the three children who were still unaccounted for. Grid references and a photocopy of an Ordnance Survey map of the area were added, the areas in question having been examined after tourists and local residents had reported some unusual activity. Lights at night, cars parked in odd situations at unusual times, a woman seen digging on the moors in the early hours of the morning by the light of the moon – these and similar reports had been a consequence of the publicity surrounding Potter's trial and conviction and a spate of such sightings had led to weeks of intense police activity at several locations. But apart from the known victims, no other bodies had been found.

The bodies of the three victims for whose murder Potter had been imprisoned were found by a combination of thorough and sustained police work, the sensitive noses of searching police dogs and more than a slice of good fortune.

In one case, a moorland gamekeeper had remembered a patch of freshly disturbed earth near a boulder, where he had thought someone had buried a pet dog – but the body had been one of the children.

Mark's police instincts told him that the three missing girls must be buried in the vicinity; somewhere within those thousands of wild and desolate acres, there lay three small bodies which had been denied a Christian burial. Their remote and unknown graves had never experienced the loving attention that came from a grieving parent or a caring family; there was nothing to mark their final resting place. Even with his police experience, he found the entire scenario ghastly to comprehend and he sympathized with the bereaved parents – how *had* they been able to cope with such a tragic loss?

But there was worse to come. The next page contained a transcription of the sounds from six tape recordings found in Potter's room upon her arrest. The resultant allegation was that she had tortured each child before killing her and had tape-recorded their cries for mercy and their dying screams. The tapes had been played many times, both by the police to their own officers during the investigation, and to the jury during the trial. Mark had never listened to the tapes although they were stored in the offices of the CID at Force Headquarters, and he knew that he might have to steel himself to hear them. In his file, however, he found there was an attempt to put the sounds into words.

Each of the six tapes had a different girl's voice upon it, and although it had been impossible to prove that they were indeed the voices of the deceased or missing children, the circumstantial evidence had been sufficient to convince the police, and then the jury, that three of those children had been cruelly and systematically tortured before death and that these were indeed their dying voices. Butchered alive was one term used by the press. There was the inevitable speculation about the fate of the other three. Everyone believed they knew what had happened but there was no evidence to sustain their suspicions.

The file acknowledged that the sound reproduction was of poor quality, possibly due to the microphone being too far from the source at the time, but after long periods of silence words like 'No . . . please, don't . . . no . . . I don't know . . . please . . . no . . . help . . .', accompanied by piercing, agonizing screams, could be discerned. In the case of the three bodies which had been found, according to the forensic pathologist, the girls had died from multiple stab wounds, the earliest being insufficient to cause death although they would have caused severe pain. He had implied that, before death, the girls had been systematically stabbed, cut or sliced on different parts of their bodies as a form of continuing torture . . . No other voice was upon any of the tapes, the long silences carrying their own particular horror.

Mark was repulsed and put the file to one side.

Although he struggled to remain detached in his studies, his mind dwelt on the knowledge that the woman who had done those things was soon to be released. She would walk among the public, talk to children, mingle with society, go shopping, visit places of interest, go on outings . . .

The British system of justice meant she had paid the penalty for those actions. But had she? Would she ever? Could she ever?

He abandoned his reading for a while and decided to make himself a coffee, telling himself that the crimes had been committed a quarter of a century ago . . . it was all over . . . he must treat his subject as a human being. He must protect her. That was his duty.

He turned again to her modern photograph. She looked utterly normal, she could be any middle-aged woman, just like any mother or grandmother. In fact, her roundish face with its dark eyes, quiet smile and rimless spectacles was welcoming and warm. He tried to tell himself that she was not the woman who had tortured and killed the children; that woman had been a younger person, an evil, misguided, mad youngster, a different personality. Mark accepted that people could change, they could put evil behind them and forge ahead with new, fulfilling lives. But had that kind of transformation reformed Louisa Mary Potter into a calm and gentle Kathleen Hicks?

As he closed the file, Mark tried to visualize his forthcoming task.

It seemed very odd that the Home Secretary in person had seen fit to approve Potter's release, especially in view of the public outcry that would surely arise. When she gained her freedom, the ghastly details of her crimes would again be digested by the horror-struck public. And knowing the powers of the press, some investigative journalist would ferret out her new name and her present address . . . then his headaches would truly begin. Mark began to appreciate that this was no ordinary protection duty. He realized just what an enormous and impossible task he had been set, and just how little he really knew about it all.

But orders are orders, he told himself. Even though complete protection was impossible, he would do his best in the circumstances and would strive to neutralize or prevent any assassination attempt. He would also learn more about the victims' families and relations.

He would start tomorrow morning by talking to former Detective Chief Superintendent Adrian Kenworthy.

4

The contents of the grey file and his own worries about coping with what appeared to be an impossible task conspired to rob Pemberton of a good night's rest. He slept fitfully, enduring long periods of wakefulness when it seemed his mind would not halt in its detailed consideration of his imposed duties. Even so, he rose at seven thirty, had a light breakfast of porridge oats, laid his fire, polished his shoes, dressed in a clean shirt and a smart dark suit, then drove to his office in Police Headquarters at Great Halverton.

After dealing with the morning mail, dictating letters to the CID secretary and conferring with Detective Chief Superintendent Foulds on routine matters, Mark obtained Mr Kenworthy's address from Personal Records. He rang to arrange an appointment and Mrs Kenworthy answered. She said that any time this morning would be fine because her husband always welcomed visits from serving members of the force. He loved to chat about old times and so when Mark suggested 11.45 a.m., this was agreed.

Mr and Mrs Kenworthy lived in a bungalow opposite the Grammar School, as the campus was still known locally, and Mark arrived on time.

The front door was opened by Mrs Kenworthy even before he could emerge from his car and she held it open for him as she smiled a warm and genuine welcome. Petite and grey-haired, she said, 'Adrian is so pleased to have a visitor, Mr Pemberton, do go through, he's in the lounge.'

Mark entered to find a plump-faced, ageing man seated in a comfortably large armchair beside a glowing fire. He said, 'I can't stand up, gammy knees you know. Arthritis.'

'Don't try.' Mark went across and shook him by the hand; it was a strong handshake accompanied by a warm smile. He noticed that his host wore carpet slippers and that a walking frame stood beside the chair.

'Sit down.' Kenworthy indicated a chair opposite. 'Alice will organize coffee. She's a treasure, looks after me well.'

'Sugar and cream?' Alice was now at Mark's side, smiling.

'No, thanks. Black will be fine, no sugar.'

As she went away to organize the coffee, Mark said, 'I'm Mark Pemberton, Headquarters CID. I'm a Detective Superintendent.'

'Alice said you were coming; business, she said. I don't recognize you, you must have been a young lad when I packed up. I got to sixty and thought what the hell – pack up and enjoy life before it's too late, I told myself. So I did.'

'I've just got nineteen years in,' Mark told him. 'I remember you at Headquarters, I think you were D/C/I when I joined. Special Branch.'

'That's going back a bit, Mr Pemberton. Aye, well, I've been out of the job about twelve years now. I must say I miss it – you're all computerized now, eh? The PNC was just getting established before I left, and the Command and Control system in the Control Room. Now you've got something called HOLMES that helps you solve murders! To me, they all resemble magic machines that try to do the work of real police officers!'

'Call me Mark, please. But nowadays, it's not quite like that, Mr Kenworthy. HOLMES is just an aid to our work, it hasn't taken over major enquiries. Our officers still have to do all that foot-slogging to gather the right data, then feed it to the computers without making mistakes . . .'

'I'm only joking, I don't criticize progress, things have to move on even if old codgers like me don't understand the way things are going.'

They chatted about life and developments in the force, with Kenworthy asking about colleagues who were still serving, then Mrs Kenworthy brought in a tray of coffee and some biscuits. Mark had given up eating pastries and biscuits in an attempt to control his cholesterol level, but decided to enjoy these. They looked home-made, so he made an exception. Alice smiled and told him to help himself, then, like a wise wife of any senior police officer, she disappeared to permit them to talk business.

She knew that even retired policemen had a role to fulfil, her husband's vast knowledge of crime and criminals often being called up, and she also appreciated that there were still lots of things she must not be allowed to know.

The introductory chatter over, Mark began his story.

'I'm here because of the Potter case, Mr Kenworthy, Louisa Mary Potter.'

'The most evil woman I have ever had the misfortune to meet,' said Kenworthy with venom in his voice. 'She should have been strung up, Mark, I mean that. The world would have been well rid of her.'

'She's coming out of prison next week,' Mark told him quietly. 'She's persuaded the Parole Board to let her out on licence.'

'She always was persuasive, she could charm the birds from the trees, she could convince you she was an angel, she could have been a first-class con woman too. I'll bet she's fooled the Parole Board into thinking she's genuinely reformed. She'll have been working towards this release for years, scheming, doing all the right things, never stepping out of line. Didn't I read she'd turned Catholic? She's no Christian, that turn to religion is all part of the act, part of her grand plan. I know how she thinks – whatever she's done recently has been done to create the right impression. She'll have been working on this for years, plotting and scheming the best way to secure her freedom, making herself look good.

'She knows how to manipulate people, Mark, and she knows how to win their warm feelings. But caution yourself that she's mentally unstable, evil, wicked, depraved, diabolic – you can feel it in her presence. I suppose I mean *I* can feel it. I can sense evil, Mark, smell it even, which is why I was such a bloody good detective even if I say so myself. I always knew a real villain when I was confronted with one – I still do. And that woman is a villain and always will be, make no mistake. She did them all, you know, all six kids.'

'She was convicted of three murders, Mr Kenworthy.'

'I know that, you know that and the whole bloody world knows that, but I know she killed those other bairns and buried them on the moors, but what I have never discovered is why or where. And she did it alone. She was a butcher. She'd knifed fish as a job and knifed those kids just as efficiently. But why did she do such bloody terrible things to them? I've no idea. The question of her sanity was raised at the trial, but the jury reckoned she knew what she was doing. You've heard the tapes?'

'No, I know about them, but haven't heard them yet. It's on my list of things to do. We've still got them.'

'You must listen to them, Mark, all of them. They'll make your blood run cold. I've seen hardened detectives weep at those kids pleading for their lives ... bloody awful case, it was. I wept afterwards, I don't mind admitting, cried my eyes out when it was all over. Emotion, distress, frustration or whatever. It all got to me. I think she was trying to copy or even outdo the crimes of Myra Hindley and Ian Brady.

'God knows why she'd want to do that. Anyway, it's all over now, so what's your interest? She's not claiming she's innocent, is she? Is that she-devil trying to say there was a miscarriage of justice? She never admitted anything, you know, not a thing. We had to prove the lot but we did make out a watertight case against her. She's not saying I bullied or beat her to get a confession out of her, is she? That I denied her her rights . . . Rights! A bitch like that . . . Why have criminals more rights than victims? Answer me that. But you lads have had a bashing lately, haven't you, what with the Blakelock fiasco and the Birmingham Six, the Guildford Four and the rest of them. That seems the latest fashion – criticizing the police by saying you were pressured or beaten into making a confession. The public can't see that there's a hell of a big difference between being innocent and not being found guilty . . .'

Mark let him ramble on, an old man saddened by modern lawlessness and the failure of the criminal justice system to deal adequately with the hardest of villains, and when he'd finished Mark continued.

'My reason for talking to you, Mr Kenworthy, is because we've heard, in a roundabout way through an informer, that someone, even a relation of one of the dead children, intends to kill her when she's released. It's more than just a threat, so we believe; we're taking it seriously. My job is to prevent that killing.'

'If I was you, Mark, I'd let the bugger kill her. It would be rough justice, but nobody could blame him.'

'We can't allow that, Mr Kenworthy.' Mark laughed with the old man. 'And you know it! But I wondered if you could remember anything that might lead us to that person. I mean, could a member of one of the families really be intent on killing her?'

'They all had reason at the time. I thought they were all very restrained about it. You know that two of them have made shrines to their lasses?'

'Yes, I know that.'

'That's a starter for you. And Tom Waterhouse always said he would never see her released alive. He didn't want the death penalty, but he did want her locked up for ever. He said no punishment was sufficient to make her pay for what she'd done but I never heard him threaten to kill her.'

'He's living in Scotland now,' Mark added.

'That doesn't stop him having a go if he really wants to. She'll come out under an assumed name, will she? Be given a job and a new start? That'll keep her secret safe, surely?'

'Yes,' said Mark. 'The reports say she is reformed . . .'

'Reports! What do the experts know about these sort of criminals? She's conned them, good and proper, as I knew she would.

No, lad, let the buggers get to her, let them kill her. That's what I say.'

'Have any other members of the girls' families threatened anything? Apart from the parents, are there any others who are likely killers?'

'There's Andrew Stabler, brother of little Helen. Her body was never found and her parents made a shrine of her bedroom. Well, Andrew was ten years old when his sister disappeared, and when he was in his late teens, he got himself into a lot of bother with the local law. Shop-breakings, punch-ups, drunken behaviour, that sort of thing. Nothing too serious, the sort of thing he got probation for, although he did a short stretch inside, two months in a juvenile detention centre for burglary. If he had a real problem, it was that he could be uncharacteristically violent after a few pints. They put it all down to the stress of having to cope with his missing little sister. It was tough on the lad, I'll accept that. I tried to help him but he blamed the police for not finding Helen, dead or alive. He seemed to be having a go at us, using us as his excuse for being anti-social and getting himself into trouble.'

'Are you saying he could be a threat?'

'Of course he could, you know he could. I'm talking about many years ago, remember, so he might have mellowed a little. But imagine him nursing a grudge all these years and now wanting revenge, probably for his own messed-up life as well as for his dead sister. Years of bitterness could come to a head when she's released. Imagine him with a belly full of beer and a head full of hate, then imagine what he'd do upon hearing that Potter's been released . . .'

Mark had taken out his pocket-book and was making notes of these details. As the two men talked, Mark realized that Kenworthy had a remarkably clear recollection of events, not surprising when it must have been his most dramatic and memorable case. High spots from the investigation would be permanently imprinted upon his brain, an indelible part of his police career. Mark therefore took this opportunity to explore the old man's memory.

'I've not read the case papers yet,' he admitted. 'That's my next job. It'll take weeks to go through the files completely and I haven't that amount of time. I rely on my officers to abstract information. But in a résumé I've studied, I didn't see any mention of a man friend in Potter's life at Rainesbury.'

'When we checked her antecedents,' Kenworthy told him, 'we did discover she'd had several boyfriends. None was relevant to the case. They were mainly casual acquaintances and we found no serious romance or permanent relationship. She was a pretty girl, even I can't deny that, and she did attract a lot of attention when she went out. So far as we could determine, none of those lads was involved with her in the murders, if that's what you are implying.'

'Not necessarily that.' Mark shrugged. 'It's just that I thought it odd they weren't mentioned.'

'They were never suspects, Mark,' the old detective admitted. 'She had one steady boyfriend, an Irishman called Balleen. He lived in the same digs and worked in the building trade, labourer or something, on the Lump. He did a bit of second-hand car dealing on the side. He went back to Ireland before she was arrested. He wasn't involved in the crimes, he'd gone before the first murder was committed, but you could do worse than look him up. I made reference to him in my files even though he was never in the frame.'

'Can you remember his Christian names? I'll check to see if we've anything else on him,' Mark said. 'He might have kept in touch, she might have confided in him. Perhaps he visited her in prison? If he was close to her, he might help us discover if anyone said they wanted to kill her at the time, whether she got any threatening letters in prison or whatever.'

'You can always ask her various prison governors about visitors. Anyway, Balleen was called Joseph Patrick,' smiled Kenworthy. 'One of many Joseph Patricks from across the Irish Sea. He had no record. We checked him through Special Branch records because the IRA was busy then, the Provisionals were being formed about that time and the IRA needed cash to set them up, but we couldn't prove anything about Joseph Patrick. He had no known links with any terrorist activities although he did come into our sights for a major series of robberies.'

'Robberies?'

'Building societies mainly, some small branches of banks and post offices. There was a sudden spate of them throughout the region while he was living here, large sums stolen by an armed raider over many months. They stopped when he returned to Ireland. We quizzed him before he left, but we got nowhere. But the main thing for you is that he was clear so far as the murders were concerned. He'll be in his early forties now.'

'Younger than her?' Mark commented.

'Yes, by a few years. I remember Potter's landlady once commenting on the age gap; it was odd then, a woman of twenty-five going out with a lad of eighteen. But they never slept together, at least not so far as Miss Clayton knew.'

'Miss Clayton?'

'Potter's landlady at Rainesbury, their landlady in fact. It was a very large boarding house, bed-and-breakfast only, cheap and cheerful sort of spot but run with a hand of iron and kept meticulously clean. Lino on the floor instead of carpets, dining tables covered with blue checked oilcloth, no flowers in the house, hot water bottles instead of central heating. Electric fires on meters in the bedrooms. Bare, no real comforts. That sort of place. Miss Clayton wouldn't have any sort of hanky-panky there, especially so far as her regular residents were concerned. No unmarried couples sharing rooms either, that was forbidden! And Potter could cope with those conditions, she'd had a spartan sort of upbringing.

'She didn't touch alcohol or have a bet on the Derby. She secured work at the boarding house when she came to the area, and she lived in. Even out of season, she lived there while working at other places. It provided company and a little income for Miss Clayton out of season. Balleen came to stay too, working on the Lump, doing casual building work and his car dealing. He was always flashing cash about, always busy, rushing about. He and Potter became pals; pals, I'm sure, not lovers. I think they were pretty close for a time, lost souls together in a strange place. I never met him but got the impression he was a strange lad, Mark, a weird mixture of personalities. I can tell you more if you're interested.'

'Not really, not if we can rule him out of this enquiry.'

'You can't really rule him out, can you? He might have had a grudge against her, eh? He might be the chap you're seeking. Anyway, he went back to Ireland before she committed her crimes. I doubt if he ever knew what she'd done – he wouldn't unless he read the English papers.'

'I wonder if those digs are still there?'

'I'm sure they are, Mark. It was a big house, like a private hotel really, with seventeen or eighteen letting rooms; it was called Mermaid Villa and stood on a big site in Beach Road. Miss Clayton was in her forties then, a confirmed spinster, so she should still be around, retired maybe. She'll know more about Potter's boyfriends.'

'I wonder if Miss Clayton visited her in prison?' Mark asked. 'It seems her own relations didn't.'

'It's the sort of thing she might do. She and Potter had become good friends, by the way, they'd go for long walks on the beach or have trips out to York or up to the moors. Potter might even have confided in her, although we got little information out of Miss Clayton. At the time, she couldn't believe Potter would commit such awful crimes, but she did become very supportive, more so than Potter's own family as you've said. They weren't very supportive to her during our investigations either – I did wonder if they knew more about her than we did! It wouldn't surprise me if she'd killed the pet cat when she was a kid or put the budgie in the oven, it's the sort of thing evil kids do. She had a very cruel streak in her and she was cold and calculating. I got the impression that her parents were quite happy about her living away from home. They never came to visit her in Rainesbury even though Miss Clayton extended an open invitation to come and stay.'

'You've a very clear recollection of things,' Mark smiled.

'She was an enigma, Mark, such a bloody puzzle. Charming, beautiful, clever, capable – but utterly evil. She fascinated me – and still does. And I still want to know why she killed those bairns – we never did find out. I could not establish her motive for such sustained and awful bloody cruelty. Is that something you might do after all this time?'

Mark smiled. 'I'm considering reopening the case, Mr Kenworthy. It might help in what I'm doing, open a few doors.'

'Good idea, I'd welcome that. The case of those missing bairns was never formally closed, you know,' the old man said. 'There are still three little girls unaccounted for, probably three more murders that could still be detected if you do reopen your enquiries. Although we let the enquiries lapse, I did have several attempts at reviving the investigation, but we failed to come up with any new evidence. I know it all happened a long time ago, but the case could do with a new brain, a fresh approach, maybe even your computers would help!'

'We and the computers would be relying heavily on your past work,' Mark reminded him.

'Fine, but a fresh approach might produce results. There are three more bodies waiting to be found, Mark. They'll be in a hell of a state by this time, of course, but something identifiable might be salvaged. There might be remnants of clothing, shoes, buckles from sandals, teeth, bones, one kid wore specs, so they must be somewhere. And if you did find any remains, it might put that she-devil back behind bars where she belongs. It would give you a bloody good reason for interviewing the parents all over again.'

'I'm going to start reading the murder file when I get back to the office,' Mark promised. 'But I am engaged in a protective role now, that's my priority.'

'Then listen to all the tapes,' suggested Kenworthy. 'Read the case file. And then decide which takes priority.'

'I'll think about it. I must be off. You've been most helpful, Mr Kenworthy. Can I come again? I might have more things to ask once I get my teeth into this one.'

'Please do. In the mean time, I might just find my old notebooks. I've stuff recorded there that was never placed in files or given as evidence. You're welcome to look at it. It was good to talk, Mark. I'm always pleased to see former colleagues. Alice . . .' he shouted. 'Mr Pemberton's leaving. See you, Mark, and the best of British with this one. If you can find those three bairns, you'll make me a very happy man before I pass to the great CID office in the sky.'

During the short drive back to the office, Mark told himself that if he did recover those corpses, Potter could feasibly stand trial for the additional murders, provided that other supporting evidence was available. That would provide him with the satisfaction of having her incarcerated for the rest of her life. That could be his true objective – he would protect her from assassination so that she might answer for three more murders. In that way, he could justify his protection of her. He warmed to the task.

Back in his office, he called in Gill, secretary to both himself and the Detective Chief Superintendent, and asked her to bring him the Louisa Mary Potter tapes and the case file after lunch.

Now it was lunchtime, so he took the lift down to the canteen. It was Tuesday so it must be steak and kidney pie with chips and peas followed by rice pudding, not the best of diets for cholesterol control. He hoped they had salad as an alternative.

He'd listen to those tapes this afternoon.

5

Mark listened to just one part of one tape. It was horrendous, nauseating, deeply disturbing and obscene. He did not have the time to listen to all six, but that snippet was sufficient to spur him into a desire to reopen Kenworthy's inconclusive enquiries. Anyone who could inflict such pain upon another human being did not deserve any freedom.

Unfortunately, there was no means of identifying any of the screaming children. It had been impossible to allocate names to those whose pleas for life had been recorded, but a glance through the transcripts made him appreciate the utter evil of Louisa Mary Potter. He wondered if the Home Secretary, or any members of the Parole Board, had heard the tapes. He thought not; if they had, it was doubtful if they would have ever allowed that woman to resume a normal life.

Reeling from the experience, Pemberton inspected Kenworthy's case file. There was so much material; there were four cabinets full of files comprising statements from hundreds of people who had been interviewed, notes made at the time by Kenworthy and his teams of officers, official reports from various sources, copies of newspaper cuttings, forensic science analyses, scenes of crime reports, photographs of the sad remains of the dead girls and the locations at which they had been found plus copies of the response from the DPP.

In addition, there was that host of theoretical paperwork and material evidence which goes to make up a comprehensive murder file. There was also an explanatory note which said that bulky items associated with the enquiry were kept in the CID stores – they included several card index systems and items of real evidence such as the butcher's knife used by Potter and later found on a rubbish tip, and a collection of assorted objects which had been subjected to forensic examination.

Mark made no attempt to digest the entire contents of the massive file; it would take weeks to examine just one drawer full, but he asked Gill to tell Filing that he would be examining some of the papers over the coming weeks. He would need to dip into sections of the file as he worked and he would steel himself to listen to more of the tapes from time to time in the hope that they might provide some clue to Potter's terrible behaviour.

He next settled down to draw up his plan of action which would include a request for officers to be written off their normal duties to assist him. At this stage, he did not know how many he would require – there'd be those needed to make enquiries into the background of suspects in addition to those necessary for round-the-clock covert surveillance on Potter alias Hicks, plus a HOLMES data processor and secretarial assistance. He'd need teams to reopen enquiries too, not the full complement of a murder room but enough to digest the contents of the old files and apply the data to their new task.

He began to jot down the names of several officers in whom he could place his trust, including the tall and slender Detective Constable Lorraine Cashmore. She had a gorgeous figure, a lovely smile and a very fine detective brain aided by feminine intuition. As he made his preliminary notes, Mark realized that it would be difficult to interview people like Miss Clayton, Patrick Joseph Balleen, Tom Waterhouse and the others while struggling to maintain secrecy. If he reopened enquiries, he would be able to gain legitimate access to the families and all the others he had to interview. He would therefore ask the Chief Constable for formal permission to do so. He rang the Chief's secretary.

'Is he in?' Mark asked.

'Yes, Mr Pemberton.'

'Can he see me – now?' was his next question.

There was a pause as the Chief's secretary spoke to her boss on the intercom and she responded by saying, 'Yes, you can come up now.'

Mark climbed to the top floor, knocked and was admitted.

'So, Mark, what's all this about?' Charles Moore produced one of his dashing smiles as he indicated the chair before his desk. Mark sat down.

'Louisa Mary Potter alias Hicks,' he said, and then explained his actions so far, concluding the account by saying, 'I've decided it would help if we could reopen the file on the missing children, sir.'

'You realize that your enquiries could reach the ears of journalists and that would result in some unwelcome publicity about Potter, Mark?'

'Yes, but it would be very difficult for anyone, even the press, to link Potter with Hicks, and Hicks with our renewed enquiries, wouldn't it? She'd be leading her new life, under her new name, and I could tell those of my team members who are guarding her that Hicks is a potential victim. There is no need to give reasons, but we could spread a rumour among our own people that Hicks had been in prison with Potter and was a close friend. I could tell my team that she is known to have knowledge of Potter's whereabouts, Hicks and Potter being released at the same time. I would continue to stress that Potter is living in the south and imply that someone aims to get at Potter through Hicks . . .'

'In that case, Hicks might have to be prepared to talk to the press, Mark, to talk about "Potter" . . . You'd need her co-operation, not the easiest of achievements if you're reopening the files.'

'I bet she'd rather pretend she was Potter's friend than admit her real identity, sir! And we are protecting her, that should result in some co-operation. It's a good cover story and no one need know that Hicks and Potter are the same woman.'

'This isn't quite what I envisaged, superintendent, I'll be honest. I wanted a low-key, secret operation to protect her. Softly, softly, no fuss, certainly no publicity.'

'That can still be achieved, sir. I'm confident I can separate our supervision of Hicks from our reopening of the file on the children. If the press do hear about our renewed enquiries, there'll be no way they can associate it with our guardianship of Hicks. They won't know about that side of our operation. We can divert all their enquiries towards a reopening of our investigations, even to the extent of digging up the moor if necessary. That'll draw the press to us, we can steer things our way, we can gain control.'

'If you start digging, you might even find something . . .'

'It's always possible, sir.'

'Let me sleep on this one, Mark,' Moore decided. 'I need to

think it through in a little more depth before I give my go-ahead. I suppose, if I do agree with you, that you'll need to establish an incident room, make use of HOLMES and other computers, and you'll expect the usual trappings of a modern murder enquiry with an increased number of personnel, and of course, more expense?'

'Yes, but on a fairly modest scale. I reckon I'll need something like a dozen officers – perhaps fifteen or sixteen at the most.'

'Right, leave it with me. I'll be in touch in the morning.'

When Mark left his office, Charles Moore lifted the handset of the secure telephone and dialled a London number.

'Moore speaking,' he said. 'About Potter. There's been a development.'

He outlined Mark's suggestion and then asked, 'So, is this a feasible scheme? From a purely selfish point of view, I'm sure he'll not prove the outstanding murders which is a pity – I refer to them as murders even though they were never formally declared as such, there being no bodies. We could do with having the mystery cleared up, no one likes unsolved crimes on their books, or missing children.'

The anonymous voice replied, 'I understand, but on the positive side, it would get the families and the public on the side of the police, eh? As you know, Charles, we were planning to organize a leak of information as Pemberton's work got underway, but in view of your proposals, that might not be necessary. So yes, authorize the reopening of the missing children file but do not make any public announcement. Wait for the press to find out what's going on and then confirm your actions if necessary. But make no public link between Hicks and the investigations – I'll make sure she's briefed too, she'll co-operate, I'm sure, she's gone along with us so far. I think our scheme will draw our fish to the bait, eh?'

'Right, thanks, let's hope it does. I'll be in touch.'

'Do make sure your superintendent is aware that Hicks is in real danger, Charles. He must regard the reopened enquiries as a diversion. Her protection is his real duty.'

'I'll warn him.'

Mark spent a second evening poring over more mountains of paperwork. He found no obvious fault with the earlier investigation and no readily apparent opening for new lines of enquiry, but did make copious notes which would serve to provide his teams with lines of investigation should Moore agree to reopen the case. Finally he drew up the draft of a schedule of duties to provide full twenty-four-hour supervision of Kathleen Hicks for the next six months in addition to coping with the extra enquiries. One benefit was that the officers guarding Hicks could be changed more frequently, thus aiding their cover and providing them with a refreshing change of duty. Discreet observation, over a long period, could become a very boring chore and sloppiness could follow. He was pleased with his ideas and read through his notes to find they did make sense. Satisfied with his progress, he placed them in his briefcase in readiness for tomorrow then decided to listen to some Chopin, enhanced by a glass of brandy and the flickering of the logs blazing in his grate.

At eleven the following morning, he was called to the Chief's office and given the necessary approval. But Moore cautioned him. 'Mark, I know you are a very seasoned detective, but remember that this business with Hicks is primarily protection duty. Your priority is to protect that woman. She is in genuine danger, I must stress that. Reinvestigation of the missing children is, in fact, a diversionary tactic, almost a public relations exercise, a way of opening doors and mouths.'

'I understand, sir.'

'And furthermore, Mark, I do not want you concentrating exclusively on the investigation as a means of getting Hicks put back inside; I'm not blind, I know how you feel about her crimes and I know you'd love to get her put away again . . .'

'I'll protect her, sir, I'll do my duty.'

'Well, that's it then. Provide me with an outline of your plan and then you're in action. The sooner the better.'

'It's being typed up for you now, sir, under personal and confidential cover.'

'And good luck, Mark,' smiled the Chief Constable.

Mark was allowed his sixteen officers and that afternoon each received a telephone call. It was an instruction to report for special duty at Room 207 at Force Headquarters by no later than nine o'clock the next morning.

6

Mark arrived just after eight thirty and was pleased to see that Barbara Meadows was already there. She was organizing coffee for the influx of officers. By nine o'clock, everyone was present and he asked them to gather some chairs to form a large semicircle in front of the table he would use as his desk for such conferences. Each officer was in civilian clothes and the group comprised one detective inspector, three detective sergeants and a dozen detective constables, men and women. And to make the office procedures run smoothly, there was the efficient and trustworthy civilian typist, Miss Barbara Meadows.

Everyone was showing a keen interest in their unknown duties but waited patiently until Pemberton was ready. Some were guessing loudly, others remained silent as they awaited enlightenment from their smartly dressed superintendent. Smiling and pleased at their eagerness, he squeezed through a gap in the chairs and stood behind his desk, rapping upon it to gain their attention. Then he began.

''Morning all,' he smiled. 'Welcome to Room 207.'

He was greeted with good-humoured responses ranging from ''Morning, sir' to 'Where's the body?' and then he asked if everyone had secured a mug of coffee. They had, and so he began.

'You've all been specially selected for this job.' They all groaned at this opening remark. They were accustomed to hearing such words which usually meant there had been no choice; such 'specially selected volunteers' were often pressed men. But not on this occasion.

'I mean it,' Mark continued. 'This is no ordinary job; each of you has been specially recommended, hand-picked by me for this task, selected for your professionalism, your reliability and your skill!'

'We believe you, sir, many wouldn't!' laughed Detective

Sergeant Ian Wrigley as the others booed and cheered in good humour.

Mark enjoyed the banter and continued, 'Most of you are younger than me, and so the name of Louisa Mary Potter might not mean anything . . .'

'It bloody does, sir!' cried Detective Constable Harry Ward, a crumpled man in his late forties. 'The child killer, she killed three bairns at Rainesbury and buried them on the moors. Sliced them into little bits with knives, tape-recorded their cries for mercy. She got life three times and keeps trying to get parole. I was serving at Rainesbury at the time, a probationer constable with just three months in. I was a green youngster then, full of idealism and thinking that criminals weren't really bad, just unfortunate. But that woman made me realize just how bloody evil some people can be.'

Mark held up his hand. 'OK, Harry, so you know her. How about the rest of you? Anyone *not* know of her crimes?'

No one responded. They all knew who she was. The crimes of Louisa Mary Potter had become part of the force's own folklore and aspects of the case were featured during training courses. Even the youngest recruits knew something about the Rainesbury Murders.

Mark now had their close attention and went on. 'OK, so I needn't go into too much detail here. It's all in the files for you to check if you need to, but I'd like you to acquaint yourselves with the background and personalities. Those murders are behind the reason we're all here today. So, working as a team, we've got three things to do. Task Number One – we're going to reopen the file into three missing children. Three youngsters, all girls, disappeared at the time Potter was committing those other crimes in 1967. Their bodies were never found. Everyone believed Potter had killed them. I believe that too. We're going to re-examine those old files and reopen enquiries by using modern techniques, such as HOLMES and up-to-date incident room procedures. It'll be a small, low-key enquiry. If anyone asks what you're up to, especially the press, refer them to me for an official statement. I'm not courting publicity for this one, not yet anyway, but I will tell the press if they ask. No more than that. Now, Task Number Two – Louisa Mary Potter has been granted parole.'

There were loud cries of 'Shame,' 'I don't believe it,' and 'They must be bloody stupid,' so Mark called for silence.

'OK, I know how you must feel, but the Parole Board, in its wisdom, has agreed to release her on licence. She comes out on Monday. She will not be living in our patch, you'll be pleased to know. She'll live in the south of England under an assumed name. I might add that her release has nothing to do with our decision to reopen the case – that decision was taken before news of her release was given to us. Her release is therefore a somewhat remarkable coincidence. Whether it is a fortunate coincidence remains to be seen, but her freedom is of no direct concern to us unless she returns to this force area, say for a visit to old friends. We shall be informed if that happens. I must add that there is no reason to think she will kill again.

'Task Number Three – a woman called Kathleen Hicks served alongside Potter and befriended her. She's also being released at the same time. The release of both women is to be regarded as secret, so I want no one talking about it. Hicks did a stretch for manslaughter of her lover but we've discovered, through an informer, that someone intends having a go at her, at Hicks that is, hoping, we think, to persuade her to release details of Potter's whereabouts with a view to murdering Potter. We don't know who's going to try it on, but it is sound intelligence and the Home Office has a very good reason for keeping both women, Potter especially, in the land of the living.

'I'm not saying they'd go as far as killing Hicks, but we don't want any unsolved murders on our patch, do we? Think of the crime figures! So our job is to protect Hicks from attack, to prevent a murder happening. There is just a possibility that the attempt might come from a member of the families of the dead children and so we must get among them. Potter, at her new home in the south, is also being protected because of the same threat – she, too, will have a different name. Here in Yorkshire, it is our job to provide round-the-clock protection for Hicks. She will live at Swandale in a safe house. I'll provide details shortly and a photograph will appear on the notice-board, along with duty rotas for observation duties. They're boring, I'm afraid, but necessary.

'So,' he went on, 'we have decided to merge these duties. We hope that our enquiries into the missing children might tell us who's going to try and kill or harm these women. For that reason, we shall combine the revived missing children enquiries with our surveillance duties, using the same personnel so that the boredom of doing prolonged observations can be reduced.

'Detective Inspector Paul Larkin will be in charge of the incident room. We shall run it as an incident room which is serving a murder enquiry, and we shall conduct our investigations along the lines of a modern murder hunt. Paul, can you see to that? You know the routine and the setting-up procedures. I've got part of the old murder file out of CID storage, it's in my office.

'You'll need the rest, piles of it, and you'll need good statement readers to go through the papers to abstract data for HOLMES. It'll be a chore to start with, but once we start getting the basic data logged, we can begin to interview members of the families, old witnesses and so on, to see if they can remember anything of interest. Their memories will be jolted next week when it's officially announced that Potter has been given parole. Hicks' release – and that's not her proper name – will hardly merit a line in the papers. But Potter will be out of prison and in her new home by the time the news is broadcast. I hope all the families on our list will want to talk to us then, but do remember that some might not want old wounds reopened. We need to be careful the way we approach this one. When we reach the stage of talking to members of the families, I want each of you to be alert to the possibility that one of them might be planning to bump off Kathleen Hicks and/or Potter if they can find either of them. In spite of our own feelings about Potter's crimes, we can't allow murder to happen, so keep alert for evidence of any attempts. That is very important.

'We shall not work overtime on this one, except during the observation duties or unless something abnormal happens. Normal hours will be from nine each morning until five o'clock, a straight eight-hour shift. Weekends will be free, unless there's drama, or unless you're on obs.

'The presence of Hicks within our patch, I repeat, is top secret – I must emphasize that. No one outside this room must know who she is or where she is, not even other officers. And if we are told where Potter is living, then that too will be top secret. We are engaged on reopening an old missing children file, that's the official line to adopt if anyone asks what you are doing. Any leaks from here which say otherwise will result in disciplinary proceedings. Need I say more?'

There were muted murmurings of understanding from the group and Mark thanked them.

'Thanks,' he said. 'So, our first job is to get the incident room up and running, that's your immediate task. When that's done, Detective Inspector Larkin will allocate the first actions. OK? Let's get the show moving! Paul, a word with you please.'

Mark led his D/I into the small ante-room at the end of Room 207; it was the room he would use as his own office and its glass-panelled door overlooked the floor which would soon be full of busy desks and glowing VDUs. Mark closed the door.

'So, Paul, what do you make of this job?'

'Dunno, sir, to be honest.' Paul shrugged his shoulders. 'It seems a strange sort of duty to me.'

'The missing children enquiry is to be reopened because the threat against the released women is real enough,' Mark told him. 'We need to get close to the parents and relations to find out who's behind the threat. By reopening the old case, we should be able to do that – sadly, and being realistic, I don't think there's a cat in hell's chance of finding those missing bairns after such a lapse of time, but I do hope we can achieve our real purpose.'

'It's been done to death over the years, sir, even the press and television have tried to discover those bodies and to get Potter to admit she killed them, without success.'

'I wanted you to know why we've taken this course. So we need one hundred per cent co-operation from our teams.'

'No problem, sir, they're all good officers, willing, discreet, hard-working.'

'So, any idea how you'll tackle this?'

'Once the incident room is functioning, sir, and HOLMES is operating, I'll select a team to begin to log in data from the key statements. I'll be able to allocate some action from that.'

'OK. I'd like to make personal contact with the parents, Paul. I must prepare them for what's going to happen and I'll need to do that before our teams visit them, and before anything appears in the press. That's my personal duty, at least for those living nearby . . .' and he began to outline his view of the forthcoming investigations, highlighting Andrew Stabler's trouble with the police, and the untouched rooms which remained as shrines to two of the children. Then he said he was going to Swandale to visit the landlady of the safe house, and then to Rainesbury to visit the victims' parents.

'I'll come back here before you despatch any of the teams to their actions,' he assured Paul Larkin. 'So, this is what I want you to do now.'

Having briefed his D/I, Mark knew that a drive out to Swandale would be a good start to his own work. He wished to establish contact with Mrs Agnes Dawson. Her home was a modest semi-detached house built of brick with a bow window protruding into the lawn at the front, and a patch of ivy climbing the side wall above the drive to the garage. The wintering garden looked neat and well tended with its rose bushes pruned and the dead vegetation removed. He could see a light burning in the lounge as he rang the bell and waited.

A small grey-haired woman in loose blue slacks and a floppy white sweater answered. In her early seventies, she seemed very agile and alert.

'Mrs Dawson?'

'That's me.' She didn't smile. She didn't know whether this man was genuine or not.

Mark introduced himself and showed his warrant card.

'You'd better come in, then.' She was abrupt in manner and there was no warmth in her voice. She bade him be seated in a comfortable chair and invited him to have a coffee which he accepted, specifying black. Then she sat on the settee to listen to him.

'It's about Kathleen Hicks,' he began.

'She'll be safe enough here, Mr Pemberton,' she almost snapped at him. 'I've taken other women in like this, put them on the road to self-reliance, given them a helping hand. Friendship an' all, if I might say so.'

'I know,' he said. 'You've a tremendous reputation.'

At this praise, her face relaxed the tiniest of fractions.

'In this instance, things are slightly different, slightly more difficult,' he said. 'I know you are aware that there might be an attempt to injure Kathleen. I'm in charge of a small group of officers who will be keeping a discreet eye on her; I understand she knows of our interest. It might be a false report of course, but we take it seriously. We shall be very, very discreet. But I wanted you to know of our interest, Mrs Dawson, so that if you do see anyone hanging about, watching her, watching or calling at the house or whatever, then I'd like you to inform us. I'll ask my officers to make themselves known to you. They do not know Kathleen's true identity, by the way. I do. Now, I have no wish to pry into Kathleen's private life but I do wish to make sure she comes to no harm. I need to strike a balance and might want your help. You agree to that?'

'Of course,' she said. 'I had this carry-on once before. I know what you need. Yes, all right. Leave me a number where I can get you. If that woman's in my care, then I don't want her harmed either, no matter what awful things she might have done. Let bygones be bygones, that's what I say.'

He gave her a brief outline of the plans he proposed and she listened with alertness. This was no senile old woman; she was alert and intelligent, probably the ideal person with whom to lodge someone as vulnerable as a released long-serving prisoner.

'You'll be wanting to see her room?' she suggested at length.

'Thanks.'

'I always put my special ladies in this room,' she said, leading the way to the foot of the stairs. 'It's quiet, private, safe from prying eyes and it's got its own loo and shower.'

The house was surprisingly large with four bedrooms and a huge landing. Hicks would occupy a middle room which overlooked the drive to the garage; her window looked upon the wall of the adjoining house which was not a pretty view, but it was secure. The room was nicely decorated and very clean.

'Thanks,' said Mark. 'Have you anyone else in?'

'A lady who's been with me for over a year now, since her husband threw her out, Mrs Eden. She's been checked, by the way, by the security service and your Special Branch before the Home Office agreed to Kathleen staying here. She has no job, she has a modest income of her own and spends time rambling and exploring the moors and doing bits of charity work. She's in her room now, if you'd like to say hello. She's not an ex-prisoner, by the way, just an ordinary lodger.'

'I'd like to see her, so I know who she is,' Mark replied.

'Right, well, I'll show you round next. That's the only resident here at the moment, except for me, of course.'

'Thanks. I'm sorry to be a nuisance. I'm pleased you can cope with rather troublesome needs.'

'Don't apologize. Hicks got herself into that mess, not you and your officers. I just hope things work out for her, maybe she deserves a break. No one's all bad.'

After inspecting the main bathroom, toilet and loft space with its ladder and solid flooring, Mark waited as Mrs Dawson tapped on Mrs Eden's door. The door opened and Mark saw a woman in her middle thirties with blonde hair piled high on her head. With a slender figure in casual jeans and a sweater, she had a long, intelligent face with blue eyes and an easy smile.

'Hello,' she said.

'This is Mr Pemberton.' Mrs Dawson made the introductions and said that Mark was just looking around because a friend of his was coming to stay.

'It'll be company for me,' said Mrs Eden. 'My name's Rebecca.'

After a short, pleasant chat with Rebecca Eden, Mark thanked the severe Mrs Dawson, left her the number of the dedicated telephone line into the incident room together with his own private number, then left. Mrs Dawson was a bossy old mother hen, he decided, but she'd probably be very good for Kathleen Hicks. He wondered how Rebecca would get on with her.

Having met her future landlady, he decided it might be sensible to visit her former landlady, Miss Clayton of Mermaid Villa, while he was visiting the families at Rainesbury. The seaside town was almost an hour's drive away and as he left the safe house, he switched on the radio to listen to some classical music *en route*.

7

Finding himself driving past Mermaid Villa on his journey through Rainesbury as he sought the Stablers' shop, Mark decided to make this his first call. He found that twenty-five years after the Rainesbury Murders, Miss Brenda Clayton was still running Mermaid Villa as a boarding house.

Neither she nor it had changed very significantly in that time, he guessed, save that each was correspondingly older. Mermaid Villa remained a bare building on the corner of Beach Road with pink and pale green woodwork upon whitewashed walls devoid of ivy or climbing plants. The overall appearance was one of candy floss colours with a lack of adornment; the large entrance hall had a tiled floor with an umbrella stand at one side, above which was a mirror with protruding hat pegs down each side, while the lounge into which Mark was steered had an old mock-leather settee and several equally dated easy chairs. An antiquated gas fire, devoid of even one flame on this winter day, occupied a space in the wall and a small table in the corner contained lots of ancient magazines. There was a fairly modern television set while the pictures on the walls were portraits of some anonymous and sepia Victorian people, perhaps Miss Clayton's ancestors. As Mark Pemberton took stock of the room, the maid asked him to wait while she sought Miss Clayton.

Now in her early seventies, Miss Clayton was a tall, severe woman with iron grey hair neatly trimmed and well cared for; he could imagine it tied in a bun. Perhaps it once had been but not now. It was like a mop of tight curls which left her ears on display and was above the clean white collar. Brenda Clayton's rounded cheeks were as ruddy as if she had an outdoor job, the veins clearly on show for she used no make-up to disguise them. She wore a flowered pinny over a plain pale blue dress with a white collar, somewhat reminiscent of a nurse's uniform, and her sleeves were rolled up to her elbows. Her large, strong hands were covered in dough and she was wiping them on a towel as she stomped into the room. Even with her soft moccasin shoes, she looked massive and threatening as she halted in the doorway.

'Yes? What is it?' Her keen grey eyes took in every smart detail of the man now standing before her.

'Miss Clayton? Brenda Clayton?' he asked.

'That's me.'

'And you are the proprietor of this boarding house?'

'You sound like a policeman,' was her retort.

'I am.' Mark introduced himself, showing his warrant card.

'So what have I done? Accommodated a criminal last night? Somebody dumped a stolen car in my car-park? Or is somebody doing the rounds and leaving without paying their bills?'

Mark smiled. 'None of those this time,' he smiled. 'I'm here on a totally different matter.'

He paused, hoping she'd invite him to sit down and have a coffee, but she didn't.

'Go on, then,' was her response.

'It's about Louisa Mary Potter,' he began.

'They won't leave that woman alone, superintendent. God knows she's paid for what she did. More than twenty years locked away is enough for anyone.'

'You thought a lot about her?'

'She was a fine girl and a good worker when she was here, superintendent. I could have loved her as a daughter; she's done me no harm. I've been to see her, you know, in prison. She's coped well, she's not let the system get her down. There's still a bit of sparkle there.'

'She's being released on parole, next Monday,' he told her.

'And about time too. She'll do no more killings, superintendent. She'll not be a danger to children, or anyone else. I'd have her back here, you know, to help me but folks wouldn't give her any peace, would they?'

'Some of the families hereabouts might not agree with your sentiments, Miss Clayton. They might not be so happy that she's coming out,' he said. 'We must keep her whereabouts a secret; we don't want trouble upon her release.'

'She's not coming back here, is she? To Rainesbury?'

'No, she's beginning a new life under a new name, Miss Clayton. I'm not allowed to acquaint you with that, but if Louisa feels inclined to tell you, then it's up to her. I do know she respected you, Chief Superintendent Kenworthy told me that, he said she liked living here.'

'But you haven't come here just to tell me all that, have you?' Her eyes were almost smiling at him.

'No, I'm afraid not. We're reopening the files on the three missing children. My officers might have to talk to you at some length, when we've gone over your earlier statement.'

'Why can't they leave her alone, superintendent? She's paid her penalty . . .'

'We're not accusing her of anything,' Mark pointed out. 'It's not an enquiry to trap her. We're simply reopening the files on the three missing children, in the hope we can find the bodies to give them a decent burial. I know that after all this time it would be welcomed by their families.'

'I can't say I feel that's all you're doing,' she said. 'You'll be trying to pin those kids' deaths on Louisa. Kenworthy was angry that he never got her for those.'

'That's not our prime objective. I can tell you this, that we've reason to think that someone, even a member of one of the families, might attempt something silly against Louisa,' he said. 'Our investigations are to prevent that. We must find out more about the families as they are now, with youngsters grown up and full of hate.'

'Aye, well, any of them might have killed Louisa given half a chance, when they knew what she'd done. It was a good job they put her away. She was safer inside.'

'Those feelings could be resurrected when they know she's been released. Was any particular person threatening her then?'

She shrugged her big shoulders. 'Not really, everybody was up in arms, the whole town, parents of kids, dads going to pubs threatening to get her when she came out. It was widespread, the hatred. It seems such a long time ago, looking back.'

'Has it faded away now?' he asked.

'I thought it had, but I agree with you; when she comes out it might set things off again.'

'I'm going to see some of the victims' families when I leave you, to explain the developments. Do you see any of them now?' he put to her.

'No, never set eyes on them, never a word, never a whisper. We've lost touch, they've aged now, they've forgotten it all by now. I hope you don't go stirring things up.'

'We'll do our best not to, Miss Clayton, we are keeping our role very quiet,' he said. 'But there is one thing I must ask you. Louisa's Irish boyfriend. When she was living here she was friends with Joseph Patrick Balleen.'

'Your men weren't interested in him before, not for the murders, he'd gone home before it all happened.'

'His home was in Ireland, was it?'

'Yes, he was a good family man, and he was no trouble here

either. Paid his bills, never caused me any worries. A real nice young chap.'

'Our files say very little about him, Miss Clayton, because he was not implicated. But I'd like to know more, I need to know everything about Louisa's background if I'm to protect her properly. I really do need to find him. Do you know if they fell out just before he left? Could he want to harm her, do you think?'

'You're not thinking he might want to kill her, are you?'

'We've no evidence of that, I just want to eliminate him.'

'You're a strange breed, you policemen; years ago, you'd have welcomed Louisa dead, folks were calling for the death penalty for her. Now you want to keep her alive and are thinking an old and dear friend might wish to harm her!'

'Our job's to protect life and property, Miss Clayton, and I don't want anybody having a go at Louisa. So I must try and find out as much as I can about her past. If she was close to Joseph Patrick, she might have confided in him, or any other of her male friends.'

'He was the only one she showed any real interest in, but even he never visited her in prison.'

'If he was in Ireland, maybe he never knew about the crimes?' suggested Mark. 'Was he ever in touch with her? Did he write or ring her?'

'I don't know, I never saw any letters from him, I'd have known his writing. He just went back home, later she cleared his things out of his room and life went on as normal.'

'Has he ever been back here? Have you seen him in recent weeks? Heard from him?'

'No, not a word. He's gone completely.'

'How close were they? Was theirs a romance, do you think? Or just friendship?'

'Well, I'm not one to say, superintendent. They went around a lot, they even had a joint account with the Country and Coast Bank and shared costs of outings and the cars they ran. I thought they were going to marry, but I never saw an engagement ring. There was no row, I'm sure of that, he wanted to go home because of some family reason involving his mother. Louisa had a chance to go with him, but didn't like the thought of living in Ireland. I think she thought he'd come back and resume the friendship.'

'Which part of Ireland did he come from?'

'Wexford, a small place called Enniscorthy. I forget his exact address. There was a big family of them, eight lads and two girls by all accounts.'

'And he was younger than Louisa?'

'She was twenty-five, he was only eighteen when he was here, so I suppose there was a bit of a gap, especially at that time, people were more conventional than they are now. I thought he was a bit young to be away from home, but he said he was glad to get away from the family house, with noise and the overcrowding. He was clever, a real smoothy, if you know what I mean. He could talk the hind leg off a donkey and was charming to everyone, a lovely lad. He could have been a confidence trickster, superintendent, but he was honest as the day he was born. He always paid me on time, and paid his other bills, the garage, the paper shop and so on. He liked touring England, especially Yorkshire and the north-east, and he would sometimes take Louisa with him in one of his cars – he bought and sold cars on the side, you know. Once he asked me to have a day out with him in Keswick, but I was too busy, too tied up here. He was a good car salesman, he could sell a car to anybody, he had the gift of the gab all right. He'd kissed the Blarney Stone, make no mistake.'

'Thanks, Miss Clayton, this is a good start. I'll find him and see what he can recall about Louisa. I wonder if he ever met the families of those dead girls?'

'Oh, yes, he lodged with one of them,' she said. 'It was just a coincidence, him being gone before she killed the bairn – well, to be precise, before the bairn went missing – but it was odd. He came to me from there.'

'Did he?' This was news to Mark, although he reckoned such a snippet would be in the file; if so, it would emerge in the data to be logged into HOLMES. 'Which family?'

'The Stablers. They still run the grocer's shop as they did then. It's a big house, with the shop underneath; they took in lodgers and bed-and-breakfasts, lots of people did, and still do, in this town. Joseph lived there for a time, then moved in here. Their Helen vanished, you know.'

'I'm going there next,' Mark told her. 'So he'd left the Stablers' digs before the killings? Was that long before?'

'It depends what you mean by long before. He was going out

with Louisa for a year or so, I think it was; they went out together before he moved in here, then I said he could come here, I had space in the winter and the Stablers were wanting more room for their family, so he came here. He'd have been here, oh, six or eight months before he went back to Ireland.'

'Can you remember dates?'

'I can get my registers out, superintendent, if you really must know.'

'I would like to know,' he persisted.

'Then sit down, I'll wash my hands and get them.'

She returned with a large tray bearing two mugs of tea, two scones and the relevant register.

'You pour while I find the place,' she said.

He obeyed, pouring a generous mug as she flicked through the pages of her tidy register, eventually halting.

'Here we are, 1966–67. He came to me in the October of 1966, when the summer season ended, and he stayed until February 1967, the first week. He left on the 6th. Paid all his bills. He had come to England in the spring of 1966, I think, and I believe he got digs somewhere else before he arrived at the Stablers'.'

Mark took notes of the dates and asked her to keep the register safe. She retorted that it had been safe for the last twenty-five years!

He chatted a while longer to Miss Clayton and felt he had, for the time being, exhausted his enquiries, but made a vow to return. A thorough scrutiny of the file at Headquarters would surely raise further questions for her to answer. He was in no doubt that there was a lot more to ask and now a major question loomed – was it a coincidence that Balleen had lodged with the Stablers? The name of Andrew Stabler had already come into the frame for his new investigation and his sister, Helen, was one whose body had never been found.

Mark now had two men to trace and eliminate. He left Miss Clayton after asking for directions to the Stablers'.

8

As it was lunchtime, Mark found a small snack bar where he had a tomato sandwich in brown bread and a glass of blackcurrant juice before arriving at the Stablers' shop. He walked along Pier Road, sampling the saltiness of the chill breeze which came off the North Sea and feeling the occasional sting from a grain of sand blown in the wind. Winter in Rainesbury was never a cheerful time; the holidaymakers had gone and the entertainments were closed. After the summer season, the town literally died, and it was dead now. Doors were closed, amusement arcade windows boarded up, the promenade deserted and the sea-front buildings in dire need of coats of fresh paint. The effects of sea spray were rapid and ruinous if left unchecked and these buildings would need attention before Easter. Stabler's Grocers, on the other hand, was clean and freshly painted with a defiant air of efficiency. As Mark entered the shop, a bell rang, upon which a smiling lady appeared from a curtained section at the rear.

'Can I help you?' she asked.

'I'm looking for Mr Stabler,' said Mark.

'Who are you from? Most of our reps make appointments . . .'

'Detective Superintendent Pemberton,' Mark smiled. 'I'm not selling anything. Are you Mrs Stabler?'

There was a worried look on her face as she nodded her head, then called through the curtain, 'Hugh, it's the police.'

Hugh Stabler was well over six feet tall and broadly built; he had neatly trimmed fair hair going grey at the temples and his square face with its blue eyes looked fresh, pink and healthy. Now nearing his sixtieth birthday, he had owned and run his small grocery shop in Stewart Drive, on the corner with Pier Road, since it had been left him by his own father almost forty years ago. Stabler's Grocers was almost an institution in this suburb of Rainesbury, an old-fashioned shop where personal service counted and which, even now, had defied the trend towards self-service. If you wanted something, you had to ask for it and it was obtained for you. Thus shoplifting and theft were rare on these premises.

In recent years, however, Hugh had changed, albeit in a modest way. He had expanded his range of goods to include an off-licence and a video tape library as well as small items of stationery, greetings cards and frozen foods. To achieve this, he had incorporated the old garage adjoining the shop, and now parked his car and his small delivery van behind the premises, on land purchased from next door. That expansion had been the only extension of the business this century.

Throughout the quiet but efficient running of his business, his wife, Eileen, had been his partner, assistant and bookkeeper.

She'd worked in the shop as a girl, being an assistant to Hugh's father and mother all those years ago – which was how Hugh had met her. Their married life had been one of contentment without ecstasy, and they'd had but two holidays overseas, both obtained through business contacts. They'd managed to produce a son and a daughter, yet now had but one son, Andrew; after the tragic disappearance of Helen, they had decided not to have any more children.

'Yes?' The big blond man did not smile a welcome.

'I'd like a quiet word with you,' Mark began. 'And with your wife too, if that's possible.'

They looked at one another, each wondering what the other had got involved in, then Mrs Stabler said, 'You'd better come through, superintendent.'

He was led into the tiny rear room which had a table surrounded by four dining chairs. Stabler pulled one from its position and invited Mark to be seated. Mrs Stabler went over to the counter at the side of the room, switched on the kettle which was already warm and asked if Mark would like a cup of tea or coffee.

'Coffee, please,' he said. 'Black, no sugar.'

On the wall above, Mark recognized a portrait of Helen in a Brownie uniform; he noticed that it was positioned below a crucifix. Also on the wall was a miniature ceramic piscina bearing a portrayal of the Blessed Virgin Mary. He guessed the family prayed for Helen every day . . .

'I came in person, rather than telephone you,' Mark began, and then the bell rang. Mrs Stabler abandoned the coffee-making and went to attend to the customer.

Her husband said, 'Go on, superintendent, this will happen all the time, I'm afraid. We're used to it.'

'There are two things I must tell you, Mr Stabler.' He looked steadily at the stolid man. 'We are reopening enquiries into the disappearance of your daughter and the other little girls. I know it's been a long time, but . . .'

Stabler let out a huge sigh; it was almost a sigh of relief and he allowed himself a small smile. 'We've been praying for that.' There was excitement in his voice. 'We'll help all we can, of course. Has some new information come to light? New evidence? Something to prompt you to do this?'

'I'm afraid not,' Mark had to tell him. 'But it is associated with the second piece of news. You won't be pleased to learn this, but Louisa Mary Potter is to be released from prison on Monday, on licence of course, and with the consent of the Parole Board.'

'Oh my God . . .' His face now changed. 'This is terrible news . . . I'm a Christian, superintendent, and I know all about forgiveness, but I can't feel it in my heart to forgive that woman. God knows I've tried, I've prayed for her, we've both prayed for her, but . . . well, you know . . .'

'We are led to believe she has totally reformed, Mr Stabler, and the Parole Board, after a lot of consideration, feels she deserves an opportunity to begin a new life.'

'She's not coming back here, is she?'

'No, she's been given a new identity and she will live in the south of England.' Mark had to follow the official statement for this. 'She is not regarded as a threat any more, Mr Stabler. She is now a mature woman in her fifties.'

'She's never admitted killing Helen, you know. She did it, but I wish she'd just say where she was buried, that's all, just so as we could give her a proper funeral. It's not a lot to ask, I hold no hatred for her any more.'

'Can I ask about your son? Andrew? Didn't he express his hatred of Potter?'

'He did, poor kid. He went off the rails; it was all due to the pressure of losing Helen. He works away now, he's with a paper manufacturer in Manchester on the marketing side. He's got a good job. I think he's got over his problems. He was only ten when Helen disappeared but, well, he's thirty-five now and has got the anger out of his system. He's kept out of trouble for years now, we're proud of him, the way he's rebuilt his life.'

'We might have to talk to him,' Mark said. 'We'd like to talk to everyone, I'm afraid; it'll open a lot of old wounds but I feel sure we can find those children even after all this time.'

It was a lie, and he hated himself for having to say this, but he knew he must show confidence if he was to secure the co-operation of this family and all the others.

'He won't mind, not if he knows you're trying to find Helen,' Hugh Stabler said, and then his wife returned.

'Sorry about that,' she said, going to finish making the coffee. 'So what's happened?'

Hugh Stabler gave her a calm and brief résumé of Mark's news and she smiled too; Mark noticed just a hint of a tear in her eyes as she brought his coffee over.

'I know your men have tried and tried,' she said. 'I just hope you can do something this time.'

'We've got computers now.' Mark hoped this would imply that their efforts would be extensive. 'We're going to feed all the data from the original enquiries into the computers to see if it throws up any new lines of enquiry. It will take time, of course, but we hope it will produce results. I might add that we are not necessarily trying to convict Potter all over again, we just want a solution to the problem of the missing children, that's our chief aim.'

'It would serve no purpose, sending her back to gaol,' said Mrs Stabler. 'She's been caught and she has served her sentence. I will pray forgiveness for her.'

'You are very generous,' was all Mark could think of adding.

'We are Catholics,' she said if that explained everything.

'She became a Catholic in prison,' Mark told them.

'I read it in the papers,' said Mrs Stabler. 'I do hope it was a genuine conversion, not one of convenience – and I'm unchristian by suggesting that!'

'You are realistic,' Mark said. 'But who knows? Perhaps she has had a total conversion for good. I hope she has.'

'What happens next?' asked Hugh Stabler.

'My officers started work only this morning,' Mark said. 'There will be a few days of familiarizing themselves with the material in the old files and then they'll have to log the data before we can do much else. Once we begin to analyse the old statements and the information they produce, then we might have to return to you – and the other parents – for a deeper discussion.'

The bell rang again.

'I'll go,' said Hugh Stabler.

As Mark sipped the coffee, he turned his attention to Mrs Stabler. 'Before I came here, I had a talk with Chief Superintendent Kenworthy, he's retired now, of course, and he told me you've kept Helen's room as it was.'

Mrs Stabler nodded. 'We always thought she might come back. If she did, we wanted her room to be exactly the same as it always had been and, well, the years slipped by and we never altered it. I know she won't come back now, but I can't find it in my heart to change it. Would you like to see it?'

'If it's not too painful for you.'

'No, it's not, not any more. But it does symbolize our hope that, one day, she will be found. Come along, I'll show you. Bring your coffee with you so it won't get cold.'

The room was neat and tidy with a child's size single bed covered with a colourful bedspread adorned with Disney characters. This matched the curtains, while the wallpaper bore scenes from Beatrix Potter's Peter Rabbit stories. Mark wondered if the Potter coincidence of names had occurred to the family.

He made a conscious effort to memorize every detail of the room, although Kenworthy had probably taken photographs of it at the time. The bed bore several soft toys all reclining near the pillow – a teddy bear, a kitten, a pink monkey and a nightdress case in the shape of a fluffy pink pig. The dressing table was full of childish things too, small trinkets, notebooks, a Brownie cap and some badges, a purse with pre-decimal money still inside, a school exercise book and some dried flowers.

'She made those flowers at Brownies,' her mum said with pride. 'She liked being a Brownie.'

Mark smiled and looked towards the window. It overlooked the rear of the house and shop and he saw two statues on the window sill, the sign of a Catholic household.

'She was keen on her religion?' he asked.

'Yes, she went to St Peter's Catholic Primary School, they made the faith enjoyable, fun but serious, if you can understand.'

'So who is the saint? That other statue is the Sacred Heart, isn't it?'

'Yes, and the saint is St Patrick. One of our lodgers gave it to Helen.'

'Would that be Joseph Patrick Balleen by any chance?'

'Yes, it was. You know him?'

'I knew he lodged with Miss Clayton after he left here, she told me. I've not met him, but I believe he was a friend of Louisa Mary's.'

'Yes he was, they were good friends. He was a good Catholic too, superintendent, that's how we got to know him. Through the social club at the church. When he arrived here from Ireland, he stayed in digs at the other side of town, and when we met him, at the club, we offered him a room. He stayed for a while, then went to Miss Clayton's – he'd met Louisa, they became friends. He was a nice boy, very good with our children, he helped Helen learn about the countryside for her Brownie badges and taught Andrew how to tie knots like they do in the Scouts.'

'Has he been in touch since he left?'

'No, not a word. We've never heard from him or seen him since he left.'

'Did you find that odd?' he put to her.

'Frankly, yes. Well, at first I thought it odd, but looking back, not many former lodgers did keep in touch. Some would send Christmas cards for a year or two, but he didn't even do that.'

'Did he say why he was leaving?'

'It was something important concerning his family, superintendent, but I don't know what. He went before Louisa did those awful crimes, though.'

'So I understand.'

'I wish he had kept in touch, but you know what young men are, the world's worst letter writers.'

'When I joined the police and went to live in digs, my mum nattered because I never wrote!' he laughed.

'And I natter at our Andrew for the same reason!' She smiled at him.

'Is Andrew married, by the way?' He suddenly thought of the question. 'Your husband says he works and lives in Manchester now.'

'Oh yes, he's married a lovely girl from York, they've got two children of their own now. I've a picture in the lounge if you'd like to see it.'

'Thanks,' he said, and after a final look around the quiet room, Mark followed her downstairs. The lounge contained several family portraits and snapshots in frames, and he was shown one of a tall, fair-haired man who was undoubtedly the son of Hugh Stabler.

He was standing beside a dark-haired girl and two children, a boy and a girl, stood before them.

'He's doing real well, is Andrew.' Mrs Stabler was clearly proud of her son. 'His daughter is called Helen and she's so like our Helen; they'd have been aunt and niece by now. Andrew had a tough time as a young man, perhaps you knew?'

'I talked it over with your husband,' Mark said. 'But he's got over his problems now, has he?'

'Oh, yes, totally; he loves his family and he loves his job; he's a delight now, superintendent, although I must admit we almost despaired of him at one stage.'

'One thing has just occurred to me,' Mark said as he prepared to take his leave. 'Were all Potter's victims Catholics?'

'No,' she said. 'Three of them were, our Helen, Clare Wiles and Rachel Waterhouse. Rachel's body was found, Potter was charged with killing her, but Clare was never found. The other girls weren't Catholics, they went to non-Catholic schools, but all six were friends, through Brownies. They became friends there, and played together away from Brownies, that's how she got her hands on them.'

'We never knew why she killed them,' Mark said.

'Neither did anyone. Six little playmates . . . why them? Why all six, superintendent?'

'I intend to find out,' he said. 'Now, we might have to talk again, perhaps one of my men will visit you or I might return. Thanks for your co-operation. My next call is the Wiles family.'

'Clare was Helen's best friend,' said Mrs Stabler.

9

William and Jean Wiles lived on a vast council estate to the west of Rainesbury and as Mark drove between the rows of old cars and unkempt gardens he became aware of hostile looks. Small scruffy children stared at the smart man in the well-groomed car, doubtless having been trained by parents to look out for men who might be debt collectors, bailiffs, income tax men, council officials and anyone else with a formal role to play or money to collect, and that included plain-clothes police officers. Adults stared too, some standing morosely on street corners and others peering through curtainless windows as they pondered upon which of their number was to receive a visit from this official-looking man in the smart car.

Mark knew the estate well; he also knew some of its inhabitants because, in the past, he'd been here while making crime enquiries. This was no inner city estate however; there were no tower blocks and concrete jungles because the well-constructed semi-detached houses were neatly arranged in sweeping crescents on a hillside site. It overlooked Rainesbury Bay well over a mile away and the views from some of the houses were stunning – as a private estate, the sites would have commanded high prices and the resultant homes would have housed well-heeled occupants, but few of the present residents seemed to appreciate the benefits of their superb location.

Many of the gardens were unkempt and filled with the detritus of ill-disciplined people – old prams, cookers, settees and chairs, litter, plastic bags, bottles and beer cans; all of this and more had been deposited on lawns whose grass had never seen a mower, while many houses were in need of a coat of paint and the services of a competent window cleaner. The place was like a gigantic rubbish tip. Mark, the epitome of tidiness, felt sad that people allowed themselves to descend to such depths when so much had been done for them. From his long police experience, he knew they would never learn better behaviour and he could guess what the interiors of these houses were like. He'd been in several . . .

But not every house was in such a state of neglect or despair. Some were beautifully maintained and well furnished, and he wondered how they could maintain their own living standards among such squalor. It was akin to a badger, the cleanest of animals, having to live in a pigsty . . .

As he pulled up outside 42 Crompton Road, he found himself looking at a smart, tidy garden with clipped hedges and neat footpaths, while the front door to the house was clean and nicely painted. Two tiny children on battered old metal trikes stopped their race along the footpath and watched him leave the car; he wondered if they would vandalize it or snap the aerial and did not tempt fate by looking back as he went to the front door.

When there was no reply, one of the children yelled, 'He'll be in his shed round the back, mister.'

'Thanks,' smiled Mark, who then went along the passage at the side of the house and found himself crossing a well-tended back garden with a large vegetable patch. Now, in winter, it was almost empty save for a few Brussels sprouts and cauliflowers. There was a large wooden shed at the bottom and a light brightened its only window. Mark went towards the door and knocked. It opened outwards and a shirt-sleeved man in his early sixties stood before him. He had dark, thinning hair, a heavy moustache, horn-rimmed spectacles and a rather gaunt, sallow complexion; he was dressed in overalls and his demeanour was that of a man who worked with his hands.

'Yes?' he demanded.

'Mr Wiles? William Wiles?'

'Who wants to know?' asked the man, suspicious of smart, official-looking men.

'I do. Detective Superintendent Pemberton.'

'I've done nothing wrong, mister, and I know nothing.'

'You are touchy, Mr Wiles! Can I come in? I want a chat, but not out here.'

Already, Mark could see two female faces, their hair still in curlers, peering from behind the curtains at two separate kitchen windows across the garden, people watching the mysterious visitor to number 42. Wiles retreated into his shed and Mark followed, closing the door.

Inside, it was cosy and snug, with an electric heater throwing out waves of warmth. There was an old dining chair minus its back rest and this served as a stool; Wiles pointed to it and Mark sat down. His trained eye absorbed the flavour of the shed. It was a workshop full of electrical equipment, some new and some old, with several items in various states of repair lying among other pieces which were untouched as they awaited the skills of Bill Wiles.

'You look busy,' said Mark, eyeing the plethora of goods. Tools had been neatly arranged along the walls; he noticed a soldering iron, clippers, plugs, fuses and wiring charts.

'Keeps me occupied,' acknowledged Wiles. 'They made me redundant six months back. I earn a quid or two doing repairs, fixing things. There's no law against that.'

'I'm not here to harass you, Mr Wiles.' Mark tried to convince him. 'I'm here to give you some information and to ask for some help.'

'Help? Me help the law?' There was scorn in his reply.

'Louisa Mary Potter.' Mark spoke the name with deliberation. 'She's been given parole, she comes out next Monday.'

Wiles sat down on the edge of his bench. 'God, that's all I need! First redundancy, now this.'

'The Parole Board's let her out on licence. She'll be living in the south of England, under an assumed name. We don't regard her as a danger any more.'

'She killed my bairn, Mr Pemberton, you know that. They've never found her neither, nor the other two.'

'That's the other reason I'm here. I want you to know that we're reopening enquiries into the disappearance of your Clare, as well as Helen Stabler and Suzanne Hayes.'

'Well, I suppose that's good news, although it seems odd after all this time. They've tried before and got nowhere. I can't see you getting anywhere after all this time, but I do appreciate you trying. If you do find the bairns, it'll mean she stands trial again, will it, and goes down for another stretch?'

'That depends on all sorts of things, Mr Wiles. The DPP – the Director of Public Prosecutions – will have to decide whether or not we prosecute, even if we do find enough evidence to justify a trial – and that could be very difficult after such a length of time. But I just wanted you to know, from me, what's happening. Our men might want to come for a chat with you and Mrs Wiles. We'll have to re-read your old statements and see if there are any new lines of enquiry.'

'Well, yes, I'll help. I don't normally help the law – you don't, living in a dump of an estate like this. Help the law here and you're cut dead, like scabs in a strike. Bloody strange people, I'll tell you. But this is different, isn't it?'

'It is, but you're not helping the law, Mr Wiles, you're helping yourself and you're helping the others who suffered like you. The police are just the middlemen in all this.'

'You've told the others?'

'Just the Stablers so far. We are telling them all. I believe the Hayes family have gone overseas.'

'Australia. They couldn't face living here, not knowing where their Suzanne was buried. You'll be telling them?'

'We'll have them told by their local police force,' Mark assured him. 'Now, while I'm here, does the name Balleen mean anything to you? Joseph Patrick.'

'He was that Irishman that lived at the Stablers' for a bit, eh?'

'You knew him?'

'Not really. When our Clare went to Brownies, she called for Helen Stabler at the shop and they walked around to the Brownie hut together. It was the Scout hut they used. Sometimes that Irishman was there. He was only a lad but he was good with kids, boys and girls; he could get on with them, unusual for a lad of that age, but he came from a big family himself and showed the kids tricks with things, bits of string, how to light fires and cook sausages, make whistles out of hazel sticks, dinner forks out of bits of wood, secret signs, animal tracking, trail laying, all Scouty sort of things.'

'He was a Catholic, I'm told, and first met the Stablers through the church social club.'

'We're Catholics, well, in name. We don't practise now, not after the farce of Vatican II which turned us all into bloody Protestants. Clare always went to Mass, made her first confession and first holy communion and we supported her by going to Mass with her . . . but since she died, well, there seemed no point in it any more. Mebbe we'll resume when we get older, before we head for our great garden shed in the sky, eh?' and he laughed. It was a bitter laugh, devoid of humour.

'You've no other children?'

'No, Jean, that's my wife, couldn't produce any more. She works now, at Barlow's Estate Agents, helps us pay the rent and keep ourselves in clothes. I'll never get a new job at my age, Mr Pemberton, so I do odd jobs. Funnily enough, I never saw myself being self-employed yet here I am, and I enjoy it, doing things my own way, in my own time. It's good, I keep busy.'

'Can I ask what are your feelings towards Potter, especially now that she's being released?'

'Feelings? Nothing really. I don't hate her, if that's what you're suggesting. No, I don't, not now. I did then, when it happened, and I just want our Clare found, nothing more. I don't want revenge, not after all this time, and if that woman's served her time and it's reformed her, well, I'm not one for wanting her back inside. Maybe it's my Christian upbringing, being taught forgiveness and all that, or maybe I'm just getting old enough to know that folks can make mistakes and can change.'

'You're very generous.'

'Well, that bitch that killed them bairns was only a lass, now she'll be a grown woman, old enough to be a granny. She'll have learned a lot now, wisdom, forgiveness, compassion. She'll never do the likes of that again, even if she does come out.'

'And Mrs Wiles? How's she feel? Any idea?'

'The same, Mr Pemberton. We used to talk it through for hours on end, coming to terms. It took a long time, Jean not being able to have more children, but she's got on with her life and she's closed the door on Potter's crimes. We don't keep Clare's room as a shrine, not like the Stablers do, we couldn't cope with that. It's over, that's our attitude, finished. Talk to her if you want, she'll be in the office.'

'Later perhaps. One of my officers might want a chat once we've delved into the files. Anyway, I won't keep you any more, Mr Wiles, thanks for talking to me.' Mark rose and prepared to leave. 'We might want another chat, depending on what we discover.'

'Feel free,' said his host, opening the door. 'I just hope we can find those lasses even if it does make us all weep.'

'Thanks,' and Mark let himself out, closing the door to retain the heat that Wiles had so carefully nurtured. The curtains on several neighbouring windows fluttered and Mark smiled.

Everyone on an estate like this knew everyone else's business, but if the police called to ask if they'd seen anything, they always said they hadn't; they'd seen nothing and they knew nothing . . . unless they wanted revenge on a neighbour. Council estate culture was a study in itself.

The only other victim's family still living in Rainesbury were the Hallidays, parents of Tracy for whose death Potter had been convicted. Mark drove to the outskirts, through rows of select, executive-style houses as they were known, and found himself in Beehive Lane seeking Ashdale Cottage. It was a large stone house of imposing appearance, more of a mansion than a cottage, and there was a small blue Fiat parked in the drive. He looked at his watch. Three thirty, teatime perhaps, for the lady of the house?

The chimes brought an elegant, smartly dressed woman to the door and it was evident she had just returned from the hairdresser's. The perfume wafted about her as she smiled at the smart gentleman on her doorstep.

'Yes?' She inclined her head, probably expecting him to launch into a sales routine for something like double-glazing or encyclopedias.

'Mrs Halliday? Una Halliday?'

'Yes?' The head inclined again, waiting.

'Detective Superintendent Pemberton,' and he showed his warrant card.

'Oh dear, is it something to do with Eric? He's not in trouble, is he?'

'Eric?'

'My husband . . . in his business, he's a bookmaker, you know, turf accountant, well, people with accounts tend not to pay on time and if the bank's pressing us, he presses them. He can be a bit heavy-handed when he goes after slow payers . . .' She grinned sheepishly. 'I just wondered if there'd been a complaint.'

'Not to my knowledge. It's not about that,' he told her. 'It's about Louisa Mary Potter.'

'Oh, God, not her again! She never goes away, that woman, she's always plaguing us . . . always there . . . wherever we go, whoever we talk to about Tracy . . . You'd better come in, I was just putting the kettle on. I've just come in – hairdresser, you know,' and she stroked her new hairdo.

Mark said it looked nice as he followed her into the splendid house. She led him into the fitted kitchen. Pointing to a high stool at the counter, she asked him to get two mugs off the shelf while she boiled the kettle. He obeyed, she was that sort of woman. As she prepared the tea, she chattered about the problems of coping with her daughter's death, with people always asking about it, always showing concern when all she and Eric wanted was to forget about it . . .

'So,' she said eventually, settling at his side, 'what's happened to bring you here today, superintendent?'

'Potter is being released on licence on Monday,' he explained. 'I wanted you and your husband to know before the news is made public.'

'Well, I suppose she had to come out sometime, I did read she's a reformed character, whatever that means.'

'The second thing, Mrs Halliday, is that we are reopening enquiries into the three girls who are still recorded as missing. Our officers will be starting their investigations early next week and we might want to talk to you and your husband, I'm afraid. It could open old wounds. I wanted to tell you what was happening.'

'Our case was closed, superintendent. They found Tracy.'

'I know, but three others are still unaccounted for, we need to explore every avenue.'

'I fail to see the point after all this time – you'll only stir up memories that need to be left alone, and surely if you can prove she killed the other girls, they'll not incarcerate her all over again, will they?'

'That's a matter for the DPP, Mrs Halliday. We just want to have one final attempt at finding those missing children, by using modern and very sophisticated techniques.'

'Well, if you must, but I know if I had my way, I'd say let things remain, leave things alone, don't go stirring up trouble, not now.'

'What are your feelings about Potter?' he asked her as they enjoyed the tea.

Mrs Halliday was an attractive woman, he realized, although she must now be in her fifties. She looked younger, her hair was blonde and beautifully coiffeured, her skin looked fresh and youthful, her clothes were expensive and there was clearly money in the household. In spite of Eric's financial worries, he seemed capable of making a good living, and his wife was not a brassy woman. She had real style.

'When Tracy was killed, I was devastated. We'd tried for years to have a child, you see, and Tracy was everything to us, a late arrival. You can imagine how I felt about Potter, taking her away from us like that. I'd have disembowelled her alive if I'd had the chance, Eric would too. He was mad; I think if she hadn't been put away, he'd have killed her, he's got quite a temper when he's roused. But now, well, we've mellowed. We still remember Tracy as she was, a happy, lovely little girl and we've often thought we had some lovely times with her, and through her. Fun times, happy memorable times. But she could have died another way, she could have had an accident on her bike, or a car might have knocked her down or she might have got a disease ... Fate is cruel, superintendent, so we are now resigned to a life without her, but one with happy memories. We remember her how she was, a lovely girl.'

'You've kept her room unchanged, I was told.'

'My, you have done your homework! We did keep it like that for a while, but it's changed now, superintendent.'

'Mr Kenworthy's notes said ...'

'Yes, well, we did keep it unchanged for a lot of years, perhaps hoping she might suddenly return home, but, well, she's not a little girl now. Even if she did return, she'd be a woman in her thirties and I might not even know her ... so we changed the room on her thirtieth birthday. Everything went. I cried, but it did me good. It was almost as if we had exorcized her ghost. Eric was marvellous throughout, a real tower of strength. He's forgiven Potter now, I have too, I think. Time is a strange healer. I feel whole again, I've no wish to harm that woman, not now. She needed help, I hope she got it.'

'You're not Catholics, are you?'

'Us? No, we're not. Is that important?'

'Some of the victims were, and their parents have found solace in their faith. And the name of a Catholic youth has surfaced in my enquiries. Balleen. Joseph Patrick. Does it mean anything to you?'

'I knew about him, from the other parents,' she said. 'But I never met him.'

Mark explained in detail Balleen's links with the enquiries and Mrs Halliday confirmed that Tracy had been in the Brownies along with the other victims; sometimes, the Brownies had their meetings in the Hallidays' large garden, but she could not recall Balleen ever attending. Potter had come, however, sometimes, with Brown Owl.

Mrs Halliday could not help much, but as Mark left the house, he felt that his day's visit to Rainesbury had been successful even if it had been little more than a public relations exercise. He had found no new evidence nor had he really sought it, but of some importance was the fact that he had not found any hint of threats against Potter; indeed, he had encountered a definite aura of forgiveness which appeared to run contrary to the warning supplied by the anonymous informer.

One mystery was the Irishman, Joseph Patrick Balleen. Mark hoped the fellow wasn't going to become an obsession, but the name had surfaced several times today and it did seem odd that he had never kept in touch with his friends in Rainesbury. If he was such a nice young man, why had he not maintained contact?

Already, Mark had actions which would engage his small team and he began to sing to himself as he drove back to the incident room. One priority was to find Balleen, and he began to wonder just what had transpired between that man and Potter. Had he done something which had triggered off her violence towards the children or was Balleen now waiting in the shadows to wreak his own revenge upon her?

10

Mark wondered whether he would return to the incident room before his officers finished for the day. They were entitled to go home on time, but as he drove into the parking area at twenty past five, he was pleased to see the lights of Room 207 still ablaze. Inside, he found a buzz of activity with the place now fully operational. Three blackboards dominated the wall at the far end, each containing details of one of the missing girls. There were photographs too, enlarged and enhanced from 1967 negatives; they depicted the children, the moorland areas where searches had already been concluded, and objects found in earlier searches which might or might not be relevant. There were also pictures of the three girls whose bodies had been found, and a 1967 portrait of Louisa Mary Potter.

Maps of the original search areas had been located and were displayed on another wall, the areas ringed in red being the graves of Rachel Waterhouse, Tracy Halliday and Michele Brown. Areas searched for the other children were also marked, this time in green. He was pleased to find that a separate map indicated Rosebay Avenue in Swandale where Hicks would be resident; the surrounding countryside had been ringed and he knew that Larkin would despatch a team to make a survey of the land from a security aspect.

Natural cover or sniping positions would be identified, whether they consisted of old barns, quarries or dense woodland.

In the body of the room, VDUs flickered upon desks piled high with photocopies of statement forms; a glass cabinet, secured from the Force Museum, contained artefacts which had been used as evidence in the original trial; and as Mark walked through the assembled officers and equipment, the entire surroundings oozed an aura of efficiency. He experienced a feeling of contentment; already, the room bore the atmosphere of a realistic murder investigation and he knew that each of these officers had the necessary commitment.

That was why they had not gone home at five o'clock.

He banged an ashtray upon his desk and called for silence.

'It's gone five,' he reminded them. 'No one's asking you to work overtime on this one.'

'The job's got to be done, sir,' smiled one of the detective constables. 'We'll go when we've finished what we're doing – and we won't claim overtime.'

'Thanks.' Mark spread his hands in a gesture of warmth towards them. 'I'm in your capable hands. Now, before I settle down, I'll tell you what I've done this afternoon.'

They ceased their activities for the moment as he moved behind the table he'd earmarked as his own.

'Barbara, can you take it down in shorthand?'

She hurried to find a notebook and settled at the end of his table as he began to outline what had happened both in Rainesbury and at the safe house. Experienced in this kind of detailed work, she noted everything. She would type up his report, photocopy it and make sure copies were placed in the general files for everyone to read. Everything in this room, everything that was said, every interview and every piece of information had to be readily available to every detective . . . Sometimes this was best achieved on paper, and sometimes it was wise to record it as computer data; sometimes it was logged in both media. When he'd finished his address, he told his officers that there were certain actions that now required their attention.

'Paul,' he addressed Larkin, 'make a note of these and allocate them tomorrow. Action: trace, interview and eliminate Joseph Patrick Balleen. See if HOLMES throws up any more references to him from the old enquiry. Action: trace the movements of all six little girls for at least a month before their disappearance. Establish, where possible, those occasions they had all been together, for example at school, at church, at Brownies, birthday parties or whatever. If we can't place them all together, try to establish other group contacts in say threes, fours or fives giving dates, times and places. Action: establish the precise timing of Balleen's return to Ireland and also establish the precise timing of the disappearance of each girl – this should be easy, our records will already show that. Action: trace and inform the Waterhouse family of Potter's release and our reopening of enquiries – they're living in Scotland. Action: do likewise for Margaret Brown, mother of Michele. Potter was convicted of Michele's murder. Mrs Brown's husband, John, died afterwards and she is now living in Middlesbrough; she's now Mrs Harper. Address not known. The electoral register might be a start. Action: do likewise for Brian and Jean Hayes, parents of Suzanne. They live in Sydney, Australia, so get the local Australian police to check them out, and establish that they are still living there. Action: in all cases where parents or families are interviewed, establish their current feelings towards Potter, especially in the light of her impending freedom. Action: trace and interview Andrew Stabler, brother of Helen, now married and living in Manchester. So, that's enough for now. Other actions will arise as the statements are read and as interviews are made. Now, any questions?'

'Sir,' asked Woman Detective Constable Lorraine Cashmore, 'will anyone be interviewing Kathleen Hicks? If she was a friend of Potter, Potter might have confided in her, about the disposal of the other children. Prisoner's confidences, that sort of thing.'

'Thanks, Lorraine. We've got to be careful in our dealings with Kathleen Hicks.' Mark spoke quietly. 'I'd like to have her interviewed, but I think I'll wait to see what our other avenues produce first. Can we keep her in reserve? But Paul, make a note that Hicks will have to be seen in due course, that's an action for a volunteer, I guess. Or the boss! Or both.'

There followed a few more questions about his impressions of the parents to whom he had spoken, and he referred to the atmosphere of forgiveness he had already discovered. He told how they were not ecstatic about the missing children case being reopened but that he'd not encountered any open hostility. His visit had produced one more action – it would be necessary to interview Eric Halliday, the bookie who would forcefully press his customers for payment. His views on Potter might be worthy of closer examination. Larkin made due note to arrange an action which delved into his background, with particular emphasis upon his violent streak.

'Right,' said Mark. 'It's six o'clock, I'm going home. Remember what they say about all work and no play . . .'

He knew that his departure would encourage the others to go home too, for he had no wish to pressure them, however unintentionally, into working late into the night. As he prepared to leave, Barbara, with one of her beautiful smiles, presented him with a thick file of photocopied statements.

'There's lots more to come,' she told him almost apologetically. 'But this is just to keep you busy tonight!'

'I do love a spot of light reading in front of the fire!' He smiled with mock regret. 'But thanks.'

He had been tempted to have his supper in the canteen but decided to leave the premises as a means of showing his men that he did not require them to show their loyalty by staying at work. He went home, lit his fire, washed, changed and made himself dinner. Tonight's reading would be the file given to him by Barbara but there was a lot of thinking ahead too.

When Mark arrived at the incident room on Thursday morning, there was a note from Paul Larkin asking him to report to the Chief Constable at 9.30 a.m. He therefore delayed the morning conference until after that meeting and occupied the waiting minutes by chatting to D/C Young, the programmer of HOLMES.

'Anything of interest turned up yet, Duncan?' he asked.

'We've only processed a fraction of the entire statements, sir, so nothing of real significance has emerged. I did run a check on Balleen's name, though, after your talk last night. He shows up in some of the parents' statements, coming over as a friend of the girls. I've logged the references. There's never a question of him harming them, none of this child abuse that's so prevalent now, but he did join in their games a lot. It seems he was very much a family man, good with young children.'

Mark responded, 'Last night, I read a transcript of Kenworthy's interview of Potter and she mentioned him.'

'Yes, she did, but only when pressed, sir; we've several statements from her, some prior to her arrest when we were at the investigation stage, and the major one after she'd been arrested on suspicion of the Halliday murder. It was Mr Kenworthy who asked her about Balleen. He knew about Balleen through his enquiries at the lodging house, Miss Clayton's place, and wanted to get him out of the frame. There's some suspicion he was raiding banks and building societies.'

'Yes, Kenworthy told me. I think we should dig very deep to learn as much as we can about this Irishman, Duncan. Are we sure he did go back to Ireland and if so, when?'

'He left his digs on 6 February and sailed to Ireland on 10 February 1967. Mr Kenworthy got a copy of his ticket from the ferry office at Holyhead. He booked on the ferry to Dublin, as a walking passenger, a single ticket. No car or motor bike accompanied him. There is no record of a return ticket being issued. He was out of the country a week before the first child went missing. The first to be reported missing was Michele Brown. Her mother rang Rainesbury Police at six o'clock on the evening of 17 February 1967.

'She reported that Michele hadn't come home from school. I've looked at Mr Kenworthy's statement of evidence; in it, he says that several sources confirmed that Balleen was out of the country a week before the first murder. Kenworthy didn't put him in the frame at all and there was no evidence that he'd been involved in the murders. The overwhelming evidence showed only one person was responsible.'

'Was Balleen ever interviewed about the murders, Duncan?'

'No, sir, enquiries were made at his home address, and his parents claimed they hadn't seen him. They maintained he was still in England; he was never traced, and so he was never interviewed. There is nothing in our files to show whether he ever did return home, but there was no trace of him in and around Rainesbury, or in England even, after the crimes.'

'That's bloody odd, isn't it? If I'd been in charge, I'd have been wanting that man found. He could well have been in England the whole time, which means he could have been implicated, he could even have killed the other three children. It's easy to buy a ferry ticket and not use it, that's an alibi of sorts and as there was no return ticket, it's possible he never even went. If that was the case, where was he? Where is he now? We need to find him, high priority.'

'Yes, sir. There is an action for that.'

'Thanks. Well, I'd best be off to the Upper Floor to see what the Chief wants.'

'Good morning, Mark.' Charles Moore was in an affable mood as he waved Mark to a chair. 'I thought I'd have a word about progress in the Hicks affair. What have you to report so far?'

For the second time that morning, Mark related current developments and Moore listened calmly, sometimes asking the occasional question. He appeared very satisfied with the way things were progressing.

'So, Mark, is anything bothering you at this stage?'

'One niggle has arisen, sir,' Mark decided to inform his boss. 'My own belief, from talking to the parents, is that there is no open hatred by the victims' parents against Potter; it's gone, evaporated, expired, certainly among those still living in Rainesbury. I was wondering if you had any more information about the supposed plan to kill her? How genuine is it? It had come, so your informant said, from Rainesbury, possibly from one or other of the parents or relations. My enquiries, shallow though they are at this stage, don't support that.'

'I was given information by MI5, Mark; they'd picked it up in town and passed it on. They heard it in Rainesbury, in the Smugglers' Arms on the sea-front, and passed it to us because they felt it was genuine. There is a real threat, Mark, make no mistake, even if we're not sure where it's coming from.'

'Sir, have we access to the source?'

'Not the source, Mark, but I do have access to the MI5 officer who overheard it.'

'I need to trace and interview the source, sir, I need a description along with date, time and place. If I get that from MI5, I can put a team into Rainesbury to trace him. And while we're talking about MI5, can I ask if the name of Joseph Patrick Balleen is relevant in all this? He's an Irishman who came here in the mid-sixties, a youngster, no criminal record but suspected of bank raids here; he seems to have vanished. I want to delve into his life a little more, if only to eliminate him. He might want revenge on Potter.'

'You might have zoomed into the right man, Mark,' smiled Moore. 'I'll ring now, wait there.'

Moore dialled a number from his secure telephone and said, 'Moore here.'

There was a short pause and he continued, 'I've got my Detective Superintendent Pemberton with me, on the Hicks business,' and Moore then explained the situation as Mark had described it, finally raising the question about the authenticity of the supposed threats to Potter/Hicks.

In return, he had to listen and Mark watched him nod from time to time. Eventually, he said, 'Fine, thanks. I'll tell him.'

After replacing the handset, Moore said, 'The threat is genuine, Mark, as I said. And it did come from Rainesbury. The conversation in question was overheard in the Smugglers' Arms at lunchtime, about one thirtyish last Sunday, the day before I called you in. Two men were talking in a carrel, behind a partition. Carrel number four. But we have no description of the speakers. The threat-maker may not be from one of the families – that, I think, was speculation – but was definitely someone in that town. It is being taken seriously enough to justify the exercise you are engaged upon, Mark. And the name of Balleen is significant – his family, who live in southern Ireland, are IRA supporters and have been for years. They were supporters when he was in England. Joseph Patrick's whereabouts are unknown; he's not been seen by anyone, not even his family, so they say, since he left here in 1967. So, there you are. Somebody in Rainesbury is gunning for Louisa Mary Potter. If it's not one of the victims' relations, then who is it? It's down to you, Mark, it's your job to stop him.'

'Yes, sir,' said Mark Pemberton.

11

Mark's brief meeting with the Chief Constable reinforced his belief that the answer to his questions lay in Rainesbury. The Security Service, which until recently had not involved itself with intelligence matters relating to the IRA, wouldn't have passed on the information if they'd not considered it genuine. What was required now was a team of detectives with a thorough knowledge of the criminal classes in Rainesbury; he knew just the men.

When he returned to the incident room and assembled his officers, he said, 'I've just come from the Chief and there's one or two actions to establish before I outline developments. So, Paul, can you fix these? Action: we need to locate Louisa Mary Potter's brothers and sisters; they lived in Derby when she was nicked. Trace, interrogate and eliminate each of them. Establish their whereabouts and their attitude towards her. Action: we need to find out more about Balleen when he was working in Rainesbury – second-hand car dealings, involvement in crime, bank raids and so on, more about his job, any friends he made. Old Mr Kenworthy might be able to help in that.'

He next explained how the MI5 contact had overheard the conversation in the Smugglers' Arms and how that incidental chat had found its way to this incident room.

He also aired his view that it was odd that the threat should surface at this particular time; could the threat have come from someone with whom Potter was associated, perhaps in prison, someone in whom she might have confided? Someone who knew she was about to be released? Or was it merely a loud-mouthed braggart with no intention of doing anything?

'Detective Sergeant Agar and D/C Holdsworth?' As Mark mentioned their names, he sought the two officers among their colleagues. Each raised a hand.

'Sir?' one of them asked.

'You know the town well; you know the villains, don't you? Winkle out their secrets. Your time on Regional Crime Squad should be useful. Have you any good contacts there now?'

Derek Holdsworth, long-haired, scruffy and unorthodox, nodded. 'Yes, I've some useful snouts there, sir, and I'm not known as the fuzz.'

'The same applies to me,' agreed Agar.

Mark knew their work. Each man had been in the Drugs Squad too and was accustomed to undercover work. Holdsworth in particular was the last man on earth, judging by his appearance, that anyone would associate with the police service. He looked more like a gypsy or a scrap-metal dealer than a police officer and had enjoyed a lot of success in undercover operations; not even members of the local force knew who he was. He was ideal to probe beneath the less savoury surface of Rainesbury.

'Good, then we need to use your acquired knowledge. I want the pair of you to concentrate on Rainesbury, leave the other aspects to the rest of us. I'd have given you more teams but we've a limited number as you know. Now, this is a double-barrelled action. First, I want you to find the man who was overheard in the Smugglers' Arms last Sunday, around lunchtime. See if the landlord can help. We need to link him or them to Potter or Hicks, or to the victims' families or to the old crimes, and we need to know exactly what they're up to. Is it known that Hicks and Potter are about to be released? If so, how? Why issue the threat at this time, only days before the release dates? How will the threat be carried out? We might have to put a watch on the prison gates when the women emerge . . . so that's one of your actions. And while you are getting under the skin of the Rainesbury people, I want you to carry out the second action. I want you to ferret out as much information as you can about Joseph Patrick Balleen's second-hand car dealings, bank raids and so on. Find the criminal side of him.'

'Is there much in the old files, sir?' asked Agar.

'A little but not enough. The murder file doesn't seem to say much about his criminal activities. Kenworthy might have something more; I intend seeing him this morning so I'll pass on what I get out of him. Make sure everything you learn is logged into all our systems; report here each morning to update us at morning conference.'

'I understand,' said Agar.

'Good. Now it's my belief that we have a mystery man in Balleen, particularly as his family has links with the IRA –

although, at this stage, I fail to see what the IRA or any terrorist unit has to do with Potter or her release. But violence is threatened and there is something nasty in the wind. Balleen's not been seen in this country for more than twenty-five years so he could be a grey-haired old bugger now, but shortly before the killings, he was associating with both Potter and some of her victims. Kenworthy cleared him, he said Balleen wasn't in the frame for the murders. Well, perhaps not, but *I'm* interested in him and I need to know more about him. I have some brief details but', and he addressed this remark to Paul Larkin, 'I want good men put on to Balleen's background, on to his life away from Rainesbury. Liaise with Jim and Derek. We know his home was in Wexford in Eire so it'll mean enquiries through the Garda Siochana in Dublin. Be careful there, establish a safe contact before you start ringing up. Wexford has a divisional headquarters so you could make contact direct, rather than through Phoenix Park. I don't want the whole of Eire to know we're interested in Balleen. Don't underestimate him either, he could be our lurking assassin. Watch yourselves at all times, be always on your guard. So, this is a good action, plenty of meat in it. I'll be doing my own investigating of him too, so liaison between us all is vital.'

'Sir,' acknowledged Detective Sergeant Agar on behalf of himself and his colleague.

'And now, Tony Ashton?'

Detective Sergeant Ashton raised his hand. 'Here, sir.'

'Today, Tony, immediately after this conference, I want you to visit Mrs Dawson at our safe house in Swandale. She's an ex-prison matron. As our firearms tactician, I want you to examine the house and its surroundings, get to know it thoroughly inside and out in case we need to stage any kind of operation – siege, rescue, armed guard duties, security check or whatever. Log the outlying ground too, for cover, sniping positions and so on. We might even have to live there, some of us. Mrs Dawson has been alerted to something of this nature, so make yourself known to her. And later, if you take a team there, make them known to her. Draw up a contingency plan for me, one which ensures Hicks' safety. Confer with me over the details if you need to. OK? I want our plans finalized before Hicks is released.'

'Fine, sir,' acknowledged the sergeant.

Apart from those specific tasks, the day ahead for the rest of the officers meant further boring perusal of the old files and the abstraction of data, but the matters already highlighted did serve to add some sparkle to their duties.

After answering several routine questions, Mark said, 'Now, Jim Agar and Derek Holdsworth, I'd like a chat before you vanish in darkest Rainesbury. Come into my office.'

As there were no questions from the floor, he said, 'OK, folks, conference dismissed. Back to work! D/I Larkin will sort out the details for today's actions and some further ones I'm sure he needs to allocate. See him about any expenses.'

In his office, Mark told Agar and Holdsworth everything that he had gleaned about Balleen and suggested that, in addition to their own enquiries, they speak to the victims' families and to Miss Clayton.

'I'm going to Rainesbury,' he concluded. 'I'm going to talk to the Country and Coast Bank to see if I can find out more about the account Balleen jointly held with Potter. I also want to know about the finances of his car dealings. You stir up the underclass, get them restless, get them edgy, get them talking. If they think they're involved in a murder enquiry they'll co-operate. I'll be on radio if I need to chat with you there. Call me if you need anything. OK? And if I'm there at lunchtime, I might even buy you a pint apiece!'

'You're on, boss!' grinned Holdsworth whose idea of heaven was a pint of Guinness and an open prawn sandwich for lunch.

When they left to go about their actions, Mark had a word with Paul Larkin who cheerfully confirmed that he was completely *au fait* with his role and so Mark said,

'Fine, I'll leave you to it, Paul. I'm off to see Mr Kenworthy first, if he's in, and then I'm going over to Rainesbury. I'll be on the air if you need me.'

'Understood, sir,' and so Mark collected his briefcase, opened it to retrieve a clothes brush with which he tidied his suit, and then left the incident room.

Adrian Kenworthy was delighted to see Mark again and when Mrs Kenworthy showed him into the lounge, he found the cheerful old detective surrounded by his notebooks, all in their red leather bindings.

'Ah, Mark, come in, lovely to see you again.'

'I'm sorry I didn't ring beforehand . . .'

'Nonsense, there's no need. Now, like I promised, I've found all my old pocket-books, they're the ones containing my notes on the Rainesbury Murders. Take them with you. Get your statement readers to go through them, they might find something in these, something useful they can put into the computers.'

'Thanks, they'll be invaluable.' Mark spoke the truth.

He flicked open one book handed to him by Kenworthy and found it compiled in a neat and tidy handwriting, with names, dates and places underlined in red with a summary and an index of names at the end of each day's entries. 'This is marvellous . . . I'll bring them back when we've gone through them.'

'No rush,' said Kenworthy. 'Anyway, Alice will bring some coffee in a minute, black of course, so what's the reason for this visit?'

'Balleen,' said Mark. 'Joseph Patrick Balleen. His name cropped up when I was talking to the parents of Helen Stabler and Clare Wiles, and also when I was talking to Miss Clayton. He was on the fringes of the enquiry, Mr Kenworthy, and in modern investigations, he'd have been firmly in the frame until he was positively eliminated. You didn't chase him up? He was never interviewed in depth before he was formally eliminated, was he?'

'No, I was satisfied he'd left town before the first girl disappeared. On top of that, I was totally sure that only Potter had been involved in the killings, Forensic backed me on that. So it would have been superfluous to have pursued Balleen when we had no real cause. Circumstantial evidence did tell us he'd gone. We got a copy of his ferry ticket, then his digs, his work mates and his drinking pals all confirmed he'd gone. I did try, through the Garda, to establish that he had returned to Ireland, but we got very little response. We were told that his parents thought he was still in England, but I understand they'd been told not to cooperate with the British police. They were IRA sympathizers, his parents, you know that?'

'I know,' Mark said. 'That makes it all the more interesting now. He is in my frame, Mr Kenworthy, as a possible potential attacker of Potter. I need to find him so that I can eliminate him from this enquiry. You made notes of his contacts?'

'Yes, it's all in those books, his pals over here, his firm's name, where he worked on building sites, my notebooks have got it all.'

'Thanks. Now, was he ever listed as a missing person?' asked Mark.

'No, in our country he wasn't regarded as missing, was he? He'd gone home. In Eire, he might have been reported missing, but his family never did so.'

'You must have had your suspicions about why?'

Kenworthy smiled. 'I had served in the Special Branch, Mark. Balleen had all the hallmarks of an IRA operator in this country. He was what's known as a lilywhite – they're young fanatics with no criminal record who are used for terrorist activities. Balleen was such a person, a lilywhite. He had no criminal record, he had charming manners, an affable character, he seemed easy to trust and to get on with. Everyone who knew him said that. My own opinion, although I could never prove it, was that he was a member of an active service unit over here. When he left here but wasn't seen in Ireland, I thought he'd gone somewhere else in England to undertake bombings or such work, but he was never found. We found no evidence to link him with other attacks in the UK. His parents, I suspect, considered him to be on active service and so they were never concerned about his long absences. But we never found anything to prove or disprove our beliefs. Nothing at all. He was clean and all who knew him here said what a lovely lad he was.'

'Yet you remain convinced he was here for some ulterior purpose?'

'Oh, yes, I was sure of it. He was sending money to Ireland, ostensibly for his family. I wondered if he was sending funds to the IRA – I could never prove a damned thing, Mark. Once, when I asked about the money, he said he earned it from selling cars and was sending it to his parents to help out with family commitments. I told you we suspected him of robberies? He could have been staging those for the benefit of the IRA, that was a common practice.'

'Did you keep him out of the limelight for that reason? So that deeper enquiries could be made?'

'Yes, I must say that was a factor. I do know the Special Branch was interested in him, they'd clocked him into England when he arrived and I do know they were keeping tabs on him. Without specific evidence against him, we wanted to keep him in a low profile so we could continue to observe his movements.'

'How can I get access to the necessary files, Mr Kenworthy?'

'I think your Chief might have to do that for you. Security won't have a lot, but your Special Branch might.'

'Thanks, I'll ask him to dig out what he can while I ask around more locally. Now, how deeply did you examine his local background? Car dealings? Bank account?'

At that point, Mrs Kenworthy came in with two mugs of black coffee and more of her home-made biscuits.

Mark thanked her and relented by having a large biscuit of oatmeal and chocolate.

'Pretty thoroughly. We did obtain copies of his bank statements, Mark, they'll be in the file somewhere.'

'*Touché!* I was heading for Rainesbury now, to try and persuade the bank manager to let me see them.'

'Have a look at the files first, it might save you a lot of work and hassle. We did it through official channels, we had to, in view of the murder investigations. But we did look into all that aspect of his life because we found it odd that he had a joint account with Potter, that's what prompted us to search his account. It seems he needed an adult, that was someone over twenty-one at that time, to support his application for a bank account as he was under age. So he used Potter, they opened a joint account, on her recommendation, I'll bet. He paid for her lodgings, for example, out of that account, and so out of his money. He had the appearance of having plenty of ready cash, possibly from car sales, with money going in and out in large sums. I don't think he would dare nick any of the cash set aside for the IRA.'

'Could he have been a terrorist? Or become one later?'

'Yes, he could. He was an ideal candidate, young enough to be idealistic, young enough to be swayed by propaganda from home. If he was any good, they might have pulled him out of here and despatched him to some other battle zone. But why are you so keen on tracing him after all this time?'

'Someone wants to kill Potter when she's released, it's someone who knows she is about to leave prison. I did wonder if Balleen had called on her, either under his own name or another, and had been told of her impending release. I wondered whether he was still in her background, Mr Kenworthy, still waiting for her, still waiting to get his revenge.'

'Revenge, what for?'

'I've no idea. Maybe she double-crossed him. Maybe something happened between them. I might be wrong, but someone's waiting to get her for something.'

'I take your point, Mark. Now, there is one other thing, and it's in my notes. The bank also held a large suitcase in safe deposit, in their vaults. It was in Potter's and Balleen's joint names. We got access to it, but I won't say how. It was empty, Mark, except for a greetings card in Balleen's handwriting. The card had the drawing of a key on the front and inside was his message – "Goodbye." Nothing else.'

'In a bank vault?'

'Yes, it's probably still there, at the Country and Coast Bank in Rainesbury.'

'Is that joint account still operating?' Mark asked.

'Possibly. There was cash there and some of it did belong to Potter. She wrote from prison every so often to ask that the account remain open; it was functioning when I retired, I asked.'

'She'll have something to come out to?'

'I would imagine so. Any cash deposits will be earning interest and the suitcase will still be there unless Balleen's moved it. Potter couldn't move it, could she? And no one else would be allowed access, let alone have the authority to move it.'

'Did you examine the case thoroughly, Mr Kenworthy? Inside the linings? For false bottoms and so on?'

'We did, Mark. There was nothing. No trace of drugs. No trace of explosives. Nothing. Just that silly card. We took photographs of it, inside and out, including that daft card.'

Mark drew some further incidental information from Kenworthy, but in view of the information about the suitcase, he decided that he would, after all, pay a visit to the Country and Coast Bank at Rainesbury. When he left the old man, he took the pocket-books with him in several plastic carrier bags and decided to first return to the incident room. He'd deposit the books with instructions that their contents be read thoroughly and incorporated in both HOLMES and the card index system; he'd also locate the pictures of the suitcase and its contents, and then drive over to Rainesbury.

He wanted to see if that suitcase was still there.

12

The bank manager was Stanley Hart, a small balding man in his late forties. He had a round and cheerful face and when he stood up, Mark noticed he was rather plump, the colour of his suit making him look like a ripe damson.

Some two years ago, Mark recalled, Hart's daughter had been indecently assaulted by a group of drunken youths. Today, therefore, he received Detective Superintendent Pemberton with pleasure because the police had traced the youths in question and, although their attack had fallen short of rape, each had received a short, sharp custodial sentence. Mr Hart was therefore highly satisfied with his family's association with the police and as a consequence was willing to co-operate with them even if it meant bending some of his bank's rules.

When Pemberton explained his purpose, Mr Hart told him that objects lodged in the bank's 'vaults', which in a small branch might be nothing more than a room with shelves tucked away from public access, were never as secure as those placed in a Safe Deposit Centre. They were, however, much more secure than objects stored in private houses, up chimneys or under the floorboards. In the case of the banks, depositors who held accounts at a branch were able to deposit things like boxes and suitcases with mysterious contents and leave them secure in the bank's care.

The banks had no wish to know what those contents were and never opened the containers or examined their contents – to do so might cause problems with the bank's insurers at the very least. The deposits could be stolen cash, objects of immense personal or financial value, items of jewellery, art work or other secret things like love letters or photographs. Once placed on safe deposit, the containers could be accessed only by the holder of the relevant bank account – identities and signatures were checked before the deposited articles were released or made available.

In the case of a joint account, the signature of either party would suffice, although some conditions of deposit might stipulate that both account holders had to be present and that both signatures were necessary before action could be taken; in all instances, however, the account holder/s could either visit the room to examine his, her or their treasure safe from prying eyes, or remove the valuables if they so desired and take them from the premises.

'We've stored everything from secret toffee recipes to tax-avoiding cash via family heirlooms, pictures of nude wives and stuffed weasels,' grinned Hart. 'Sometimes our clients show me their treasures, things that mean such a lot to them – they've got to share things with someone, I suppose.'

'I appreciate the restrictions imposed on you,' Mark said, taking the photographs from his briefcase. 'But all I want to know is (a) whether this suitcase is still with you, (b) whether the card is still inside it, (c) whether there is anything else inside and (d) if so, what it is.'

'The joint account is still in action,' Hart confirmed. 'It's one we can hardly forget, although none of us was here when it was opened. It's one that we're constantly aware of. Miss Potter writes to us regularly from prison to ask for statements and to transfer cash from the deposit account.'

'She must have had a large deposit account?' Mark asked.

'Yes. I am not at liberty to inform you of the amount, but it was substantial, certainly enough to sustain a healthy income from interest which has accrued. Compound interest, that is. It is paid quarterly into the joint current account, and from that we pay a standing order which services the ASP Safe Deposit Centre here in Rainesbury. That's part of the Accredited Security and Protection Group – their premises are on the harbour side. Their office has that huge coiled snake logo on the building above the door; it's on all its stationery too. You can't miss it.'

'I know the place. Thank you.' Mark knew that it would have been most difficult to obtain this information officially. Hart had slipped it in most neatly without being asked and it was something Mark would never have thought of asking. Hart clearly felt it was relevant.

Mark asked, 'So she's got something held there?'

'*They* have something held there, superintendent. The account's in both names, Balleen and Potter.'

'Does Balleen ever contact you about their account?'

'Not a word, that's why I'm so familiar with it. It's a puzzle to us; here in the bank, we often talk about the account. It's of constant interest to our Regional Head Office too, our inspectors are always curious about it. After all, it is rather odd, an account jointly held by a convicted murderess and a man who shows no interest in it. We know Miss Potter's history, of course, but from Mr Balleen, there's not been a word. One of my predecessors did try to find out where he was through our southern Ireland connections, but we came up with precisely nothing. We don't send money to our Irish banks from their account, by the way, not any more. He used to have his own account here, so the records tell us, but that was around 1967. We keep the files current, superintendent, because of the peculiar circumstances; our inspectors have suggested that we do so, probably on the grounds that Miss Potter still uses our bank in the belief that one day she would be freed. But if Mr Balleen turned up tomorrow, he could continue with his account in this bank, provided, of course, we were satisfied with his identity and that his signature tallied with our specimens.'

'And this suitcase then, is it still with you?' Mark handed him the photographs.

'Yes, it is, superintendent. We have a copy of those pictures in our files, thanks to your Mr Kenworthy all those years ago. He gave copies to us and I can confirm there has been no change. The card is still inside it; our records show that no one has had access to the suitcase since Mr Kenworthy's enquiry in 1967. Miss Potter did visit the vaults in early January of that year, the register records that visit and Mr Kenworthy did note it.'

'What do you make of it all?' asked Pemberton.

'We don't know, we can only guess. The general consensus is that the pair of them deposited something of great value in that case – the handwriting on the card, by the way, was confirmed as that of Mr Balleen, according to your Mr Kenworthy. He told us so, it's noted in our files and we would agree with that. We did wonder if Mr Balleen had removed something from the case without Miss Potter's knowledge or consent, hence the cheeky card he left behind. It almost seems as if he knew she'd look in without telling him, that he'd stolen a march on her, as they say, anticipated some sneaky move by her and then frustrated it. It's just a theory, superintendent. But we never knew what he kept in the case, what *they* kept there, I should say.'

'Did anything else come to light during Kenworthy's enquiries?' Mark asked. 'I've not had the opportunity to go into his files in depth, my men are doing that right now and he has allowed us access to his notebooks of the period.'

'I was not here then, of course, but I have been through our own records of the account from time to time, I need to know what's going on, but apart from the cessation of the payments to southern Ireland way back in the 1966/67 era – Miss Potter halted those after Mr Balleen went home – there was nothing of great interest.'

'Those payments were substantial, I believe?' Mark said.

'Yes, at the time they were. Into thousands of pounds, supposedly from his second-hand car dealings.'

'You say supposedly?'

'I'm only repeating what was in our files at that time, Mr Pemberton. I do know that your Mr Kenworthy secured copies of bank statements in Mr Balleen's name, and in the joint name of himself and Miss Potter. We won't have those now, so I can't really help . . .'

'You've been of immense help already, Mr Hart; I do appreciate your assistance, it's far better than using the powers of the law to get what we need.' Pemberton rose to leave and shook the manager's hand.

Hart told him, 'I can't make an official statement about what I've told you just now, you'd have to go through miles of red tape and official channels before I could do that, and even then some of the information might never be released. Our rules are pretty stringent these days, although the new drugs legislation does allow us, indeed compel us, to assist you.'

'I know the restraints, and I'm grateful.' Mark was genuinely appreciative of Hart's openness. 'If I need to formalize things, I suppose I could say I was seeking funds which were the result of illicit drugs dealing! Anyway, you've been most helpful.' Before Mark left, he asked after Mr Hart's daughter.

'She's still nervous about walking past a group of youths, even when she's not alone, but she has made a good recovery. She's nineteen now, she's doing a business studies course at Durham, so we're pleased with the way she's put her awful experience to the back of her mind.'

'I'll let you know what develops about Potter,' Mark promised. 'You might get a call or even a visit from her sometime after next Monday.'

'Well, she's got a useful cash deposit to help re-establish herself,' said Hart. 'It would be unethical to inform you of her private business, I'm sure you realize that, especially as there'll be no suggestion she's doing anything illegal. Mind, I'm not sure how I would react if I met her face to face across my desk or over the counter. I was only a lad at school when she killed those children.'

'Me too,' Mark said. 'But I won't put you into the awkward situation of having to consider spying on her. We would know her movements anyway, we'll be keeping a fairly close eye on her, especially if she comes into this area. So, thanks again – your co-operation has been most valuable.'

When Mark left, he made contact with Agar and Holdsworth over his car radio and arranged to meet them for a pint and a sandwich. Agar suggested the Smugglers' Arms; they'd called there earlier but the landlord had been in Hull and the barmaid had been unable to assist them. She'd not been working last Sunday lunchtime. She told them he was expected back before one o'clock. Mark said it was a good idea to meet there and agreed to see his men at twelve thirty.

As that was almost an hour away, Mark decided to visit the lofty patch of moorland where the bodies of Rachel, Tracy and Michele had been found. His briefcase contained maps and photographs of the locality, albeit taken in 1967, but he hoped this was sufficient for him to identify the area. It was a ten-minute drive out of town and he parked on a large gravelled area beside the road; with expansive views, this was now an official car-park with a free parking sign whereas in 1967 it had been just a patch of flat turf beside the road. Had Potter parked here, he pondered? Then he wondered whose car she had used. Could she drive? If not, how had she transported the bodies to this lonely place? They were further questions he must answer. Armed with his maps and photographs, he trudged along smooth grassy sheep tracks which led him through the thick wintering heather and it was then he realized just how difficult it was to pinpoint the burial places accurately.

He found Michele's grave with surprising ease – a huge granite boulder stood guard over it.

Carved with countless initials of lovers and passers-by over many centuries, it was readily identifiable from the photographs. The earth at the foot of its southern slope was soft and sheltered. The boulder stood about four feet high and was some ten feet long by five feet wide, probably the residue of a passing glacier aeons ago. Michele had been buried beneath one of its sheltering sides but the location was otherwise unmarked. He double-checked with his map and photographs and nodded with satisfaction. From here, he noticed, the car-park was visible and so anyone digging here could have been within sight of passing vehicles. In summer, though, thick bracken growing the height of a man would obscure the rock from the road – but not in winter, so she must have dug the graves at night. As Tracy, Michele and Rachel had disappeared in February and March, it would be dark quite early those evenings. But it was speculation on his part, and now there was nothing to indicate the site's role in Britain's most horrific series of child murders.

The burial places of both Tracy and Rachel were likewise adjacent to towering boulders, each rock being unique in shape and size, and each easily recognizable from the photographs. In all cases, the grave had been in a soft portion of earth close to the base of the rock, fertile ground where, in wet weather, small pools of water gathered, and in cold, dry weather sheep would shelter from the chill northerly winds.

Although the first three girls had vanished within a couple of weeks between 17 February and 1 March 1967, their bodies had not been found until June. Rachel's had been found first, and this had rapidly helped to locate the others.

Of Suzanne, Helen and Clare, there had been no trace. Suzanne had been reported missing after Sunday school, around 4 p.m. on 1 April, with both Helen and Clare being missed after their confirmation class on 6 May, their absences having not been reported until six o'clock, each mother thinking her child had gone to the home of the other.

Why were the little girls allowed to go out alone at a time when there'd be maximum distress and alarm? With the papers full of stories about the kidnapping of little girls, there'd have been warnings about not going off with strangers, about the need to remain in groups, about the need to be accompanied by parents where possible . . . but inevitably, in spite of the warnings and the dangers, children did go out alone. But Balleen and Potter were not strangers to the little girls or to their parents – in spite of the warnings, those parents would have trusted both Balleen and Potter to care for their youngsters. As Mark stood on this lofty, open site with the wind of the moors making his cheeks tingle and his eyes fill with tears, he could see the North Sea in the distance. It looked a dull grey in this light with one or two steamers moving steadily along the horizon and some white horses dotting the expanse of water which was closest to the shore.

All around was another sea – in autumn it would become England's largest area of open purple heather but in winter the dead plants were a dull brown among patches of short green grass mown smooth by free-ranging blackfaced moorland sheep. He could see tiny villages in the dales below, sturdy places built of stone surrounded by acres of green grass and some ploughed fields showing signs of cultivation among the massive expanse of open moor. Upon these heights, there was solitude of a kind rarely found anywhere else in England. If he'd been here for any other reason, it would have been an enjoyable experience. He walked among the massive rocks and the rough heather, using the narrow sheep tracks as footways, and wondered whether three more small bodies lay buried nearby.

As he scanned the seemingly limitless expanse of open moorland stretching inland before him, Mark knew that any searchers would face an impossible task. Indeed, Kenworthy's men had faced the same intractable problem all those years ago. They had spent weeks digging in this area, searching with dogs capable of finding human remains, but they had never found any sign of the missing bairns.

In brooding over the events of that time, Mark felt sure that the killer would never have returned to this place to bury the additional victims; surely, having already interred three bodies here, their killer would have gone elsewhere to repeat the procedure? But where else could she have gone? Anywhere within the two million surrounding acres, he told himself!

He qualified his own thoughts by wondering whether Potter had indeed killed the other three. Was it feasible that two independent killers had been operating? It was a sobering thought and one that could not be ignored in spite of the certainties expressed by Mr Kenworthy. Shaking his head with dismay at the improbability of ever finding those girls or producing an answer to all the nagging questions, he retraced his steps to the car, wiped a tiny amount of earth from his shoes and drove back into town. Looking at him, no one would have known he had just tramped several hundred yards across the moors, for he was as immaculate as ever. The bracing moorland air had given a touch of colour to his cheeks, however, and an appetite to match. Mark looked forward to lunching with his colleagues.

The Smugglers' Arms was a stone-built sea-front inn perched on the edge of the harbour. Only the width of a narrow road separated it from the water while the smell of salt air and wet fish wafted around the premises. Some two or three centuries ago, the inn had served as a clearing house for a range of illicit imports which were part of the culture of any coastal town or village. Hereabouts, brandy, tobacco and even dried fruit had been among the more popular of the incoming goods. Deep cellars, thick walls with secret cavities, hidden doors and even a secret room had all been part of this establishment when it was operating to defeat the revenue men.

Some of those smugglers had operated well into the last century and, today, reminders of those times had been preserved in an acceptable modernization of the old inn. It now catered for tourists during the summer and some local imbibers or day trippers during the winter months. For them, it still looked like a smugglers' den but the hiding places and secret rooms were now corners and alcoves with lights and dusty old brandy bottles to provide atmosphere and effect.

Mark entered to find a row of wooden carrels along the rear wall, each containing a table and short wooden benches, while the centre of the floor contained old treadle sewing machines minus their working parts so that they now formed tables. Other tables occupied the end walls, while a door led through into other small rooms. He wandered through each room seeking his colleagues, but failed to find them and so adjourned to the bar where he ordered a pint of apple juice in a big glass. The barmaid smiled and dealt with his order, asking, 'Will you be having a snack, sir?'

'Shortly,' he said. 'I'm waiting for some friends. I'll study the menu in the mean time.' He found an empty table in one of the carrels with a view of the door, picked up the handwritten menu in its plastic laminated cover and waited. A figure 4 in a plastic holder stood on his table. Agar and Holdsworth arrived within a quarter of an hour, apologized for the short delay, and accepted a drink apiece, Agar asking for a pint of bitter and Holdsworth opting for his Guinness.

Mark ordered a prawn sandwich for himself, but they each settled for a home-made steak and kidney pie, chips and peas, Holdsworth forsaking his passion for prawn sandwiches on this occasion.

'Working lads, sir!' Holdsworth grinned. 'We've big appetites – especially when the boss is paying!'

Mark's hunger had been sharpened by his short trek across the moors, and when he noticed the delicious smells of cooking he decided to swap his sandwich for something more substantial. Another day of cholesterol control gone!

He changed to steak and kidney pie. As they settled down to await their meal, Detective Sergeant Agar, speaking softly in spite of the hubbub of conversation around them and looking more like a press photographer in his jeans and worn leather baseball jacket than a policeman, explained how they had separated to locate their own contacts from the past, who comprised informers in the drugs world and petty villains with something to hide. Their morning's work had produced a smattering of information.

'No one's heard any local threats against Potter, sir,' was Agar's conclusion. 'Leastways, not that we know of.'

'I go along with that, sir,' agreed Holdsworth. 'I've found nowt, not a whisper, and some of the lads I've talked to would have known about it if it was common gossip.'

'Then we must see if the landlord remembers those two who were overheard by our security shadow.'

'What was he doing here, sir, the security man?'

'They're not saying, but this place, this pub even, is still in the smuggling game, eh? Drugs now, isn't it? They pass through here off ships, hard and soft drugs, and there was a hint of someone smuggling in people, boat people, others from the Middle East, putting them ashore here.'

'Rumour, sir, most of it. We never caught anybody. I'm not saying the pub is a hundred per cent clean, but if drugs are passing through, they're in a fairly small way.'

'But a pub on the harbour side is always a good bet for goings-on of that kind, test runs for bigger intakes, eh? And even for assassins coming in to do a job?' Mark planted the idea in their heads. 'Hello, food!'

As the waitress placed their meals before them, Mark realized that it was possible to overhear conversations in the adjoining carrels. If one was talking to friends, then it was not likely, but in the silence of one's own company, one could catch words from both sides. As the waitress attended to their table, laying the mouth-watering pies in their place settings, he heard a girl in the carrel behind him talking about her work in a solicitor's office, while a man in the carrel in front of him was grumbling about the poor car servicing he got from his garage. So the man from MI5 could have been right – the sound carried well.

'Thanks.' He paid her and they settled down to eat, and then a man emerged from the rear of the inn and walked behind the bar. 'Hi, Sharon, any messages?'

'The landlord's back,' noted Holdsworth with a nod of his head. Sharon had clearly remembered their first visit because she indicated their presence and the man acknowledged her message. But food was more important just now. The landlord ordered himself a plate of plaice and chips, pulled a pint and said, 'I'll see them in half an hour.'

13

The landlord's name was Doug Weston and when Pemberton approached him as he paid for the lunches, Weston seemed reluctant to talk. Mark asked if they could go somewhere private and so the three police officers found themselves being taken into Weston's tiny office on the first floor. There was no room to sit down and the place was cluttered with paperwork and unopened boxes of potato crisps.

'You'll remember the Rainesbury Murders?' was Mark's opening speech. 'Louisa Mary Potter killed three children here, in '67.'

'Yeah?' Weston was a large man, a surly, unshaven individual with a mass of thick curly hair in need of a wash and a cut. He was untidily attired in a heavy loose-fitting woollen sweater, worn corduroy trousers and unpolished brogue shoes. If he'd kept himself clean and smart, he would have been a presentable and impressive man. His clothes did look expensive.

'Two men were in here on Sunday,' Mark told him. 'Having lunch, in that same carrel where we were. Number four. We'd like to know who they were.'

'Search me. I don't know everybody who comes in here. So what's that to do with them killings?'

'They were overheard planning to kill Potter if she comes out of prison.'

'Every bloody parent in town wants to kill that woman, superintendent, loads of them sound off in here every time the story's in the papers. Surely that's not a crime?'

'We've reason to think this was a serious plan, Mr Weston; we feel it wasn't an idle threat, it wasn't just parents and townspeople sounding off, otherwise we wouldn't be here now, troubling you, would we?'

'Look, I don't know who they were . . . I can't even remember them.'

'What about the waitress? We've had words with the barmaid, who can't help us. Make no mistake, Mr Weston, this is important. If they were eating lunch or a bar snack . . .'

'It would be a bar snack in there, lunches are in the restaurant.'

'So they'd pay and you'd place it in the till – a computerized one, I noticed just now.' Mark waved his own receipt. 'It shows the date, the time, your VAT number and the table we used. So your till records will show that somebody did occupy carrel four and did buy a meal last Sunday. And your order forms would identify the table number too? While I'm on this topic, the carrels next to it, on each side, interest me as well. A lone person was there at the same time – I'd like to confirm that.'

'Connie, the waitress that's on now, well, she was on lunchtime on Sunday. I'll call her up. She might remember them. Now, till receipts, they're here somewhere, rolls of 'em, all kept for the VAT man.'

He pressed a button on the intercom and asked Connie to come up to the office while he rummaged through the papers on his desk. He did find the till receipts for Sunday and began to unroll them, feeding the reel through his thick fingers as he sought the lunchtime period. By the time he'd found the right sequence, Connie had arrived, looking worried.

Weston said, 'Here we are, table four. That's in carrel four. Two snacks, Sunday, paid for at 1.58 p.m. £10.65. Gammon and chips one of them, the other sausage, egg and salad, two coffees and drinks.'

Mark jotted the details in his notebook and turned to Connie, explaining his interest.

She frowned as she struggled to recall the customers, so Mark said, 'Salad with sausage and egg, Connie? Not the most normal of requests . . .'

'Ah!' She smiled. 'Yes, you're right. I took his order and the kitchen forgot what I'd said, they put chips on the plate, so I had to take it back and get salad. He was allergic to potato, he said, gave him stomach pains. I remember him.'

Mark beamed. 'This is great. Now, can you describe them, both of them? It is important.'

'I'll get coffees,' volunteered Weston. 'I haven't had mine yet. Connie?'

The policemen expressed their preference and Connie added, 'Thanks, Doug, white, no sugar.'

As the landlord went out, Mark inclined his head towards Holdsworth; Holdsworth recognized the reason for Mark's silent gesture and said, 'I'll give you a hand to carry the cups.'

And so the scruffy detective accompanied the equally scruffy landlord out of the room as Mark began to question Connie. He was soon probing her memory in the absence of her boss and drawing from her far more than she realized she had recalled. There were two men, one considerably older than the other. She guessed the young one was in his late twenties with the elder one getting on for fifty. It was the elder one who was allergic to potato. He had thick grey hair, slightly curly with no sign of balding, and spoke with an Irish accent; he was clean shaven, had good teeth and did not wear specs. He was tall too; when he stood up, he was about as tall as Mark, so the girl said. She couldn't remember what he was wearing, except that he was neither very tidy nor very untidy. His companion only said 'Thank you' and so she couldn't say whether he was Irish or not, but he had short cropped dark hair and a gold ear-ring in the pierced lobe of his right ear. He had a solid round face, slightly florid, with dark eyes and stubble about his heavy jowls.

He was wearing a white T-shirt or vest which could be seen beneath a heavy navy-blue sweater, and she did remember he wore jeans and trainers. One of his legs was sticking out into the aisle, she recalled. But she did not recall any names being mentioned.

During his quizzing of Connie, Weston and Holdsworth returned with the coffee, and each remained silent as Pemberton began to question the girl about the man in the adjoining carrel. Again, the till roll had to be resorted to, but it did help in producing the required answer.

Carrel five had contained a party of four – a family, Connie recalled – but she did remember serving a solitary person in carrel three. It wasn't a man, she said; it was a woman. A smart young woman in her thirties, with a pile of thick blonde hair, and she wore modern clothes, well cut – a dark skirt, high-heeled shoes and a patterned woolly jumper. Connie had noticed she was very slender and quite attractive. She'd had a bar snack, paying for it at 2.09 p.m., and it had cost £5.20 in total. Connie remembered giving her a receipt. Mark smiled. If this woman was the MI5 informer, then she could reclaim her expenses if she kept the receipt. No further description was available.

With both the girl and her boss present, Mark asked if the two men had been in before; they shook their heads.

'I'd have remembered the no-potato thing,' Connie said. 'I've not seen either of them.'

'Me neither,' said Weston.

'Any chance of you ringing me if they do come?' Mark had noticed a blank piece of the inn's headed paper on the desk so he picked it up and scribbled down the incident room number. 'Quietly, so as they don't know? It's important to us, it could stop a killing.'

'Sure,' shrugged Connie.

But Weston was not so enthusiastic about becoming a copper's nark. 'I don't want my customers thinking I'm an informer,' he grumbled.

'If there's a killing by those men, I'll remind you of that.' Mark left the piece of paper on the desk and tapped it with his forefinger. 'The number's there, Mr Weston.'

After the meal, Mark joined his men for a walk along the seafront, the powerful sea air clearing his head and bringing a tingle to his face.

'Well,' he said. 'What do we make of all that?'

Agar spoke. 'It suggests the intelligence was right, sir. We know there was someone there.'

'And it means we've got to find those men. I'm not too happy with Weston, he was nervous about something, reluctant to talk.'

'Maybe he thought we were after him for something else,' suggested Holdsworth. 'He's no angel, sir, he's on the wrong side of the thin blue line, I'm sure about that.'

'So we can't expect him to ring us if those characters do return; you might have to keep popping back in there. You know what I think?'

'Sir?'

'I think we should see if Joseph Balleen was allergic to potatoes.'

'An Irishman allergic to spuds? Now there's a laugh, sir. But sure, I'll check it out. You don't think that was him, do you? In that pub? The grey-haired Irishman?'

'It's possible, the age and the accent were about right. Now, what have you discovered so far?'

'Not a lot, sir, but I did find a man who knew Balleen when he was here. He's a small-time builder, he used to sub-contract labour to the firm Balleen worked for, and he's still in business doing small construction work, jobbing repairs to houses and farms, that sort of thing. Mind, he hasn't seen Balleen for years, or heard of him.'

'So what did he tell you?'

Detective Sergeant Agar said Balleen was known to be a good worker and a pleasant character, always cheerful and full of fun.

He worked on sites across a wide-ranging area, and was happy to be a hod carrier one day and a bricklayer's mate the next. He always used his own car to travel out to sites, saying he liked to be independent and also liked to see something of the locality after work or during his meal break.

With work finishing at 4 p.m., he could have returned on the battered old works bus, but said he preferred to have the time to tour the district. He would sometimes rush off while the others had lunch in their huts, saying he wanted to see the castle or the abbey or some other local place of interest. He was always on the go, always rushing about, always busy with one thing or another. Agar said that Balleen had been described as a bundle of energy, a real go-getter, one who seldom sat down and did nothing. He made use of every spare minute.

'And his car dealing? Anything on that, Jim?'

'Not a lot at this stage, sir, but he did quite a good trade, so my contact said. He'd have a different car for himself every few weeks, keeping the good ones that came his way and selling the others.'

'How did he advertise them?'

'In the *Evening News* mainly, or in shops and on notice-boards in town. Or by word of mouth among his building mates; lots of them worked for cash and had money to spare for old bangers.'

'So his work was all honest?'

'As far as I can tell at this stage – mind, I'm not saying he was honest so far as the tax man was concerned, or the National Insurance scheme. He worked for cash, on the Lump, like a lot of Irishmen who came here.'

'Worthy of further delving, you think? In spite of the time lapse?'

'Certainly,' Agar said. 'We haven't really got under the skin of the underclass yet, but people have long memories. If there is any useful information, we'll find it.'

Pemberton recounted his morning's activities, particularly his discussion with Hart in the bank, and asked them both to bear those factors in mind when making their enquiries about Balleen around the district.

Mark's immediate work over, he bade farewell to Agar and Holdsworth and said he was going to call on Miss Clayton at Mermaid Villa before returning to the incident room. He wanted to know a little more about Balleen's association with Potter, whether there had been a serious rift, and felt she might be the one to tell him. She might also know if he'd been allergic to potatoes. He promised to keep Agar and Holdsworth informed of any new information.

Miss Clayton, severe as ever, sat him down at one of her bare tables in the dining-room. Mark explained that he was interested in the financial association between Potter and Balleen and wondered if she knew anything about their arrangements or whether there had been a disagreement of any kind.

'For example, cars,' he asked. 'Did Louisa have a car? If so, who paid for it?'

'Yes, she did. She passed her test here in town, first time, superintendent, and Joseph gave her a car. He had lots, he bought and sold them, you know, so there was always a car or two spare. He paid for it all, he liked to impress her.'

'Did he give that impression? That he was out to impress a woman older than himself?'

'I think that pleased him, superintendent. He did take her out to some smart places in town, upper-class restaurants, the theatre, night-clubs, he was always saying he could afford it.'

'And Louisa? Did she like that kind of treatment?'

'Oh, yes, she loved it. She hadn't had much of a home life, you know, a large family living on a low income, and so these outings by Joseph really impressed her. I don't think she loved him because of it, but she did go along with him, and he was always keen to show her something new. He once took her on a day trip to London from here, by train, that sort of thing. He bought her flashy presents too, nice jewellery, good clothes. In some ways, he spoilt her.'

'At eighteen?'

'He was knowledgeable for his age, he was a bit of a show-off, superintendent. There were times I thought she was taking unfair advantage of him, you know, pretending to like the high life just so he would pay for her. She hadn't much money of her own, she never earned a lot. She always got her way with him.'

'And he always had plenty of money?'

'Always, and he always paid his bills. He did work hard, and I do know his car dealings earned him quite a lot, he had a knack for finding bargains and selling them for a profit. He could persuade people to sell cheap and buy for a lot. A real charmer.'

'Last time I was here, you mentioned their joint account. Did you know he was sending money to Ireland?'

'To his family? Yes, he told me. He said they weren't well off and he felt he should repay his parents for bringing him up. He would sometimes tell me he'd sent hundreds of pounds, especially after a good spell of selling cars. I think his mum put some aside for him there, for when he returned.'

'A nice gesture on both sides, eh?'

'He was a very nice man, superintendent. I think he came from a nice family too.'

'Did you know about the suitcase they'd deposited at the bank?'

'Good heavens, that again! Your Mr Kenworthy went into all that when he was investigating the murders. He asked Louisa about it and she just said she had no idea what it was, or what the silly card meant. He'd left a card inside it, hadn't he?'

'Yes, he had,' Mark agreed. 'I can't fathom it out either.'

'I'm guessing it's still there?' she asked.

'Yes, Balleen has never been in touch about it; Louisa does keep in touch about the account.'

'I'm sorry, superintendent, I can't help you about that.'

'One final question, an odd one,' he smiled. 'Was Joseph Patrick Balleen allergic to potatoes?'

'Allergic to them? Good heavens no, he loved a pile of chips!' she laughed. 'Whatever makes you ask that?'

'There's a man living somewhere in Rainesbury who we feel might be Joseph, but this one's allergic to potatoes.'

'Well, he ate plenty of them when he was living here,' she said. 'And I don't think he'd visit the town without coming to see me! I think you are wrong there, Mr Pemberton.'

'Thanks. Well, I'll let you get on. I must return to Headquarters and see what my men have been up to while I've been away.'

When Mark returned to Police Headquarters at Great Halverton late that afternoon he found that the incident room was still humming with activity. One success was that Margaret Brown, the mother of Michele, had been traced in Middlesbrough where she was now called Margaret Harper. She had been informed of developments, but had shown little interest. Her attitude was that Potter had been found guilty of murdering Michele, and she had no further interest in the case. She knew of Joseph Patrick Balleen and how he'd taught the girls during Brownie sessions, but she'd never met him nor had she seen him since that time.

Similarly, Andrew Stabler had been traced to an address in the Greater Manchester police area; a very experienced officer had interviewed him and had faxed a statement for Pemberton's information. The message was clear – Andrew had no further interest in the crime; he had overcome his wild days and was now happily married with a family of his own and a good job. He told the visiting officer that he had no animosity whatever towards Potter and did not care what she did, where she went or whether she came out of prison or she didn't. He'd met Balleen but they'd never become friends; Helen had thought a lot of him, responding to him as an eight-year-old would when befriended by a knowledgeable man more than twice her age.

Two further reports had traced one brother and one sister of Louisa Mary, the brother in Lichfield and the sister in Bristol, but neither expressed hatred of Louisa, nor did they express any real interest in what she did upon her release. They had nothing to offer.

'So I reckon if anybody's going to kill her, it's that Irishman who hates potatoes, or his mate, or Balleen', said Mark to Inspector Larkin.

'Yes, sir,' said Paul Larkin, who added, 'I wonder how we'll find him before he finds either Louisa Mary Potter or Kathleen Hicks?'

14

Sitting alone in his small office overlooking the activity of the incident room, Mark Pemberton pondered upon Paul's remark. Early indications, often very accurate, did suggest that the townspeople and the victims' families were not inclined to wreak vengeance upon Louisa Mary Potter, certainly not to the extent of killing her. The only known threat had come from the man in the Smugglers' Arms. The fact that his unguarded remarks had been heard by a member of the Security Service was fortuitous to say the least – a member of the public or even a police officer might have regarded such remarks as empty words, boastful threats or idle chatter. Had that been the case, the threat might never have reached the knowledge of the police.

So why had the woman in carrel three considered the threats to be genuine? And what was she doing in town that day? Why was she in that very pub lunching at that highly convenient table? Were the men known to her? Had she followed them? Was she in Rainesbury on some mission which entailed their supervision? Was there some security operation afoot about which the police had no knowledge? Mark knew that that was always possible. MI5 was under no obligation to notify the local police of its movements or even to announce the presence of its officers in an area.

The fact that the security woman had chosen to remain anonymous did indicate an undercover operation. The major query was how the Irishman and his mate knew that Potter was about to be paroled. Other than a few officials, no one knew. Had they come to Rainesbury solely with the intention of locating her and destroying her? If so, why? Why Rainesbury? Did they *know* she would one day return to this town? And how seriously should the Irish links be treated? There was even an IRA link; was the IRA wanting to wreak revenge on Potter? If so, why? What had she done to upset them? And what had been in that suitcase in the bank; what was the significance of the silly card inside it . . . and what now lay hidden in the ASP Safe Deposit Centre? For Detective Superintendent Pemberton, the questions seemed endless and without answer.

The involvement of the Security Service, however innocent it appeared to be on the surface, did add aspects of wider concern. For one thing, the involvement of MI5 in covert operations concerning the IRA had been nil until 1992, that role being played jointly by the military and the police. But now they were known to be involved, could that involvement in fact have begun many years ago with sleepers and informers waiting in the wings? Mark was very suspicious about the 'accidental' overhearing of the death threat and began to suspect that his reopening of the missing children case was indeed a useless exercise so far as the threat was concerned. He began to feel that he was being used.

He was beginning to feel that his work was nothing more than a cosmetic exercise to disguise the real purpose of some obscure operation. If so, he disagreed with the moral of that – by investigating a case of missing children, he would be encouraging the families to place their faith in him. He must honour their trust and do his best to locate the missing children. He decided that he did owe a duty to each of the families and became determined not to be diverted from his endeavours to find the remains of Suzanne, Helen and Clare. At the same time, he knew he would have to delve far deeper into the peculiar circumstances which had led to his present assignment. Fortified by his own thoughts, he went into the body of the incident room and hailed Inspector Larkin.

'Paul, do we have the date of the Parole Board meeting which sanctioned the release of Potter and Hicks?'

'I'll check, sir.'

Mark watched as his inspector accessed HOLMES for dates relevant to the enquiry and it did produce a date – Thursday, 12 December. Beside it, it said, 'Potter granted parole.'

'Is that significant, sir?' Larkin asked.

Mark explained the tumble of thoughts which troubled him and said, 'I was pondering the possibility that there has been a leak from the Parole Board's secretariat or the Home Office. This date is some weeks before I was given this brief, which means someone had the time, about three weeks in fact, to inform interested parties about the release of those women. It could have been done before our involvement. And there's more than a month between the Parole Board's decision and the actual release date, giving plenty of time for someone to stir up trouble and set unwelcome things in motion.'

'What you are saying, sir, is that if there was a leak about Potter's release, someone has alerted her intended assassin who's waiting to deal with her. If it's not an aggrieved relation and it's not that Irishman Balleen, then I reckon we do have problems.'

'There's worse, Paul. If there is a mole in Whitehall, that same mole could tip off the press when the release occurs, and also provide them with Potter's undercover name and address. Apart from the assassin, the whole bloody world will know who she is, where she is and what she did.'

'We'd better alert them down south or wherever she is.'

'Down south?' asked Pemberton.

'Didn't you say Potter was in a safe house down south?'

'Oh, yes, sorry, I was miles away . . .' Mark had almost slipped up; momentarily, he'd forgotten that Hicks was Potter. He recovered in time to continue. 'I'll see to that. Can you ensure that our plans for the safe house in Swandale are watertight? If our mole is intent on giving information to the press or to assassins, Hicks' whereabouts might have been revealed.'

'If that's the case, the assassin might have been seen in Swandale or wherever Potter is.'

'We've had no hint of bother there but check it out. That makes me think that the key to our problem lies somewhere in Rainesbury, Paul. And that brings me right back to Balleen, the bank and the objects in the safe deposit.'

'Sir, does this mean the Chief hasn't been straight with you? Is he concealing something?'

'That's more than possible, Paul. He's done this before, he seems to give all the knotty problems to me. I reckon he thinks I'm spent, that I've blown my chances of promotion because I keep losing my bloody temper! He gives me all the dirty jobs now. Maybe I'm wrong, but there is something not straight with this one. I know he would tell me only what I needed to know, no more, no less. Besides, he might not be fully *au fait* himself with the underlying situation about Potter's release.'

'I think we are handling a red-hot potato here, sir!'

'And we're looking for a bloody Irishman who dislikes potatoes,' laughed Pemberton. 'Come into my office, Paul, let's talk this one through from another angle, shall we?'

As the other members of the incident room staff filtered away from Room 207 at the end of their working day, Mark and Larkin tried to establish an alternative aspect to the case. Mark began by stressing his belief that, somehow and in some way, Balleen was a factor. His name and his presence had cropped up too many times to be disregarded. And since the murders – before the murders in fact – he had vanished.

Nothing had been heard of him since but he was still required by Pemberton for interview and elimination as a suspect assassin.

Three children had gone missing and were still unaccounted for, while for twenty-five years Balleen's bank account, which he shared with Potter, had remained in action, accruing interest which was being used to fund a deposit in a Safe Deposit Centre. Now, with news of the re-emergence of Potter after twenty-five years of imprisonment for awful crimes, there were anonymous death threats to her from an unknown Irishman who just happened to be overheard as he ate his lunch in a pub next to a woman from MI5. And behind it all was the shadow of the IRA.

'It's all so bloody odd, Paul,' Mark said. 'It's very weird and most unsettling. It's like trying to retain a handful of oil. There's nothing firm to seize, nothing to hold on to, nothing solid to grip. Everything slips away to leave nothing behind, except dirt. So, having listened to me and done your part in the incident room, how's it all seem to you?'

'It's taking a long time to sift all the information in the old files and log it into the computer; our lads have worked well and Kenworthy's notebooks were marvellous, but so far – and it's still early days – we've turned up nothing of significance, no leads, no openings for new lines of enquiry.'

'All I can say is keep at it, Paul. Tomorrow, I'll ring that Safe Deposit Centre but I don't think they'll tell me what's there. Now, it's time for home. Fancy a pint?'

Larkin looked at his watch. 'Sorry, sir,' he said. 'It's gone six now, I'm expected home. I'm taking the wife out for a meal, it's her birthday . . .'

'Oh, well, have a nice time and wish her many happy returns from me.'

'Thanks, sir,' and Paul Larkin went to tidy his desk.

Mark did likewise, asking a solitary remaining detective to be sure to lock the room when he left. Mark was not looking forward to a lonely meal tonight, but there seemed to be no alternative. He could always light the fire, pour himself a brandy and read some more files. He picked up a spare photocopy of all the statements which had been processed; even now, the file filled six large lever-arch covers, and he called to the lone detective, 'I'm taking this lot home, John, if anyone's looking for it. I'll fetch it back tomorrow.'

'Sir,' acknowledged the detective.

Pemberton's perusal of the files that Thursday night was disappointing because it produced no new ideas or leads; it succeeded only in making him feel sleepy as he relaxed before his blazing log fire. The statements taken all those years ago told him nothing about the present circumstances and provided no stimulus for the current enquiry. Next morning, he returned the files to the reading table in Room 207, checked the mail and assembled his officers for their morning conference.

Agar and Holdsworth produced nothing further from Rainesbury; they had not yet found their Irishman and had no further information about Balleen. Two more sisters of Potter had been traced; each showed a flutter of interest in the news but proffered no signs of wanting to visit her or befriend her in her new life. The Waterhouses had been traced to a new bungalow in Kilmarnock where Tom now worked as the manager of a supermarket, but he expressed no horror or anger at news of Potter's release. According to the Strathclyde officer who had broken the news to Tom and Elaine, they were both very calm and Elaine said she would pray for her.

No anger, no animosity, no threats.

That morning's conference produced no new leads; it was more of a consolidation meeting, each detective confirming his actions for the previous day and announcing their thin results.

When Mark addressed his teams, he tried to show a confident approach, referring to yesterday's snippets about the Irishman in the pub and the Rainesbury team's modest success in tracing a builder who knew Balleen. But things were quiet, too quiet. Detective Sergeant Ashton added a bit of sparkle by outlining his basic plans for supervising the safe house and for coping with a siege or other incident. Mark nodded with satisfaction – the fellow knew his job and had put it all on paper, including a recommendation for an infra-red night-sight camera which would pick out snoopers in the dark.

'So it's another day of filing, I'm afraid. Logging old data, reading old statements, looking for new ideas, gaps in the sequence of things, anything that will give us a lead to take us to those missing bairns ... I'll be around today too,' he added almost in resignation.

Larkin told the conference he had arranged for photocopies of Adrian Kenworthy's notebooks so that everyone could see how he had approached his enquiries; his meticulous notes with their index and highlights might be of assistance. Mark smiled to himself – he'd probably read those notebooks after his dinner tonight.

The conference over, Mark went into his office and, after dealing with his routine paperwork, rang the Accredited Security and Protection Safe Deposit Centre. He requested the manager's name, then asked to be connected. The manager, ever cautious, took Mark's particulars, the name of his parent force and the telephone numbers of both the Headquarters and the incident room, and said he'd ring back. He did so almost half an hour later.

'We must exercise caution, superintendent,' he said. 'So how can I help you?'

Mark explained about Potter whereupon the manager, whose name was Lyon, said he knew the name and recalled the murders. Who didn't? Mark went on to tell him of the joint account and the suitcase deposited in the bank, and how he knew that the account financed a rented box in his Safe Deposit Centre.

'So,' Mark concluded, 'what I'm asking is whether there is any way we, the police, can find out what is contained in that safe deposit box. I don't want to drive all the way to Rainesbury if it's a waste of time.'

'No way,' said Lyon. 'Without the key, no one can gain access, and I mean no one, not even us. We can allow authorized representatives of the keyholder to have access, but we must be satisfied that the account holders have given such permission and that any such representative has the key. The key is the answer. Without it, there is no way, legal or otherwise, of looking at the contents of that box. It is impossible to force an entry, even with thermal lances or bombs! Our vaults are under the cliffs with reinforced concrete walls that are impervious to anything, even hydraulic rams and high explosives. To get in, you must have the key.

'We do not have spare keys or duplicates. No one here, not one member of the staff, can gain access under any circumstances – the security system is made by Rosengrens, the Swedish experts, in partnership with Chubb, and every key is an individual. Factory-sealed containers for every individual key are handed to our customers and only that key will open their box. If you can get the key, superintendent, and a signed authorization to have access to the contents, then I could let you in. And in 1967, only one key per deposit box was issued. Now, we issue two keys as well as computerized identity cards with PIN numbers.

'If anyone does walk in with a key they've found, there are added security measures to prevent unauthorized access even if they've stolen both the key and the card bearing the PIN number. In other words, we are totally secure and, of course, no one here, not one member of our staff, knows the contents of any of the boxes.'

'I think that's pretty final!' said Mark. 'So, on a more practical level, can you confirm that either Balleen or Potter, or both, has something deposited in your vaults, and that payment has been made over the last twenty-five years to keep the account in action?'

'I'll check my computer,' he offered and then, a few seconds later, said, 'Yes, a joint deposit account is held in both those names, either customer having right of access without the other; the payments are up to date. There is no identity card with that box and therefore no PIN number, as the box was first leased before we implemented those procedures. We have invited the clients to come and collect such a card and PIN number, but we have had no response. With Miss Potter in prison, that is understandable, but I cannot answer for Mr Balleen. He has never been in touch since 1967.'

'We've lost him too,' said Pemberton. 'His family in Ireland think he stayed in Britain, and his British friends think he returned to Ireland. He's gone, vanished from the face of the earth.'

'One more thing, superintendent: the box in question is one of our largest box safes – seven inches tall by just over a foot wide and a shade more than eighteen inches long. There are larger ones, but this is like a medium-sized suitcase or a rather large briefcase.'

'What sort of secrets could be held in there?' Mark sighed.

'Your guess is as good as mine, superintendent.'

'My guess is hopeless. If I knew the answer I'd be well on the way to completing my present investigation! Now, has anyone else been talking to you about these clients?' Mark asked. 'Trying to gain access?'

'No,' he said. 'No one.'

'Thanks, you've been most helpful. I might want to talk to you again about this.'

'Call me any time,' said Lyon.

As he replaced the telephone and considered wading through Kenworthy's old books, Woman Detective Constable Cashmore tapped on his door.

'Yes, Lorraine?'

'I think I've found something interesting, sir,' she announced.

15

'Sit down.' Mark pulled a chair from the desk and the young detective settled down. She was clutching a sheaf of papers and smiled rather nervously as she waited to present her thoughts. Mark sat opposite. Lorraine was in her late twenties, always smartly dressed in sober two-piece suits with white blouses and flat shoes. She was unusually tall for a woman, taller than he, probably over six feet, but she had a delightfully slender body, neat breasts and long, slender legs with a proud, erect carriage. Some tall girls tended to stoop, almost believing their height was a disadvantage and not therefore making the most of it. But not Lorraine Cashmore. In her police uniform, she had always looked splendid as she patrolled the streets head and shoulders above most other women and an object of admiration for the men. She walked tall, head erect and shoulders back, almost like a model showing off a new fashion, and in addition she was blessed with a sharp brain aided by acute feminine intuition – which was why Mark had selected her as a member of his team.

'I don't know whether this is something important, sir, or whether I'm being silly . . .'

'Lorraine,' he said, 'you are never silly. If you've brought this to me, then it's important. Whether it is relevant or not remains to be seen. So what have you found?'

'At our morning conference, you've often mentioned the word secret. Then yesterday you asked Jim and Derek to winkle out the secrets of the villains in Rainesbury.'

'Did I say that?' He grinned impishly at her.

'Yes, sir, you did . . .' She halted, blushed and said, 'I am being silly . . .'

'For heaven's sake, Lorraine, you're not! So what's so important about secrets?'

'I checked HOLMES' system of cross-referencing to see if the word was used in any of the statements. I was thinking of that deposit in the bank really – I saw it as a secret known only to Potter and Balleen. I wanted to see how HOLMES dealt with key words and – well, although we haven't got the entire case file fed into HOLMES yet, it did refer to this statement because it contains the word secret. And "Secret Seven" was a phrase keyed in too.' She held up the papers in her hand.

'Fine, good thinking – and good work by our HOLMES data input wizard! So who made that statement?'

'A girl called Jeanette McCarthy. She was eight at the time. She lived with her parents in Rainesbury and like some of the victims, she was a Catholic and she went to Brownies. But her family moved away from Rainesbury before the crimes were committed; they went to Farnthorpe, that's one of those housing developments on the outskirts of York.'

'So why was she interviewed?' Mark asked.

'All the Brownies were interviewed, sir, because all the victims were members in the same Brownie group.'

'Yes, but why would Mr Kenworthy interview this girl if she'd moved out of town?'

'She was a friend of all the others, a friend of all the victims. They went round in a little group, visiting each others' houses, going to parties and so on. They called themselves the Secret Seven.'

Mark realized what Lorraine was saying. 'Really? So when that family moved away, the Secret Seven became the Secret Six. Those six died, but number seven survived . . .'

'Yes, sir.'

'And good old Mr Kenworthy saw fit to have her interviewed and her statement recorded. That's good stuff, Lorraine, good CID work by that old team and good work by you. What's her statement say?'

'It was the bit about secrets that got me thinking, sir.' She flipped over the first page. 'When I was a little girl, six of us had a secret society. Little girls do that sort of thing, form societies and secret clubs, all very cliquish.'

'I thought girls never kept secrets?'

'Sir, that's sexist!'

'It's true . . .' He laughed. 'So tell me about the Secret Seven?'

'Well, in my own case, every member of our club had to have a secret, something no one else must know about, and it had always to remain a secret. That was a condition of membership. We had to write it down on a piece of paper and show it only to members of our club and no one else. Then we had to hide it; we all shared our secrets, that's what our club was for. It was a great privilege to be a member. We kept all the girls we hated out of it – it was one way of making ourselves exclusive, a bit superior I suppose, especially when the big girls wouldn't let us play. Anyway, sir, our secrets were always to do with our mums, mine was how many times I saw mum and dad together with no clothes on.'

'Strong stuff,' Mark chuckled.

'It was all very serious.' She was more relaxed now and was enjoying her banter with the superintendent. 'Well, sir, in this statement by Jeanette McCarthy, she said that all the victims, including herself, were members of a Secret Seven. They had secrets too, just like us, but she wouldn't tell the police what they were! It was a condition that they'd rather die than reveal their secrets, they swore to that by clenching their fists and concealing their thumbs with the fingers while making an oath. That was their secret sign. You know what little girls are, how stubborn they can be, how seriously they take that sort of thing.'

'Actually, I don't know, I've never had a sister nor a daughter.'

'Well, sir, believe me, a little girl with a secret can be very, very stubborn if someone's trying to prise it from her.'

'So Kenworthy's teams never did find out what Jeanette's secret was?'

'No, sir, and all the other little girls died.'

'God, you're not trying to say they died because they wouldn't reveal their secrets, are you? Or because this Jeanette kept her mouth shut?'

'No, at least I think not. I hope not. But Balleen is mentioned in her statement, sir, and Potter, she knew them both.'

'Now this is important, Lorraine. Well done. Let me see that statement. It sounds just like the breakthrough we need. If every victim was a member of that secret circle of kids, then that's the common factor, not school, religion, Brownies or their other activities. Secrets, eh? Tell me, Lorraine, what sort of secret would six small girls die for?'

'I don't know, sir, I just don't know.'

'Surely, though, they wouldn't die for something as silly as the secret you had?'

'No, sir, nor would they be killed for something as stupid as that. They must have known something else, something very important to Potter.'

'You could be right. Well, I must read this through. Fix me a coffee, please, and one for yourself, fetch them in here and wait till I've read this. Mine's black, no sugar.'

As her tall, lithe figure left the tiny office, Mark began to read the statement. Like all statements from children, its contents would have been abstracted in question-and-answer form, in the presence of at least one of the girl's parents, but it was written in a continuous narrative as was the prevailing custom. On a statement form bearing headings and the name and crest of the force, Mark read:

> *Name:* Jeanette Maria McCarthy, born 13 March 1959. Schoolgirl attending Bar Convent Primary School, York. *Parents:* Roy and Maureen McCarthy, 'Sandford', 66 Viking Road, Farnthorpe, York. Father's occupation – Taxi driver. Mother's occupation – housewife. Date: 18 May 1967.

The statement read as follows:

> I am a schoolgirl attending the Bar Convent Primary School, York and I am eight years old. I used to live in Rainesbury with my mum and dad at 18 Friary Street, but came to this house in the last week of January 1967.
>
> When I lived in Rainesbury my best friend was Helen Stabler because we went to the same school and Brownies, and our other friends were Michele Brown, Rachel Waterhouse, Tracy Halliday, Suzanne Hayes and Clare Wiles. Some went to our school, that's Rachel and Clare because they are Catholics, but we were friends with the others because of Brownies.

We had a club. We were the Secret Seven and we all had a secret. I'm not allowed to tell my secret to anybody, nobody could tell their secrets, that's why we were the Secret Seven.

We had a secret sign. We closed our right hand tight, like a fist, but put our thumb inside so you nearly couldn't see it. When we met, we all made that sign. It was a secret sign; if you didn't know the sign, you couldn't come to our club meetings. That was how we kept nasty girls out.

The rules were that we must die rather than tell our secrets, and the secrets of our club, that we had a meeting every Friday night, and that we always brought something to eat like a packet of crisps or a bar of chocolate.

We met in an old shed near the railway line and made scent out of rose petals and made houses for the fairies. Joseph would show us how to make things like shelters out of sticks for the fairies with big leaves for the roof or how to find footprints in the soil, like cats and dogs and rabbits make. He told us about secret signs that tramps make, and was good with secret things, like messages with codes in them and how to watch people without them knowing and how to hide things and make them look like other things. He once had a book with a hole in the middle of the pages where he kept some money. It looked like a proper book but it wasn't and he had a secret gun, at least it looked like a gun, but it was really a pipe for smoking tobacco. Miss Potter would come with him sometimes, and sometimes we would all go for a car ride to the riverside, in both Joseph's car and Miss Potter's; they both had cars and took them both sometimes, but I always went with Joseph because he drove fast and got us singing.

Mum and teacher said never to go with strange men but Joseph was not a stranger, he was our friend, and he never did nasty things to us. Mum once asked if Joseph ever did rude things to us, like asking to see our knickers, but he never did. We liked him, he was good fun, he laughed more than Miss Potter so we didn't really care whether she came or not.

Joseph's other name is Balleen, like Balloon but with ees and the policeman has told me about my friends, but I don't know who would take them away. Nobody ever tried to take me away or give me sweets and I would never go with a strange man, not ever. I never saw another man talking to my friends and they never said anything to me about nasty men trying to get them to do things.

They said when my mum and dad went to York they would keep being the Secret Seven, except there would be six, so if no one else joined them they would be the Secret Six and I could join them if ever I came to Rainesbury for a holiday or anything. But I have never been back, not yet.

The statement ended with the usual paragraph which said that it had been read over to Jeanette and she agreed that it was true; then followed her childish signature. The statement was countersigned by her mother whose addendum said that the statement had been made in her presence and with her consent, and so far as she knew, it was truthful and accurate. It was signed Maureen McCarthy.

While Mark was reading this, Lorraine returned with two mugs of coffee and sat down quietly as her boss studied the words. When he'd finished, he looked at her and said,

'This rings true, does it, Lorraine? The sort of play that a girl of eight would get up to?'

'Yes, sir, very.'

'Balleen always comes over as a nice guy, good with children, helpful and cheerful, we never hear of him playing football or having a night out with the lads over a pint or two. How's he strike you?'

'His friendship with these girls was just a small part of his life, sir; we don't know what he did the rest of the time. He had a job and a small business, he was always doing something, always on the go. I doubt if he had much time for nights out with the boys. That's why he would have money to spend on Louisa. I can sympathize with the parents, though, I understand their worries about him, but it seems he was not harming those girls in any way. I'm sure he was to be trusted.'

'That's the message that comes over loud and clear,' Mark said. 'But now I've read this, it does throw a different light on things, eh? Secrets. Dare we believe that those bairns died because of a secret – and what sort of secret would cause them to be tortured in such a blood-thirsty way, and still not reveal it?'

'If they died for that reason, sir, perhaps only one of them knew the secret?'

'Or none!' added Mark. 'And Potter tortured them all, one by one, in the hope she'd discover it? Who was last to die?'

'We don't know, sir, but the last girls to disappear both vanished at the same time, Clare Wiles and Helen Stabler. Neither of their bodies have been found.'

'You've listened to those awful tapes?' he suddenly asked Lorraine.

'No, sir. People say they are horrific. I've read the transcripts, though.'

'And do they tie up in any way with this theory about secrets?'

'One of the girls was screaming that she didn't know . . . it's in the tapes . . .'

'God, yes, I've read that. That makes those words mean something. So was that poor little kid being tortured into revealing something? If so, what? You know what I'm beginning to think, Lorraine?'

'No, sir?'

'Every piece of positive information we get brings us back to Rainesbury; we've an unknown assassin lurking in the town, we've an unknown Irishman who hates potatoes, we've Balleen who vanished while working there, and we have secrets among children who lived there and who've been killed. They were probably killed there, too – I don't think the scenes of the actual murders were ever identified. And we have a secret something-or-other hidden in a safe deposit centre, and an odd suitcase sitting in a bank vault in Rainesbury with a meaningless note inside . . . written by Balleen. All this takes us round and round in ever-decreasing circles, Lorraine, with Rainesbury in the centre.'

'We must speak to Jeanette McCarthy, sir. She'll be well into her thirties now and must remember a lot from that awful time.'

'My very next words, Lorraine. Yes, she's got to be seen. So that's a nice job for you – take that statement with you to refresh her memory. And I'll come with you. I could do with an outing.'

'Yes, sir.'

'We'll have to check that her parents still live at that address in York; in fact, they might be dead now.'

'I've already checked, sir, via the electoral register. Mr and Mrs McCarthy still live in Viking Road at Farnthorpe, but Jeanette is not listed there.'

'She'll have married and moved away. I suppose we could telephone them to find out where she lives.'

'They're not on the phone, sir.'

'You have been busy! So it means a visit, eh? A reminder of doing house-to-house! Fine, I need something to get my detective juices flowing at full speed, and this just might be it!'

'What time shall we leave, sir?'

'As soon as I've finished this coffee,' and he drained his mug. 'Come along, this is the best lead I've had so far. I'll tell D/I Larkin where we've gone and why. You've done well – and for that, I'll treat you to a lunch in York.'

She blushed ever so slightly and said, 'Thank you, sir.'

16

Mark and Lorraine arrived in Farnthorpe just before noon and had no trouble finding Viking Road. A knock on the door of number 66 quickly produced a handsome dark-haired woman in her late fifties.

'Mrs McCarthy?' Mark asked. 'Maureen McCarthy?'

'Yes?'

Mark identified himself and Lorraine, at which, instead of keeping them waiting on the doorstep, Mrs McCarthy invited them into her lounge. She said her husband was working at Rowntree-Mackintosh if that's who they wanted.

'No,' Mark said. 'I'm sure you can help,' and he explained how he was reopening enquiries into the missing girls, adding that Potter was about to be released and finally referring to Jeanette's childhood role.

'We'd like to talk to Jeanette, to see if she can recall anything about events in Rainesbury. I'm sorry if it revives unwelcome memories, but we feel it is necessary.'

The expression on Mrs McCarthy's face showed the pain of the distant memory. She sighed heavily.

'I don't hold any grudge against that woman,' she said. 'I know Roy doesn't either. He was just glad that Jeanette was spared. It was awful reading about Jeanette's little friends. We'd left

Rainesbury just in time . . . I shudder to think what might have happened to her if Roy hadn't changed jobs, if we'd stayed just one month longer.'

'We shall never know,' was all he could say before continuing, 'Jeanette will be at work? Married? We'd like to have a chat with her as soon as possible.'

'She's not married, superintendent. She does work, she teaches, but she's a nun.'

'A nun?'

'That childhood experience lingered in her mind. She was very religious as a youngster and later, after going to school at the convent in York, well, she felt she had been spared by God. She was the only survivor of those friends and felt she had some kind of mission in life, that she owed God something and that she also owed something to other children. After getting good A levels here, then a degree in theology at Bristol University, she decided to enter the convent. She's now Sister Bernadette, IBVM – that means Institute of the Blessed Virgin Mary. She teaches infants, Catholics of course, so she is doing something for children and combining it with work for God, just as she wanted.'

'Will we be able to have a chat to her?'

'Yes. Just have a word with the Mother Superior or the Headmistress. Because she's teaching, she lives a fairly normal life. Things have relaxed a lot in the monastic orders, they don't wear those long black robes any more. Not at the IBVM anyway – they dress in smart grey suits with short skirts and white blouses and don't cover their heads with wimples. They can wear their own clothes sometimes, and have nice hair-dos.'

'Thanks. We'll drive there next, Mrs McCarthy. Now, while we're here, can you remember anything about those days before the murders?'

'It's all very vague now, superintendent. Fortunately we didn't experience the full horror and so our memories might not be as vivid as they might have been.'

'I appreciate that, but did you meet Louisa Mary Potter, for example? Or Joseph Balleen?'

'Oh yes. I must admit I never liked that woman, there was something about her that made me wary, uneasy in her presence. I never knew what it was but I was always on edge whenever I was close to her. That's not hindsight, superintendent, I felt that way before I knew what she'd done. Roy said I was silly, I think he thought I was being over-dramatic or something. In fact, I think he found her attractive. Any man would, she was a beautiful girl to look at. Rather quiet perhaps, a bit distant. It might have been just shyness. But she and her friend, the Irishman, would take the girls on outings and picnics, all of them went in two cars, Joseph driving one and Louisa the other. Brown Owl would go too. Joseph was so friendly and helpful, teaching them woodcraft and all about wild birds and things. He was very talented and clever.'

'You met Joseph Balleen?'

'Yes, we liked him. Roy often worried about Jeanette and the others going out with him, but we never had reason to think he harmed the girls, he never touched them, you understand. He was a real decent boy. A lovely son for somebody, I always said. He was always called Joseph, by the way, never Joe.'

Mark looked at Lorraine. 'You've something to ask Mrs McCarthy?' he put to her.

'Yes, the Secret Seven?' she addressed Mrs McCarthy. 'Can you remember that?'

'Yes, I can. When Jeanette went out to play after school on Fridays, she always took something to eat. They had a little ritual, you know what girls are, secret signs and a symbolic meal. I knew they had some kind of secret club, but, well, most little girls have and I never quizzed her about it. I regarded it as child's play.'

Lorraine smiled. 'I did that as well when I was little, Mrs McCarthy. Now, I know the girls had their own special secrets, but was there any other secret, a big one perhaps, something that might have involved either Louisa Potter or Joseph Balleen? Or both of them acting together?'

'We asked ourselves that question time and time again, Miss Cashmore, especially after the other girls had died, but we never knew of anything. Is that something you want to ask Bernadette . . . er . . . Jeanette?'

'Yes, we want to see how much she can remember. The Secret Seven's one of the areas we'll be looking at.'

Mrs McCarthy nodded. 'Those youngsters did have a lot of secrets. Joseph seemed to live in a world of secrets. I sometimes wondered if he thought he was a secret agent or something similar.'

'Has he ever been in touch since you left Rainesbury?' was Lorraine's next question.

'No, never. Not a word, not even a Christmas card. We kept in touch with our friends at Rainesbury for a time, especially because of the murders, but no one ever heard from him. He just vanished. It was a bit odd, we thought, just to disappear like that without a word.'

Mark resumed his questioning. 'Did you ever see the old hut the girls used for their Secret Seven meetings?'

'Roy went to have a look at it, but I didn't. Once when the roof leaked, our Jeanette asked him to repair it. She took him along and he put a piece of tarred felt over the hole. It was a disused platelayers' hut built out of creosoted railway sleepers on the coastal line – the line had closed by then. Roy said it was not in a dangerous place and he wasn't worried about them playing there. He told me the girls had written "Private" on the door, followed by the words "Sanctuary of the Secret Seven". It was like a palace to them!'

'I wonder if Potter and Joseph were allowed in?' mused Mark.

'I don't know,' said Mrs McCarthy. 'I never thought to ask.'

Satisfied that she could not tell them anything further, Mark thanked her then drove through York city centre towards Blossom Street. It was almost one o'clock when he arrived at the convent and was told by a secretary that Sister Bernadette was supervising lunch for the eight-year-olds. Could he return after lunch? She would be free until ten past three and would therefore be able to spend time with Lorraine and himself. Mark asked that she be informed of their interest and agreed to return after lunch.

Mark took Lorraine into a nearby inn where they found a table with a useful degree of privacy; she chose an omelette and he opted for a chicken curry with rice. She drank half a pint of lager while he, being the driver, had a pint of apple juice. Mark had never been alone with this quiet young woman and managed to get her chatting about her background, discovering she had chosen the police force in preference to her earlier career. She'd worked for Northern Electric in their customer care department and hailed from a village near Durham City. She liked amateur dramatics and operas and one of her hobbies was embroidery, especially making scenes depicting local landmarks like Durham Cathedral, Richmond market-place, Ralph's Cross or

Middlesbrough's Transporter Bridge. Mark enjoyed her companionship and all too soon, lunch was over.

Jeanette McCarthy, in her role as Sister Bernadette, was a tiny slender woman with round granny spectacles upon her pink face.

Her mousy hair was cut very short but her cheerful face lacked any sign of make-up nor she did wear any jewellery except a watch. She was sprucely dressed in her regulation outfit with its flat black shoes, white blouse and neat grey skirt, rather like a nurse's uniform in grey. When Mark and Lorraine arrived, she was waiting in the splendid hall of the convent which now doubled as the Bar Convent Museum of Religious Life. A ready smile and happy brown eyes made her face look pretty, although she was really a rather plain young woman but by no means severe.

'They said I was wanted by the police!' was her opening remark. 'I'm Sister Bernadette.'

'They also said you'd come quietly,' returned Mark, extending his hand as he announced himself. After he had introduced Lorraine, she took them to a small ante-room where there was a table and some chairs. They settled around the bare table with its tray of glasses and carafe of water.

'Once, this was a busy grammar school and a convent combined,' she explained. 'Now, it's been reorganized on two larger sites. The main building is now a museum. We nuns must still earn our living, so we display the country's religious history – and we do a spot of teaching. So here I am, Friday afternoon and looking forward to a weekend of marking papers and organizing next week's lessons. So what can I do for you?'

For the second time that day, Mark explained his purpose and she listened intently, nodding from time to time.

Eventually, Lorraine took the old statement from her briefcase and gave a photocopy to Sister Bernadette, as a means of refreshing her memory.

'I've got over the trauma of those awful days.' She spoke calmly. 'The horror didn't register when I was little, but later, when I became a teenager, I realized how lucky I'd been. I couldn't escape from hearing about it – the case was all over the papers time and time again. Happily, no one except Mr Kenworthy came to see me once we'd moved away, the papers never came. I could have died horribly, couldn't I? I don't want to gloat over my good fortune, but I do thank God for my life; sincerely. I mean that.'

'You're our only real contact with those poor girls,' Mark said gently to her. 'You know that three of them still haven't been found?'

'Yes, I know. I've gone over it time and time again in my mind and in my prayers, but can't think where they could be. I only wish I could, I really do, I pray for that, for guidance, for some memory that will tell me where they are.'

Mark explained that he also wished to find the graves and informed her of developments so far, including news of Potter's release, then said he wished to question her about the Secret Seven club. She had a very clear memory of those childhood days which, until she had left Rainesbury, had been very happy. She laughed about the girls' own secrets – Joseph had asked them to make secret things to bring to Brownie meetings.

He'd shown them a walking stick that was really a gun, a pack of playing cards in which all the red cards were the ace of diamonds, and a pipe that looked like a pistol. She recalled his hollowed-out book and a stick of seaside rock that was really a torch, while another of his tricks was a shoe where the heel had been hollowed out to contain his money. He said they should all make or find something similar for them to hide their secrets in. He taught them how to conceal things and keep secrets.

'And did you have a secret?' Mark asked.

She blushed. 'Yes, I swore never to reveal my secret.'

'And can you reveal it now?' he smiled.

'Yes, of course. I once saw a lady stealing from our grocery shop. She was a very posh lady who lived in a big house but I saw her take some tins of salmon and put them in her bag, then leave without paying. I knew no grown-up would believe me if I told, so that was my precious secret! I wrote her name on a piece of paper, like we had to in our club, showed it to our members, then hid it.'

'Where did you hide it?'

She smiled again. 'My dad was an amateur magician and he had a special box for making playing cards vanish. I asked him to get me one and he did. He showed me how it worked, with a false bottom, and I hid my secret there. No one ever found it.'

'So that was the kind of secret you all had?'

'Yes, they're nothing now, our precious secrets, they were nothing to grown-ups and really very silly, but we swore on our lives to keep them.'

'Sister Bernadette, was the entire group ever given a big secret to keep, by either Joseph or Louisa? A group secret?'

'Not while I was a member,' she said. 'Looking back, I did sometimes wonder if they'd died because of something silly like that. Joseph would sometimes give us secrets to test us, like telling one of us something about Louisa, such as how she'd lost her purse down the lavatory or something, anything like that to see if we could all keep a secret.'

'And could you?'

'Yes, we could, individually and as a group. We became very good at keeping secrets, it was fun. We got to the stage of having a different secret every week but the silly thing was we could have pretended to have secrets because we had some personal ones that we never revealed to anyone else!'

'Would you have died to keep your secret?' asked Mark.

She paused for a long time. 'Knowing what I know now, the answer is no. But at that time, when I was only eight, well, I might have held out for an awful long time, perhaps too long, not wanting to let Joseph down. I could have died, I suppose. But when the police asked me those questions, I never did tell them my secret, the one about the shoplifter. I kept that very secret – and I was very proud of that.'

'Clearly, Joseph had trained you well. Now, did Louisa ever come to see the group without Joseph?'

'Not very often. She'd sometimes come to our room in Balfour Street and help Brown Owl when she was showing us things, but she didn't come as much as Joseph. We didn't really like her, but I never knew why. She tried to be nice to us but, well, she wasn't our favourite person. She never said much, she'd just stand around, watching Joseph from a distance, waiting for him to tell her what to do.'

'Joseph came a lot did he? To meetings?'

'Not always to weekly meetings. He came mainly when we were doing things outside, like nature trails and woodcraft lessons at weekends. He showed us how to light camp fires and build shelters out of twigs, how to make an oven out of an old tin and some clay, that sort of thing. He once showed me how to make a whistle out of a piece of hazel wood – and it worked. I think Brown Owl liked him!'

'Really? Now that's the first hint of that! Was it a romance, would you have known that at your age?'

'We all thought his sweetheart was Louisa and so we never really considered a romance between him and Brown Owl. Looking back on the way they worked together, I suppose there could have been. Maybe Louisa came along to keep an eye on him, rather than to help the Brownies? Perhaps she was jealous – but I was too young to appreciate that kind of subtlety.'

'Who was Brown Owl?' Mark asked Lorraine. 'Do we know?'

'I expect it'll be in our files, sir. I've never had occasion to check that yet but I'll be surprised if Mr Kenworthy did not interview her.'

'Her name was Mrs Aislaby, I remember. Jennifer, I think,' added Sister Bernadette.

'If she's around, we'll find her.' Mark spoke with confidence. 'Now, you said you met in Balfour Street. Where, exactly?'

'The Scout hut. The Scouts used it on Friday evenings and most weekends, the Cubs had it on Wednesdays and we Brownies used it on Mondays.'

'So when did you use the old platelayers' hut?'

'Fridays. It was our secret place, Mr Pemberton, you had to know the closed fist sign, Joseph taught us that; you had to close your fist to be allowed in. Seriously! Rachel had a lock for the hut and she was caretaker. It was all serious stuff.'

'And were Louisa and Joseph allowed in?'

'No, not even them, not even if they did the closed fist sign. It was our special place. Sometimes if Joseph or Louisa came, we'd meet outside and he'd tell us how to keep more secrets or make secret things and hiding places. Tracy's uncle found the hut for us, he worked on the railways.'

'Fine, thanks. So, in addition to that, Joseph and Louisa would take you for outings, by car. To the riverside or the woods?' Mark asked.

'Yes, to all sorts of places, up to the moors, into the woods, sometimes on Saturday afternoons or Sundays.'

'Who went? The whole of the Brownie troop or just the Secret Seven?'

She had to think about this question. 'Both, I think. I'm sure I can remember us all going in our Brownie uniforms, with some of the mums and dads coming along in their cars. We'd light camp fires and have a singsong. Yes, so it must have been the whole lot of us, all the Brownies.'

'And the Secret Seven? Can you remember if they went with him, or with Louisa?'

'Yes, we did. We sometimes went up to the moors, to where Rachel, Tracy and Michele were later found. I recognized the place from the pictures in the papers. Other times, we went along the riverside. There's a place where there used to be a footbridge across the River Raine, it was slung between two huge rocks. The iron bars are still in the rocks, with chains dangling after all those years. I go there sometimes, when I want to be alone, when I'm away from here. It's so lovely and peaceful.'

'Can I ask this rather nasty question.' Mark spoke slowly, 'Is it the sort of place your friends might be buried?'

'No,' she said firmly. 'It's too rocky, too near the footpath, it was just a short walk from Barkers Dip, that's a place outside Rainesbury. I know I wondered about that and I think Mr Kenworthy did some kind of search there.'

Mark paused for a moment, feeling sure this nun had part of the answers to his questions, and wondered what to ask next. Lorraine put her question, however.

'Sister, it's a tough question to ask a nun, but it's important; it's one which has been exercising the minds of the police and of the victims' parents for a long time. Now you're an adult, you can perhaps clarify things for us, but, well, did Joseph ever indecently assault any of the little girls? It was a question that bothered parents. I know there have been denials and I'd like to ask you because no one has ever been sure of the truth.'

'I know.' She blushed just a little. 'When Mr Kenworthy interviewed me all those years ago, he did ask but I wasn't really sure what he was trying to ask me! But no, Joseph never touched any of us. Nor did Louisa, by the way. I can say that quite categorically. Joseph was genuine, friendly, open and thoroughly decent and he never once touched any of us.'

'Thank you, Sister.' Mark continued, 'Another question that was never answered was why Louisa Potter murdered your friends. If we could answer that, we'd be well on the way to finding out what happened to Suzanne, Helen and Clare, and it would help us enormously with our current enquiries.'

'I just don't know, Mr Pemberton. Sorry, I've puzzled and wept over that question for years and years and I just do not know. The only thing that I wondered was whether it was to do with some kind of secret that one of us knew.'

'Why do you say that?' asked Pemberton.

'It's just that Joseph seemed to have this obsession with training us to keep secrets . . . and Louisa was always there, listening. Just listening, watching and waiting.'

'Listening, watching and waiting for what?' asked Pemberton.

17

The nun shook her head. 'I just don't know, but as a child her behaviour meant very little to me. Then when I started to teach, I was reminded of her actions by one of our pupils, a small boy. I don't know why I should suddenly think of Louisa at that moment, but I did. At playtimes, the boy just stood and watched the others, he never took part in their games – and then I found out he was sneaking into the cloakrooms to steal their sweets and pocket money. He was watching and waiting, waiting for an opportunity to steal. It was just like Louisa used to do . . .'

'You think she was planning something even then?'

'I don't really know, but she did seem engrossed in everything Joseph did, almost as if she was learning from him.'

'Sister, a thought has occurred to me.' Mark changed the direction of his questioning. 'Did Louisa ever try to harm you after you'd left Rainesbury? What I'm asking is, did she ever try to kill you?'

'No, I don't think so. If she did come to our house, I was never aware of it. I never saw her, my parents never had any contact, I heard them say so. They often wondered why neither Joseph nor Louisa contacted them. I was not part of her plans, you see, I'm sure of that. She could have found out where I lived if she'd really wanted to.'

'Which means', Lorraine said, 'that whatever she was planning must have been put into action after your family had left the town?'

'Yes. I have often wondered what it could be, what secret my friends held . . .'

'Did Joseph spend money on the girls?' Mark asked. 'I get the impression he was a free spender so far as Louisa was concerned. He took her out, let her use his car or even gave her one for herself, bought her treats, gave her a life-style she'd never experienced before. I know he gave presents to your friends, he gave Helen a statue of St Patrick for example.'

'He gave me a rosary once, and a book about birds. Yes, he was kind like that, often buying us things, not expensive things but useful things like books or trinket boxes. He did like giving presents. He once brought a small table to our Secret Seven hut and some old chairs.'

'Could you say whether Louisa was jealous of the way he gave all of you presents?'

'That's hard for a little girl to know, superintendent. If I'd had an adult head on those shoulders, I might have thought she was jealous, that she wondered if he was paying more attention to us than to her, a glamorous woman, for that's what she was. I can see her eyes now, watching him with us . . . Looking back, it was quite eerie, unsettling.'

'She wouldn't kill for that, surely?' Even Mark Pemberton was shocked at that suggestion. 'Not out of jealousy, not because he paid attention to children?'

'Why not?' put in Lorraine as she quoted from William Congreve, ' "Heav'n has no rage like love to hatred turn'd, nor Hell a fury like a woman scorn'd." '

'But not small girls, Lorraine. I can't believe any woman would kill them out of sheer jealousy.'

'An unbalanced person can do all kinds of strange things,' Lorraine said. 'And an unbalanced woman is capable of immense evil, total revenge, bitterness of the kind that men might find difficult to believe. I would not reject the idea totally. Even so, I do think there was another reason; I still think we are chasing some kind of secret known only to those girls.'

'And if that was the case, only those girls knew what it was,' sighed Mark. 'And they cannot tell us.'

'Louisa would know,' said the nun quietly.

'Yes, but she's not telling. She's keeping that secret to herself. She hasn't died for it, has she?'

'And she's coming out of prison on Monday.' Mark was now thinking aloud. 'If that secret lies at the hub of our enquiries, I wonder if she will follow it up? Is it feasible that after all this time, she will continue whatever quest she was about; it must have been very important if she was prepared to kill for it.'

'And,' said Lorraine, 'because she was put in prison, she might not have resolved it . . . she went to prison still waiting for an answer! That's it, sir, female cunning at its very worst. She's been waiting all this time, she's been applying for parole, she's been pretending to be a reformed character, she's done all the right things with the sole aim of getting herself out of prison. She intends to follow up that secret . . . that's what she's been plotting, sir. It would explain the supposed turn to religion, the appearance of wanting to help people. I'll bet she's been determined to get out of prison to follow up whatever unfinished business she was compelled to abandon twenty-five years ago.'

'But what on earth could it be?' Sister Bernadette looked at them in astonishment.

'If we knew that, Sister,' said Mark. 'We might have the answers to a lot of other questions. Well, I think we've detained you long enough. We must get back to Headquarters and we must get our thinking caps on. Can we come back to you if we need to?'

'Yes, of course. Did you say she's to be freed on Monday?'

'Yes, on parole. She'll be living under an assumed name and will not be in our area.'

'I shall pray for her,' said Sister Bernadette.

For the first fifteen minutes on the drive back to the incident room, Mark Pemberton was silent.

Lorraine was unsure whether or not to interrupt him for he appeared to be engrossed in deep thought. Her problem was solved when he pulled up at some traffic lights and spoke.

'Sorry, Lorraine, I'm not very communicative. I've been thinking, that chat with Sister Bernadette has helped – and I might add that your female perception might well have been so very accurate. This business about the secret is probably at the centre of everything. Let's assume that Balleen had lots of money . . .'

'Lights, sir.' Lorraine touched his elbow as a car horn behind them began to toot. 'They're on green.'

'Oh, sorry!' and he eased away to continue his journey. 'So if Balleen had money, where did he keep it? We know he sent some home, the bank statements tell us that, but he did not keep much in the bank. He used it as a clearing house, to send money to his parents, so he said.'

'He did spend freely, sir, taking Louisa out a lot, giving presents. He wouldn't have a lot of savings.'

'I think he would have plenty of cash to spend, Lorraine. He was a builder's labourer earning good money with a spot of second-hand car dealing on the side. Those two professions together, plus overtime, would provide the sort of cash that a chap would spend in the pub or on the horses. He didn't use it for that, he spent it on Louisa and the girls. Even the large sums he sent home could have come from car dealings; I do believe he had a lot of honestly earned cash.'

'He'd have few outgoings, sir, no mortgage, no wife and children.'

'Exactly. And he was suspected of robbing banks and building societies. If he was doing that for the IRA, he might have kept some for himself – and that would make him very unpopular, so I'm wondering if the car dealing was a cover of some kind, a front for some of his illicit sources of income. Now, when I looked at his bank statements, they consisted of substantial deposits and some withdrawals such as payments for car insurance, cheques to garages for repairs to cars he put up for sale and so on. That account was for that business. As a labourer, he'd be paid cash, wouldn't he? Builders' labourers in the late 1960s didn't have bank accounts with cheque books and standing orders. But he had one, a business account. There were transfers out; we know some of that went to Ireland. Some quite large sums were paid in, ostensibly from his car dealings, and I feel that was a cover story. He had lots of cash and it didn't come from mummy and daddy. So where did it come from? Was it all from honest work, or was he fiddling the IRA out of its crime proceeds? Or was he a bank raider working for both himself and the IRA?'

'Is there any evidence to suggest that, sir?'

'Not in the sections of the file that I've managed to read so far.'

'If he was a villain, sir, he was a very clever one.'

'And they're the worst kind, Lorraine. A church-going, helpful, kind, generous, personable young man couldn't be a villain, could he? That's the image he portrayed. Someone whiter than white. If he was a wrong-un, he had a marvellous cover story, hadn't he? Not one of those families who knew him said a nasty thing about Joseph.'

'If he was a villain, sir, would Louisa Mary Potter be aware of it?'

'That's a very good question. Suppose he was a baddy, and suppose she discovered his secret – that word again, Lorraine. Secret. His secret this time – would she keep his secret or would she blackmail him? Would she want cash for keeping her mouth shut? Or would she try to find out what he was up to and quietly set about her own scheme to get her hands on his wealth, his hidden wealth, his secret cache of funds, wherever it was . . .'

'Like the little boy in the playground, sir? Waiting quietly in the background, watching and planning . . .'

'And still waiting, Lorraine. Still waiting, after all these years . . . Suppose he did have a lot of money, what would he do with it?'

'Well, sir, after listening to his antics with the children, I think he'd hide it somewhere, in a secret place. He did seem obsessed with secret hiding places and implied he was something of a secret agent . . . maybe he lived in a dream world . . .'

'Precisely. But I've a feeling that it wasn't a dream world, Lorraine, I think a lot of it was real. His criminal world might have been one of the secrets kept by the bairns, eh? They wouldn't know what sort of secret it was, of course . . . but if Louisa realized what he was doing, she might get her eyes on the cash, she might want a share of it, an illicit share, especially if he'd run off to Ireland without telling her, especially if there was another woman involved . . . where's that Brown Owl now, Lorraine?'

'Mrs Aislaby? You don't think he ran off with her, do you?'

'We'll have to find out, won't we? Did she kill through jealousy? Or did Louisa kill those children because she thought they knew where Joseph had hidden his loot?'

'Wasn't it in the bank, sir?'

'No, it wasn't. There was a deposit in the bank, in Balleen and

Potter's joint name, a working account, but there is something very secret which is kept in a safe deposit centre, Lorraine, and we can't find out what it is.'

'Is it in their names, sir?'

'Yes, in joint names.'

'So Potter will have access to it, sir, when she comes out of prison?'

'Yes. And Balleen has access to it as well, wherever he is. He's not been in touch with the centre or the bank for over twenty-five years and there was only one key to the safe deposit box. One key only . . . Now, if she has the key . . . the key! That's it . . . where is the key? She won't have it in prison, so where are her belongings? Or did Balleen hide the key with one of the children? If he was going away for a short visit to Ireland, would he take the key with him? Or would he leave it here, in some safe and secret place? Is that what Potter was trying to torture out of them, from just one of them, the whereabouts of that bloody key . . .'

'Sir, but if there was a lot of money in the safe deposit centre, surely Balleen would want it? Surely he'd have tried to gain access to it before now?'

As Lorraine looked at him, he turned to face her and he knew what she was trying to tell him.

'Sir, the road . . . keep your eyes on the road . . .'

'God, yes, sorry.' He swung the wheel back on course. 'You're not suggesting he's dead, are you, Lorraine?'

'It would explain a lot, sir, his mysterious absences for example. His lack of contact with old friends, the children, his family, his lodgings, his bank manager . . .'

'And if there is money in that safe deposit, it will all belong to Louisa Mary Potter . . .'

'And she might have killed Joseph to make sure she gained access to it, sir. She now stands to get the lot.'

'Now, that is a motive, isn't it?' said Pemberton. 'Greed. Would she kill six children and a charming Irishman out of sheer greed?'

'From what I know of her, sir,' said Lorraine, 'the answer is a resounding yes. And I speak as a woman.'

'Let's call and see old Mr Kenworthy on the way home, shall we? You've not met him, have you?'

It was just after four o'clock when Mark and Lorraine arrived at Mr Kenworthy's house and they were ushered in with promises of a cup of tea and some cakes. After the introductions, Mark explained the theory that he had just produced and the old detective listened carefully. Alice brought in a tray of tea, asked Lorraine to be mum and disappeared into the kitchen as Mark completed his outline. When Mark had finished, he asked for Kenworthy's opinions.

'You've not read my notebooks, Mark?'

'My men have them – they're programming the data into our computer, so I've not had a chance to read them.'

Kenworthy told him that Mrs Aislaby, the Brown Owl for the Brownies, had been interviewed during the original enquiry. He had been satisfied there was no romance between her and Balleen. Mrs Aislaby said he was simply a very nice young man who had a remarkable rapport with children.

Sadly, no further interviews were possible because Mrs Aislaby had died of cancer about three years ago.

When Mark pressed for Kenworthy's views about Balleen's source of income, the old man laughed.

'It's in my books, Mark, it's all in my books. I did a thorough investigation, you know, without computers. It's all recorded if you care to look. As you suspect, and as I hinted when we met before, he didn't make all his spare cash by buying and selling cars. That was his cover, that was to explain to people like his bank manager where sudden large sums came from. He was a robber, Mark, he was raiding building societies, banks, post offices and even wage deliveries, and he was getting away with thousands of pounds in cash. There's a list in my notebook with dates, times, places and amounts taken. He was extremely successful. He always wore a mask, a black woollen balaclava, and blue denim overalls; he used a gun, at least it looked like a gun. We thought it was a model . . .'

'That nun saw one, sir,' said Lorraine. 'She said it looked like a pistol but it was really a pipe. And those kids probably unwittingly hid it for him . . . if there was a search, evidence would never be found on him . . .'

'My God, I've not done my homework on this one, Mr Kenworthy . . . time's been so short . . .'

'Then ask me! I don't know what you want to know unless you

ask me, do I? Isn't that the first rule of good interrogation? Be precise and direct with your questions? Ask what you want to know? I would never insult you by telling you things I thought you'd already discovered . . .'

'Twenty-five years is a long time ago, Mr Kenworthy. I can't assess all the information of the period . . .'

'Of course not. So, as I said, ask me. Ask and you shall receive, said a man with greater authority than I. When you came to see me before, you were asking all about Potter and her crimes, not Balleen, and not about bank raids that were not part of that brief.'

'So, what can you tell us about Joseph Patrick Balleen?' asked Mark, smiling at the old man who was seated before him.

Mr Kenworthy reiterated what Mark and Lorraine had discovered – the charm, the kindness, the affability of Joseph Patrick Balleen – but went on to say that the friendly Irishman was also a young criminal of considerable skill and daring. In spite of his youth, he had never been caught and never been prosecuted. He'd committed his crimes at lunchtime in and around the towns where he was working as a builder's labourer; he excused his lunchtime absences from the workmen's huts by saying he was going to Holy Mass during his meal break. And as a jobbing builder, he'd travelled across the north of England, sometimes working for one day in one place, robbing and returning to base quickly. He managed to conceal his gun, overalls and balaclava in case his car was ever searched.

Sometimes, he would work for a week in one place, committing his robbery on the last day. He was a fast operator, sussing out premises very speedily, then robbing them just as swiftly.

When he had robbed a bank or a building society, he would conceal the takings until the fuss had died down, later splitting the proceeds into smaller amounts and paying them into various building society, bank or post office savings accounts under a variety of names. If he did this locally, in banks where he was known, he would say he'd sold another car – and who would suspect this charming man in Rainesbury of robbing a bank seventy miles away in Newcastle, Leeds or Wakefield?

He used his constantly changing pool of vehicles to go to work, thus avoiding police scrutiny of repeated trips in the same vehicle. He had been questioned several times about the robberies, chiefly because of his Irish accent, but he always managed to make his pals believe he had been with them, or at Mass. He was a ubiquitous character, always making sure he was seen around, seen to be doing things, getting involved, throwing up a wonderful smoke screen, but conversely becoming invisible when he needed to.

'We never pinned a single crime on him, Mark, not one. We set traps, we carried out observations and we watched his lodgings, but he was as cunning as a fox, as slippery as an eel and as clever as a cartload of monkeys. In spite of our supervision, he was able to carry out raid after raid, week after week, in different parts of the north of England. Not once could we obtain proof against him. He could always dodge the police, even plain clothes officers, and he seemed to know when we were about.

'He was so clever, so devious, he seemed to have been brought up on a diet of spy novels and secret service dodges. I did wonder if he had been trained in these skills. He would use different clothes sometimes, sporting a lot of different caps or hats which he'd throw away when he'd used them. He was a charming young fellow for all that, the women loved him and mothered him.'

'And did he really have a family back in Ireland?' asked Lorraine.

'Oh yes, and he did send them money, legal money from his job. He loved his brothers and sisters too, he was a warm, friendly family man, a real contradiction.'

When Mr Kenworthy had finished his story of Balleen's criminal behaviour, he said that the man's sudden disappearance did not, at the outset, cause them any worries. That he had gone home did seem feasible, but as he was not suspected of murdering the girls, those leads were not pursued. When he had gone, the robberies ceased – he'd conducted them over a period of almost two years in all. There had been talk of attempting extradition if proof of his involvement in any robbery was forthcoming, but there had never been sufficient evidence to justify that; besides, he'd never been seen in Ireland since leaving home to work in England.

'I did have visits from the Special Branch,' Kenworthy went on. 'They were very interested in Balleen because of his family's IRA connections. They thought he was here as part of an active service unit, not necessarily planting bombs, but fund-raising to enable the Provisionals to be set up, armed and trained. You'll recall that they increased their terrorism from 1968 onwards. But Balleen had all the required skills and attributes to be one of their lilywhites; he had no criminal record and cultivated the appearance of being a good Catholic youth, which he was not; no killer can be. I'm not saying he was a killer at that stage, but I reckon he was heading that way. His religion was all a sham but he was idealistic, gullible and devoted to the cause which had been bred into him by his family.'

After listening to Mr Kenworthy's account, Mark asked, 'So what happened to all the stolen money?'

'A lot of it didn't get to the IRA, that's for sure,' said the detective. 'It's still in the UK. I think some went to Ireland but a lot was kept here to fund their activities in this country without the problems of transferring funds. It's probably in dozens of separate deposit accounts and now it'll be worth millions. We reckon he got away with about £360,000 all told; some did go to Ireland via bank transfers but a lot, about £340,000 we think, was kept on deposit until it was required, either in whole or in part. The building society limit for deposits was then £3,000 so we believe he opened as many as a hundred accounts in different names in different societies in different towns across England . . .'

'But if that money's still here, sir,' breathed Lorraine, 'it'll be gaining interest, as it has done for twenty-five years . . . it'll be worth millions . . .'

'Exactly,' said Mr Kenworthy. 'I did an estimate after Mark called the other day and I reckon, based on my estimate of £340,000, it could be worth in excess of four million pounds now. From our point of view, there is no *proof* it was stolen money. Plenty of speculation, but no proof, no evidence. Legally, in the absence of such proof, it belongs to Balleen and perhaps Potter. Even if we could find Balleen and prosecute him for theft, it would still be a tricky job proving that the money in those accounts was the actual proceeds of any crime. In fact, Mark, it would be impossible – and you know the limitations of the Police Property Act and the Theft Act so far as the restitution of stolen property is concerned. If we can't prove the cash was stolen or that it is the proceeds of stolen money, it will belong to Potter and Balleen.'

'Even so, I'll bet there are lots of people who would like to get their hands on that loot!' said Lorraine.

'Including the IRA,' added Mr Kenworthy.

18

Mark and Lorraine returned to Room 207 a few minutes before five o'clock and found it as busy as ever. Everyone was present, except for Agar and Holdsworth who were still in Rainesbury; they'd phoned in to say they were busy on a line of enquiry in the town and would go straight home when they had concluded it; they did not wish to interrupt it at this point.

Mark asked the others to gather around and informed them of his latest discoveries. He told them everything, including the involvement of the Special Branch and possibly MI5, plus the links with the IRA, and concluded by saying that, in view of this ominous and very real development, the protection of Kathleen Hicks assumed a higher profile. He told them that he had already warned Potter's southern guardians of the threat and that they were mounting additional protection; he hated lying to his staff, but had no choice. He reminded Detective Sergeant Tony Ashton that his responsibilities had now increased and advised him to check his plans and to call for more officers and weapons if he thought it necessary.

'If the IRA is after that money,' he said, 'they'll not kill either of those women until they've persuaded them to talk. And if they do kidnap them, I wouldn't like to be in their shoes. They'll torture them until they talk. They'll do to them what Potter did to those little bairns.'

'Does that apply to Hicks, sir?' asked one of the sergeants. 'I can't say I'll be sorry if it happens to Potter!'

'We think so, she's been Potter's closest companion and friend for years; if Potter's discussed any of her secrets, it will surely have been with Hicks.'

Mark reminded them that the women were due for release on Monday next; the release itself would be subjected to carefully planned security arrangements so that any watchers at or near the prison entrances would not be able to observe the actual departures. So far as Mark was concerned, his worries would really begin when Hicks walked into the safe house in Swandale.

Before dismissing his officers, Mark itemized the details which they must obtain from the existing files and papers, including Kenworthy's notebooks. Balleen was to continue to be targeted and any references to him highlighted; his movements, his connections and everything to do with his life in the UK had to be abstracted. And Balleen himself had to be found and interviewed – the Garda had sent a message to say he was not in Ireland and his family had no idea of his whereabouts; they'd not seen or heard from him since 1967. Of particular interest was the person who had made it known that Balleen had left the country. Who had actually told that story? How had the news been broken? Where were his belongings?

'It's more important than ever that I find that man and know everything about him,' Pemberton concluded.

He continued by instructing D/I Larkin to make sure his officers scanned either HOLMES, Kenworthy's books or the statements for all references to the Brownie group and their activities with either Potter or Balleen or both. Where were the objects Balleen had used, such as the mock pistol/pipe, the hollowed-out book, the walking-stick gun and his other belongings? He wanted every known reference to the words 'secret' or 'Secret Six' in the files, and he wanted abstracts from Kenworthy's notebooks about any robberies supposedly committed by Balleen. Dates, times and places, whether they were banks, building societies, post offices or wages snatches and the amounts taken.

'I'd like you to arrange for someone to get around the building societies, Paul,' he addressed his inspector. 'I'm not sure how co-operative they will be, especially as today's managers are more security-conscious than those in the sixties, but we need to know of any deposit accounts held since 1966 or 1967 which have not been touched since then. They could have been opened at any branch in the north of England, or even further afield, and they'll be in a range of names. Find out if an eighteen-year-old Irishman could legally open accounts or whether he'd either need some authority or have to adopt false birth particulars. If he used a false name, he might have been able to convince them he was old enough.

'The accounts will now be computerized, of course, but the old system was to issue each depositor with a simple book which recorded each transaction. You could virtually open an account in any name because it was a simple deposit of cash; overdrafts weren't allowed then, or borrowings. To withdraw your cash, all you had to do was convince the cashier that you were legitimate. If you had the passbook, that was usually enough.'

'I understand,' said Paul Larkin.

'It's more than possible that Balleen had several accounts with one society, probably under a variety of names and opened in separate branches of that same society. We're thinking in terms of a hundred or more accounts, Paul; the dates of the deposits might point us in the right direction. We need a list of all such unused accounts which are still active and we can eliminate those which are definitely not linked with Balleen.'

'I understand,' nodded Paul.

When Mark had finished talking to his teams, he thanked them and said that tonight he would be studying Mr Kenworthy's notebooks; tomorrow, therefore, which was Saturday, there might be further actions as a result of those studies. If so, he would announce them at the morning conference. If things were quiet, it might be possible for some of the officers to have Saturday afternoon off, and for half the teams to take the whole of Sunday off duty. From Monday, the level of commitment would increase with the release of Hicks and Potter.

'OK. Well, if there's no further business, you can go home and I'll see you tomorrow. We'll see what Saturday brings,' he added.

Having made himself a dinner of haddock parcels stuffed with herbs followed by spicy orange creamed rice, Mark settled by his blazing log fire with a glass of brandy. He began to read Kenworthy's notebooks, albeit in photocopy form. He'd left the originals in the incident room because they were being processed in detail for HOLMES; Barbara had had the foresight to make several photocopies of Kenworthy's neatly kept pocket-books. As Mark began to read, he realized that the procedures of a quarter of a century ago did not differ greatly from those of today. Kenworthy's notes were his and his alone; the statements taken by his teams of detectives formed no part of his own diary but would be typed, logged and analysed for retention in the murder file. Nonetheless, Mr Kenworthy's notes did contain summaries of the morning and afternoon incident room conferences plus his daily index of facts, names, vehicles and sundry subjects.

There were brief character sketches of key personalities: that of Balleen reiterated what Mark had already learned; Potter was listed as evil, scheming and untrustworthy, a suspect from the start; while Mrs Aislaby was caring and romantic, the Stablers caring and forgiving, the Hallidays tough and unforgiving . . .

As he read, he realized that not all of Mr Kenworthy's thoughts were here; the old detective probably thought that his books did contain a comprehensive record of that harrowing enquiry but in fact they did not. As a record, it was excellent and useful, but it did lack the personal touch. It contained facts, not impressions. Talking to the old man was the only real way to understand the deeper aspects of the enquiry. Mark would see him again and again if necessary.

Then the telephone rang. Mark glanced at his grandfather clock – it was almost nine thirty.

'It's the control room, sir, Sergeant Martin speaking. Sorry to bother you in your own time, but it is important. Can you ring Miss Clayton at the Mermaid Villa in Rainesbury? She called the incident room number but there's no one here, the call was rerouted to us. She did say it was very important and urgent. Her number's 824545.'

'Will do, sergeant. Thanks.'

Pondering the reason for the call, Mark rang the number and was rewarded by Brenda Clayton's voice saying, 'Mermaid Villa Guest House, can I help you?'

'It's Detective Superintendent Pemberton speaking, Miss Clayton. You wanted to talk to me.'

'Oh, thank you for calling back, I'm sorry to ring so late . . .' she began, and he assured her that it was not a problem.

'Yesterday when you called, you asked whether Joseph Balleen was allergic to potatoes . . .'

'Yes?'

'Well, would you believe it, but I've got an Irishman in now and he's allergic to them. I've just done him an evening meal, he's booked in for tonight and he said he can't eat chips or potatoes in any form because he's allergic. I thought you might want to know.'

'Is he still there?' Mark asked.

'Yes, he's gone up to his room. He said he wanted an early night and he'd see me at breakfast.'

'Can you describe him? It's not your old friend Joseph Patrick Balleen, is it?'

'Oh, no, I'd know him anywhere, even now. No, this man is getting on a bit, late forties perhaps, with grey hair, quite a lot of it, cut short. He's not particularly tall, average height for a man, and fairly thick-set. He has a strong Irish accent, Mr Pemberton, and signed himself in as Eammon Lagan.'

'Luggage? Has he any luggage? Or a car?'

'Yes, he has a large travelling bag, like a soft suitcase, the sort students often use. And he has a car, a Volvo, it's parked on my car-park. I've got the number – I thought you might need that. He's signed it in the register and I've looked at the car, the numbers do agree,' and she passed it to him. He made a note and said he'd check with the PNC to trace the registered owner.

'We'd like to see him and interview him, Miss Clayton, so don't you say a word. Don't let him know you've rung me, I don't want him frightened off. I'll have an officer come over and take a look at him, possibly without the Irishman knowing in the first instance. We'll be discreet . . . Thanks for calling, this could be very important to us.'

Mark replaced his telephone and pondered his next move. From the man's description, he did seem to be the same character who'd eaten in the Smugglers' Arms on Sunday. If he was, then he was certainly of major interest to this enquiry. Then Mark remembered that Agar and Holdsworth had said they'd be late finishing at Rainesbury. Were they still in that town? He went outside to his car, switched on the official radio and called their number, Papa Papa 49.

He had to call several times before he got the response, 'Papa Papa 49 receiving. Go ahead, over.'

'Papa Papa 2,' said Pemberton. 'Your location please.'

'Rainesbury, sir, outside a fish-and-chip shop. We got involved with enquiries into Balleen and thought we'd better finish them before we came back.'

'Good work, we'll talk about that tomorrow, but I've a job for you in Rainesbury . . .'

'It's Holdsworth speaking, sir, Jim's in the chip shop organizing our evening meal.'

Mark explained about the phone call and Holdsworth said he would happily check it out as he was already in town.

Mark added that he would like his men to have a look at Lagan; if there was any chance of a photograph, then that would be even better – they could have the picture examined by Special Branch, MI5 or even the SAS. Holdsworth said he had a camera in the car, he usually carried one, but he lacked a zoom lens. He'd try his best, although for usable pictures he might have to wait until daylight. Mark then gave him the registration number of the Volvo being used by Lagan and said he hadn't yet attempted to trace the registered keeper.

He'd do that next; Holdsworth could do likewise.

'I don't want this Lagan fellow frightened off, Derek. I need to know what he's up to and we need to keep an eye on him. But for God's sake be careful, we don't really know who he is.'

'Me and Jim can cope tonight, sir, we can keep going all night on this one if you wish. We'll need reinforcements tomorrow morning. Jim has a cousin here, we could always get a bed there – or we could book into Mermaid Villa. He could sleep while I do a bit of snooping and vice versa.'

'Right, that seems a good idea. Can you arrange something? Sort things out between yourselves and I'll send reinforcements in the morning. We'll fix overtime payments and expenses later. But remember, that man could be our assassin so he might be tooled up. Be careful, very careful, especially if you're in the same building as him. If you go to Mermaid Villa, tell Miss Clayton who you are, she's the lady who told me about this, she's expecting some response from us.'

'Very good, sir. He'll not latch on to us, though – we can disappear into the woodwork if we have to. I think we'll say we are television researchers.' Derek Holdsworth sounded confident. 'Let's hope he leads us to the other chap too.'

Mark was delighted that Holdsworth and Agar had the loyalty to remain in Rainesbury in pursuit of their enquiries; he'd get a résumé tomorrow. Had they produced anything of importance, he would have been told during their discussion. Before leaving his radio, he called up the control room and asked for a PNC check on Lagan's Volvo. The check was not particularly helpful, for it said that the car was owned by a car hire company in Liverpool. The name was given; Mark decided that one of tomorrow's actions would be to see if anyone at the firm remembered the man called Lagan. But that could wait until tomorrow. Another action for tomorrow would be for officers to visit every boarding house and hotel in and around Rainesbury to see if the potato-hating Irishman had lodged there. He must have been sleeping somewhere – and where was his young pal, the man with the ear-ring?

Mark tried to settle down by reading some more of Kenworthy's notes before having an early night.

Agar and Holdsworth arrived at Mermaid Villa shortly before ten o'clock, showed their warrant cards to Miss Clayton and explained that Pemberton had sent them.

She told them that Lagan was in Room 10 at the back of the building, that he'd booked in for three nights for dinner, bed and breakfast, and that he was alone. Holdsworth asked for Room 11, and Agar for Room 9, which were located at each side of their target's room along the rear corridor of the first floor. She had no trouble meeting their requests because there was no one else in the building apart from a regular, Mr Newman, who was in Room 4. Winter was always quiet for seaside lodging houses.

Agar told Miss Clayton that they would adopt the role of television researchers; if anyone asked who they were, she must use that explanation. They were here for the weekend doing preliminary research for a projected ITV series about the fishing industry along the north-east coast. It was a feasible story and it explained the camera and any hanging about that might be evident in town. The detectives had shaving gear and toiletries in the car – they always carried them in case of sudden decisions of this kind.

Agar settled into his room, making a show of flushing the toilet and banging wardrobe doors, just to let his neighbour know that someone else was in residence. To be too quiet would be to hint of surveillance to a man like the so-called Lagan, he believed. As Agar settled in, Holdsworth remained downstairs in the lounge; he'd already obtained a rear door key from Miss Clayton so that he could wander around the grounds in the darkness.

He'd equipped himself with a torch too, from his official car, to examine Lagan's car and generally keep observation for clandestine movements in and around the lodging house. He had not forgotten that two men had lunched in the Smugglers' Arms so the slumbering man's colleague might be around, watching perhaps, safeguarding the Irishman, checking his reliability. Like the police, villains also worked in teams, each watching the other's back.

After Miss Clayton had gone to bed, Holdsworth switched out the lights and sat in the darkness of the lounge, a chore he had done so many times during his service as a detective. Even after a full day's work, he could sit alone like this without dropping off to sleep and he had the ability to allow his mind to wander over things of interest which kept him awake while simultaneously maintaining very keen observation. It was while sitting in a comfortable chair in a corner away from the bow window that he became aware of someone outside.

It was 2.30 a.m. He heard a distinct footfall on the gravel drive and was on his feet in seconds, cat-like, ears straining for further noises. It might have been a fox or a cat out there, but it had sounded more like a human stepping on to the gravel. He moved through the silent darkness, edging towards the windows, but it was very dark out there; most of the town's street lights had been extinguished at midnight and the majority of householders were in bed.

There was no moon, but, as he stood and peered into the gloom, knowing better than to light his torch, he did begin to discern objects outside. A bench on the lawn, a sundial at the edge of the rose garden, the gateposts . . . but of anything or anyone moving, he saw nothing.

Trusting in his own senses and confident that he *had* heard someone out there, he decided to investigate. Treading silently through the large house, he made for the back door, opened it quietly and stepped into the darkness of the night. It was cold outside; there was a northerly breeze blowing off the North Sea and it made him shiver as he inched across the sandstone flags behind the house. Soon, he was treading silently over grass, a patch of lawn which separated the car-park from the house, and he found a sturdy sycamore whose trunk would conceal him if indeed there was a prowler.

Having gained the security of the tree, he halted to listen. From here, he could distinguish the lighter colour of the tarmac of the boarding house car-park for it reflected the very low light; he could see the plain police car which he and Jim used. It had nothing to indicate that it was a police vehicle although a careful scrutiny would suggest that the radio inside was not a conventional private radio.

Nearby was the suspect car, the Volvo hired from Liverpool, and another smaller vehicle occupied a far corner. It would be Mr Newman's Fiat, he knew from his earlier inspection of the register.

And then he saw a movement, a shadow, a figure moving around the edge of the car-park, partly obscured by the sheer blackness of shadows around the rhododendrons. The figure moved swiftly and then Derek saw it head for the car-park; it stopped near Newman's Fiat and moved onto the police Fiesta, where it halted. Derek heard the metallic noise, the man was attempting to gain entry . . . he was forcing the door . . .

Derek ran towards his car.

He managed to reach the shadowy figure before the man realized he had been observed; he had been too occupied with opening the locked door to notice the sound of Derek's approach.

Then Derek flashed his torch.

'Police,' he said, shining the light on to the face of a young man. 'Don't move . . . stay right where you are.'

The man froze, his back against the body of the Fiesta as Derek approached. Derek's torch picked out the short cropped dark hair, the gold ear-ring in the pierced lobe of the right ear, the solid face with a few days growth of whiskers . . .

'Don't move,' Derek warned him.

But the young man's hand suddenly moved from inside his jacket. Too late, Derek Holdsworth realized that the hand was holding an automatic pistol. There was a flash of light, a sharp retort and Derek Holdsworth fell dead with a bullet through his forehead.

Somewhere in the night, a dog began to bark.

19

The body of Detective Constable Derek Holdsworth was found beside his car at 4 a.m. that Saturday morning. The finder was a uniformed constable on foot patrol. PC 502 Tim Matthews, freshly out of his probation with but two years and six months service, was initially of the opinion that he had found a drunk, but a touch of that pale, cold and clammy skin and the sight of blood around the head and upon the ground rapidly jerked him into the realization that this was no drunk, neither was the death from natural causes. Matthews hauled his radio from his pocket, gave a succinct situation report and, somewhat breathlessly, called for assistance.

'Preserve the scene, don't touch anything and wait there,' he was instructed by Rainesbury Control.

Within three minutes, the duty inspector arrived; he was accompanied by a sergeant and two more constables who came in two separate cars. Each had its blue light rotating but they managed to arrive without sounding their sirens. Nonetheless, the dog resumed its barking and lights were switched on in one or two neighbouring houses. The inspector, John Bevin, hurried across to the anxious constable who once again shone his torch upon his discovery. Bevin knew a murder victim when he saw one and returned to his car to call out the officer in charge of Rainesbury CID, Detective Chief Inspector Howard French.

His second request was for a doctor to certify the death, a necessary part of procedures, even though Bevin knew the fellow had been dead for an hour or two by the look of him.

'Anybody recognize him?' Bevin asked his men when he returned to the body.

The darkness didn't help, but none recognized the man on the ground.

'Keep away from the body,' Bevin instructed them. 'Sarge,' he called to one of the sergeants, 'do a quick recce around the car-park, will you? I don't think for one minute that chummy will be hanging around, but we must be certain. Keep an eye open for the weapon, a firearm of some kind. And don't get shot yourselves. While I wait for the cavalry, I'll do a PNC check on this car,' and he indicated the one beside the body.

As his men vanished into the surrounding darkness with their inadequate torches lighting the way, Bevin radioed Control and asked for the necessary PNC check on the stationary car. Within seconds, the response came and Control radioed him to say, 'Sir, it's blocked.'

'Blocked! God, is this one of ours, then? Try the DVLC or our own records . . .'

Blocked was the term used to show that the vehicle in question was an official police or government vehicle, or being used by the Security Service, or engaged upon some other national, official, covert or mysterious official purpose.

Resisting the temptation to examine the car physically, Bevin waited. Scenes of Crime would play hell if he as much as opened a door. The wait seemed an eternity as he looked upon the casually dressed body and his feeling of dismay increased with every passing minute. A murder on his patch . . . questions would be asked . . . It was a relief when Control called back. But his relief was quickly dispersed when Control said, 'Sir, it's one of ours, it's a CID car based at Headquarters.'

'Oh my God . . .' he groaned.

If the dead man was a police officer he would be carrying a warrant card but Bevin knew he must not touch anything; it was vital that the scene be preserved exactly as it was and he could do nothing more until the arrival of the CID. That bloody dog was still barking too . . . and then he saw a figure walking towards him from the rear door of the boarding house.

He shone his torch upon a man who looked for all the world like an ageing university student or even a lecturer, in jeans and a heavy grey sweater. 'What's all the din?' the man was grumbling. 'Bloody dogs barking, car doors slamming, radios burbling. Some of us like our sleep . . .'

'Don't move,' ordered Bevin. 'Police.'

'Take that sodding torch out of my eyes,' cried the oncoming man. 'Who are you? What's going on here?'

'Inspector Bevin, Rainesbury Police . . .'

'I'm CID,' responded the other. 'D/S Agar, Headquarters. Sir, what the bloody hell's going on?'

'Is that your car?' The body lay on the far side as Bevin shone his light on the number plate.

'Yes, sir, well, it's our official vehicle. Why? Has somebody had a go at it?'

'Sarge, sorry.' Bevin's attitude changed. 'Look, this is bloody terrible, but there's a dead man beside your car,' and when Bevin described the victim, Agar knew who it was. He hurried towards the car with Bevin at his heels, lighting the way with his bobbing torch. When Agar saw the still form, albeit at a distance, he said, 'Oh my God, sir . . . this is my mate, Derek Holdsworth. D/C Holdsworth . . .'

The position of the body, the pallor of the skin and the awful wound in the head said everything. And then he realized the truth. Apart from the little Fiat and his own car, the boarding house car-park was empty. Lagan's Volvo had gone. He ran back into the house, galloped up the stairs and burst into Room 10. It was empty, with all the signs of a hurried departure. Bevin was right behind him.

'We've a man in the frame already.' Agar told him about Lagan. 'And a car to find. We should put out an immediate call, sir, to trace an Irishman calling himself Eammon Lagan and his car. I'll give you a description. We must preserve this room . . .'

'Sergeant,' said Bevin as they walked slowly along the landing, 'has there been some kind of covert operation in town? Something I should know about?'

'I am here on duty, sir, if that's what you are asking.'

'And does D/C/I French know about it?'

'I've no idea, sir, you'll have to speak to Detective Superintendent Pemberton.'

'I would rather our Divisional Chief Superintendent spoke to him, sergeant; this sounds as if it's rapidly developing into something beyond the brief of a humble uniform inspector.'

'I think you could be right, inspector,' agreed Jim Agar. 'Now, who's going to tell Derek's wife and kids?'

'That's a job for your Superintendent Pemberton.' Bevin spoke coldly as he hurried outside because he had heard the arrival of another car. It would be Detective Chief Inspector French.

'You'd better be available to talk to him,' Bevin told Jim Agar.

Pemberton was woken by the telephone. He had been dreaming about church bells ringing and the sound of the telephone bell on the landing was an echo of his dream. But this was no dream. He reached out and lifted the handset.

'Pemberton speaking.' His voice sounded full of sleep, which it was. He had been enjoying a restful slumber.

'Ramsden here,' growled a voice at the other end.

'Sir?' Pemberton knew George Ramsden, the tough chief superintendent in charge of Rainesbury Division.

'Have you been setting up some kind of operation on my patch without my knowledge?' he demanded.

'It's a quarter past five in the morning . . . are you ringing to ask me that?'

'Answer my question, detective superintendent,' was the curt response.

'There is an operation in hand, Mr Ramsden, but it covers a wide area, not just Rainesbury.'

'Then you've got yourself a murder investigation as well, detective superintendent; one of your own officers has bought it. Holdsworth.'

'Derek Holdsworth?' Mark was alert now. 'How, sir? When?'

'Shot in the head in the early hours by some bloody Irishman who's done a runner. You'd better get yourself over here mighty bloody sharpish and tell me what's been going on.'

'Sir,' said Mark.

As was his practice in any murder call-out, Mark did not panic into rushing from the house as if all the hounds of hell were on his tail. The fact that Ramsden was aware of the death meant that all the necessary preliminary procedures would have been set in motion and so he shaved, showered and dressed in one of his many smart suits. He had a cooked breakfast and packed himself a lunch box. Then he rang Paul Larkin. He apologized for ringing so early but told his own incident room D/I what had occurred. In view of Holdsworth's death, there would be the inevitable repercussions.

'I'm going to Rainesbury now, Paul, but I don't think there's any need at this stage to call out our own teams, it'll take time to complete the prelims. Can you inform our teams when they assemble this morning? There'll have to be a separate incident room for Derek's murder; I'm not sure whether we'll take it on board because, operationally, the murder's the responsibility of D/C/I French in Rainesbury. So the incident room should be at Rainesbury Divisional Headquarters – but with our complication, who knows? I'll try to update you by telephone when I've got more information, and I might be back in time for the morning conference anyway. And someone will have to tell Mrs Holdsworth.'

'A job for the force welfare officer?' suggested Paul Larkin.

'Good idea, that's what she gets paid for. I'll suggest that to Mr Ramsden. Right, I'm off.'

Mark's sorrow at the death of one of his officers intensified as he undertook the journey to Rainesbury. At first, the awful truth seemed difficult to absorb, but as he approached the town, he could have wept for Derek's wife and little family, and he knew that his own men must have made a terrible mistake to allow this to happen. But their mistakes were his responsibility; that's what he got paid for. What the hell had Agar been doing to let Holdsworth get himself shot? And where was Agar at the time? What had they discovered in this sodding town?

The first man he saw as he eased into Beach Road was a uniformed constable who recognized him and guided him to a parking place, and as he walked around to the rear of Mermaid Villa he saw Agar. Agar was clearly awaiting his arrival, wanting to explain things, upset and anxious.

Pemberton, his anger having increased as he approached the scene, jabbed a finger in his chest. 'You've got some bloody explaining to do, Jim, and it had better be good. I am appalled at this, that one of my sergeants could let this happen . . .'

'Sir, listen . . .'

'No, you listen. You're a sergeant, you were in charge of this team, this man, this dead man, this murdered man. This murdered policeman, Jim. So where the hell were you?'

'Sir, please, listen. Calm down . . . Don't you think I'm going through hell myself, asking myself those questions, feeling responsible?'

From the corner of his eye, Pemberton spotted Ramsden and said, 'Round here, Jim, out of Ramsden's sight. I want to hear your story before he has a go at me.'

He took his sergeant to the front of the house and his anger evaporated as suddenly as it had arisen. 'God, Jim, this is a terrible start to the day. What happened?' Even now, his voice was softer, gentler.

Jim Agar explained things as he knew them, saying he'd gone to bed after discussing their joint plans with Holdsworth. Both knew that Lagan was sleeping in the adjoining room. He explained the reason for their actions and Mark had to agree it made sense. Derek had left the house for some reason . . . and Agar did not know what that had been. Agar provided a description of Lagan, obtained from Miss Clayton, and Mark said he had heard the circulation of the details of the man and his car on the official radio as he'd been driving over.

'OK, Jim, sorry I blew up . . .'

'He was a good mate, sir, a pal really, we worked well.'

'So what had you discovered here? Why work so late yesterday?'

Agar said that Derek Holdsworth and he had split as a means of doing a series of concentrated visits to boarding houses and hotels; they'd intended spending the entire day on that chore, which was to ask everyone if they had accommodated a potato-hating Irishman with grey hair. And several of them had. In the last ten days, a man of that description had stayed at several Rainesbury boarding houses, once just for one night, usually for two, in one case for three, always moving on, and always giving a different name. The car numbers in the registers had been different too – Agar felt he'd given the real number in Miss Clayton's case simply because she had observed his arrival and his car was in her park. The names he'd used included Butler, O'Hagan, Fitzpatrick . . .

'So he was always on the move, sir, keeping on the go, but always paying his bills in cash, always cash.'

'Maybe Lagan is his real name? If he hired the car in that name, he would be obliged to use it at Miss Clayton's, just in case there was a police check, and if things tallied, it would remove suspicion, eh? Well, that's good work, Jim; I'm dreadfully sorry it has led to Derek's death. And what about the other fellow, the younger one with the ear-ring?'

'None of the boarding houses had seen him, sir. He's a mystery man, make no mistake.'

'Was he here last night?'

'I never saw him.'

'Does that mean a definite "no", or are you saying you simply didn't see him?'

'I didn't see him. He could have been here, I suppose.'

'Are you a light sleeper, Jim?'

'Fairly, yes, especially in a strange bed.'

'And you slept in the room adjoining Lagan's?'

'Yes.'

'So what made you wake up? Did you hear the shot?'

'A dog barking first. I didn't hear the shot. I think I dropped off again. There were movements on the stairs, I didn't go out, I knew Derek was around. Then the bloody dog set off again and I heard vehicles and voices. I looked out and saw the activity down here. I came out to see what was happening.'

'The first barking, how awake were you then?'

'Fairly, it was early . . . I couldn't get to sleep for a long time.'

'So would the barking have woken Lagan? Did you hear him moving, going out, closing doors and so on?'

'Not at the first barking, no . . . but soon afterwards, yes. It would be fairly soon afterwards when I heard movements on the stairs because I hadn't got properly back to sleep. I thought it must be Derek, or maybe Lagan going to the loo.'

'Did you hear a car?'

Agar creased his brow. 'Yes, come to think of it, I did . . . just after the noises on the landing . . . after the dog had barked. Yes, that car didn't set the dog off. It was the police cars coming later that set it off again.'

'Now, Derek was found lying near his car. Why would someone who had given his correct registration number on signing in here shoot a man near the man's own car? He would not know Derek was a policeman, would he?'

'Point taken, sir.'

'So, let's suppose Derek found somebody else out here, somebody snooping, somebody examining the police car to see if it really was a police car, somebody guarding the Irishman like Derek was guarding you, perhaps? And suppose Derek surprised him . . . There's a lot at stake, quick action was needed, so the man shot Derek, roused his pal in the digs almost immediately, and both then made off in the Volvo. Does that fit the noises you heard, dogs and all?'

Agar sniffed. 'It could, sir, yes. It bloody could . . . and I could have stopped it . . .'

'You could have been shot yourself, Jim, don't forget that! Anyway, I won't press you now. We'll need a statement from you, or rather Mr French will. I want you to think about the possibility I've outlined; don't agree with me just because you think you have to, but think it through. I just feel it's odd that Derek was shot near his own car. Why do that? Can we be absolutely sure the Irishman shot Derek?'

'You mean he might not have done it?'

'It could have been an accomplice, Jim.'

'I see, sir, yes. I'll think it through.'

'Have they finished with you here?'

'Not yet, sir.'

'Look, as soon as you've finished, get yourself away home. Take the rest of the day off.'

'I'd rather stay and help find these bastards, sir.'

'I don't want to compel you, you'd find it tough going, once you leave here and head for home.'

'I might go straight to our incident room, sir. I'd feel better being useful.'

'Mr Pemberton,' bellowed a voice.

Mark turned to face the wrath of Chief Superintendent Ramsden. 'Sir?'

'I want a word with you, now, in private, in my car.'

'See you, Jim, and don't take this to heart. I was a bit harsh on you,' were Mark's parting words.

As Jim Agar turned away, Mark followed Ramsden to his official car which was parked in Beach Road. Ramsden, a heavily built man who looked like a retired boxer, climbed in without a word and waited for Mark to join him. As Mark settled into the front passenger seat, Ramsden began.

'I think you have some explaining to do, detective superintendent. I do not take kindly to investigations being conducted anywhere in my division without my knowledge. It is courteous to notify me; you do not need permission to come into my patch, Mr Pemberton, but I do expect the common courtesies which are due to me and my officers. So just what the hell has been going on?'

Mark began by explaining the sensitive and secret nature of his own duties, and then provided the big man with a résumé of everything that had happened to date, including the role played by Derek Holdsworth.

When Mark had finished, Ramsden said, 'All right. I realize you could not inform me, but I shall have words with the Chief Constable about future events of this kind. I think, at the very least, any divisional commander should be aware of things happening in the area of his jurisdiction, no matter how secret and how sensitive. So, superintendent, the question now arises as to who deals with this murder? You or me?'

'It happened in your division, sir, so surely the murder incident room needs to be established in your area, with D/C/I French in charge.'

'But how the hell can we separate our murder enquiries from your somewhat odd commission?'

'We can't, sir, but I think the murder must be dealt with by you; if we divert from normal procedures, the press will smell a rat and we might blow the cover my men are operating under.'

'I don't like two incident rooms functioning together in one force area when they have a common interest. It seems cumbersome and dangerously liable to introduce inefficiency, Mr Pemberton. I will speak to the Chief and I will suggest that I establish my own incident room at Rainesbury, and that you move your enquiry to Rainesbury. Your men and the data you've collected will move over here and you will be under my command. Then I'll know what you're up to.'

'I do have a responsibility for armed supervision of a safe house in Swandale, sir, which is not in your division.'

'That is your problem, Mr Pemberton. If this murder enquiry and the exercise in this town which involves Potter are to be properly conducted, then surely I should be in charge?'

Mark made no reply.

The final decision would rest with Charles Moore, but he had to admit, however reluctantly, that it was common sense, under the present circumstances, to have one incident room to cope with all facets of the entire investigation. But common sense didn't necessarily solve or prevent crimes.

'So,' said Ramsden, 'we're both looking for an Irishman with a gun, eh?'

'There might be two suspects, sir, each with a gun. I'll be

interested to see what the post-mortem tells us,' said Mark, thinking of nothing better to say.

'Two? Bloody hell, man, what have you brought to this place? I want you to tell Mr French all you know and then you can go back to your own enquiries at Headquarters. Mr Moore has been told of this murder, and I expect he'll want a word with you too. And don't expect a pat on the back!'

'No, sir,' said Mark who had no intention of allowing Ramsden to get his hands on the Potter investigation. He would fight to retain his portion of the operation but with Ramsden's determination to take full control, that might prove difficult. Later, as he drove back to Police Headquarters at Great Halverton with his anger and frustration boiling within, his fury began to rise with every passing mile.

20

During the drive back to Room 207, Mark's anger waned. He radioed Control to ask them to arrange a meeting with the Chief Constable at the earliest opportunity and decided to be calm during the discussions. Control replied by saying that Mr Moore was already in his office and had been demanding to see Detective Superintendent Pemberton the moment he arrived.

It was a quarter to nine when Mark presented himself to the Chief Constable's secretary; he took a deep breath to calm himself and waited. Before being ushered into Moore's presence, he rang Paul Larkin in the incident room and instructed him to detain all the teams until Mark arrived – he wanted to address them before they went about their daily actions. He also wanted a meeting with the force press officer to discuss the official response to enquiries from the media so far as the murder of Detective Constable Holdsworth was concerned. Paul Larkin said he would attend to all those things.

When Mark's presence in the Chief Constable's suite was announced over the intercom, the secretary knocked, opened the Chief's office door and said, 'Detective Superintendent Pemberton, sir.'

Moore replied, 'Send him in,' and Mark entered the Chief Constable's office to find that Moore was looking resplendent in his best uniform.

He had donned his official outfit because, inevitably, he would be required to appear on television and be pictured in the press to condemn the killing of yet another police officer in the course of his duty.

'Sit down, Mark.' The Chief was surprisingly calm, but in a crisis he was always calm, deceptively so. That was one of his strengths and one of his dangers. 'You have something to tell me?'

The Chief's quiet response of pretended ignorance unsettled Mark – surely Ramsden had told him the awful news?

'Has Mr Ramsden been in touch with you, sir?' he asked.

'He has told me his story. Now you tell me yours,' and the Chief's quiet voice carried more than a hint of threat. Mark knew he must be accurate and precise in his account of Holdsworth's murder; above all, he must not make excuses nor make it appear that he had been weak or careless. Taking care over his words, Mark provided what he thought was a reliable account of the events which had led to Derek's murder and he took this opportunity to expound some of his own theories about the reasons behind the presence of the Irishman and his colleague in Rainesbury and behind Potter's repeated requests for parole. Mark also aired his opinion that the Secret Service or the Special Branch was somehow involved and expressed a desire to learn more of their background role.

Moore listened, his steady eyes upon the man before him. He recognized the superintendent's effort to remain calm.

'Mark,' he said when Pemberton had finished, 'I sympathize with you for the loss of an officer, a good officer I might add; I sympathize more so with Holdsworth's widow and family. Their loss is grievous. Jane Holdsworth has been told; the welfare officer is with her now. She's devastated, I'm told. But the murder was inexcusable, Mark. It should never have happened – so what went wrong with your sense of caution? You allowed an unarmed man to carry out observations on a character suspected of intending to kill Potter? Was that wise? Was it reasonable? Surely you knew the risks?'

'Sir, it happened so quickly, there was no time to organize

armed assistance – we needed to keep him in our sights, we couldn't lose him, not at that stage. And he was just a suspect, just a man we needed to keep our eye on. There was no evidence to suggest this man or his pal were dangerous . . .'

'Evidence? I'm not concerned with evidence, Mark, I'm concerned with common sense and professionalism. This whole fiasco smacks of sloppiness. Why were Holdsworth and Agar allowed to get so close to that man in the same bloody house even, without any armed assistance or back-up?'

Mark babbled on about instant decisions having to be made, about not wanting to lose the Irishman once they'd run him to cover, about not wanting to alert him to their interest or presence, about Agar and Holdsworth being very experienced officers, about the need to find out precisely what the Irishman was doing in Rainesbury and who he was meeting.

But as he made his points, he was acutely aware that they did begin to sound like lame excuses. Mark began to feel that he sounded just like an incompetent junior officer trying to excuse some stupidity and he could see that Moore was not impressed. Mark knew that he must not allow his temper to be fanned into a burst of rage . . . He realized that Moore had lost a valuable officer. That was of major concern to him. Apart from the horror of the killing and the personal feeling of responsibility, Moore would have to explain the circumstances to the Police Committee, the Home Office Inspectorate, Holdsworth's family, the coroner, the press and the public, not to mention the Police Federation and members of his own force.

'There will have to be an official enquiry, Mark, and you will be expected to explain your actions. If there were faults, carelessness or ignorance or disregard of established safety procedures, then I want to know. Heads might roll, Mark, yours for one. But all that is for the future; the enquiry will take a while to be established and we shall depend upon our murder teams for the basic facts. In the mean time, the job must go on. I cannot remove you from your present role and fortunately, the murder is being investigated in the normal way . . .'

'I wanted to speak to you, sir, about that. About the procedures, about setting up another incident room . . .'

'Chief Superintendent Ramsden has already discussed that with me,' Moore said.

'Ah.' Mark knew he was too late. He took a deep breath.

Moore said, 'Mr Ramsden will be in overall charge of the murder investigation and he has appointed D/C/I French to take command of the enquiry and to muster his own teams. The incident room will be established at Rainesbury – and that is a perfectly normal situation. In view of Holdsworth's duties at the time of his death, and in view of the fact that Rainesbury has featured so strongly in your own investigation, a fact you yourself have emphasized, I have decided that your teams and incident room will transfer to Rainesbury. Your incident room will close down and all files, personnel and data will be transferred to Rainesbury. It makes sense, both practical and financial, so you will work from there, Mark, until this thing is resolved. You will be under the supervision of Chief Superintendent Ramsden.'

'Sir, but mine is such a delicate enquiry, we can't risk exposure, we were just getting somewhere . . .'

'Do you call Derek Holdsworth's murder getting somewhere?'

'That was nasty, sir. But look, my work must go on. I need to talk to the Security Service, urgently . . .'

'I have an appointment with a member of MI5 this morning, Mark, at 11 a.m., at my request, because of these developments. I am very aware of their interest and involvement and in view of this tragedy, we all need to know more. I need to know more and so do you. So I want you to attend. You can ask questions, that will be expected of you.'

'Thank God for that. At least it might clear some things up. I've been floundering in the dark for long enough.'

'Yes, I think it will help. Now, Potter is to be released on Monday, isn't she? Today is Saturday, so I'll allow you tomorrow and Monday to clear up your incident room and establish some kind of working arrangement with the Rainesbury teams. You and your present teams will begin work at Rainesbury on Tuesday morning. Our priority remains the same – we must prevent Potter being killed or kidnapped – and in view of Holdsworth's death, things will be more difficult. There will be increased pressure on those we seek and besides, we need every available officer to investigate the murder of a colleague, don't we?'

'Yes, sir,' Mark was compelled to say.

In spite of Moore's calm approach, Pemberton had the feeling he was being subjected to some kind of demotion, some kind of punishment for Derek's death, and that he had lost overall command of his task. He hoped that Moore had not lost faith in him and his work. An added worry was that Ramsden would not be easy to work with or work for; he'd have his own theories and would impose French upon the whole enquiry. Mark did not relish the coming weeks and as he turned to walk away from Moore's office, his suppressed anger began to rise.

'Be back here at eleven, Mark,' were the Chief's parting words.

It took five minutes to walk to the incident room, five minutes which served only to intensify Pemberton's rage and frustration. With every step he took, he felt he had been snubbed, that his work meant nothing to anyone, that the incompetence of others was his responsibility. It was in this frame of mind that he stormed into the incident room, his face snowy white with unreleased anger and his jaw clenched in a long spasm of contained rage. He ignored a detective who said, 'Good morning, sir, I'm sorry about Derek . . .'

Pemberton marched resolutely through the room with every eye upon him; they knew he was prone to sudden rages, they knew he could be viciously wrathful, and in such a situation it was wise to say absolutely nothing. The wisest ploy was to keep out of his way. But in this one large room, there was no escape. Everyone watched as he opened a filing drawer and picked out one of the tapes of the dying girls.

Without a word, he located a portable cassette player, put in the tape and told them, 'Listen to this, all of you. Listen to what Potter did to those kids . . . listen to her . . . damn you, listen . . .'

And the room was filled with screams and pleas and desperate crying; some anonymous child was being subjected to the most horrific of tortures and every person in that room was being forced to share her torment. Mark stood and faced them as, without exception, they lowered their heads to avoid his eyes. Why did they deserve this? What had happened . . . ?

Lorraine and Barbara, huddled in a corner near the coffee-making table, were weeping as the awful cries penetrated their minds, but Mark let it play on high volume. He let the tape run, he let those who had never heard the death calls of a small girl now relive her last moments . . .

'Sir,' said Paul Larkin, 'I don't think this is . . .'

'Be quiet, detective inspector,' snapped Pemberton.

Ten minutes was sufficient. Mark switched off the tape, slid it back into its plastic container and replaced it in the file. He then walked across the room to the large table behind which he always stood to address his teams, and from there he looked upon everyone before him. Lorraine was drying her eyes, Barbara was still weeping, not only for the child or children, but for Derek Holdsworth. Some of the male officers stood in shocked silence, their drawn faces displaying horror and disbelief. Tough, seasoned policemen were devastated and puzzled by the suffering of children at the hands of adults and this was no exception.

Pemberton's fury had slipped away as the tape had been playing and he was now cool and detached.

'I played that', he said, 'because the woman who committed those atrocities did them to six innocent little girls. She might have killed a young man too – God knows what he suffered – and today we lost a brother officer because of her actions. Indirectly, yes, but it was because of her. And why? For greed. That's why. Sheer bloody greed.

'She became overwhelmingly greedy, she wanted money. That's all. That's why those children died. That blood, those screams, that agony, it was all for money, nothing else. Those agonizing screams are the legacy of one woman's monumental avarice. I want to find those missing children and that man Balleen, and I want to prove that she killed them. I want her put away again for a long, long time. But our time is running out. I believe that Derek Holdsworth was shot by the man who is also seeking Potter and probably Hicks. I think he wants to torture them too, to get his hands on the very money that Potter wanted. He's as greedy as she is and just as dangerous. My duty is to protect her so that she gets what she deserves – and no one deserves what happened to the bairns, not even Potter. I played that to remind you that I want maximum effort from you all. Maximum effort to prevent the repetition of an horrific crime; that is now more important than ever.'

There was silence among them now and, his anger spent, he wondered if he had over-reacted, whether his behaviour would antagonize the officers. He went on, 'We must protect Hicks and we must protect ourselves. Derek's death has intensified the situation and the pressure must now be on those who will be seeking Hicks . . .'

He addressed his next remarks to Detective Sergeant Ashton, asking him to speak to the officer in charge of force firearms training, Chief Inspector Farnell, to see if a complement of trained officers could be drafted in immediately. They were required for round-the-clock supervision of the safe house and of Hicks herself.

'If Mr Farnell wants to come here to discuss things with me, then ask him to call in,' Mark said. 'We need him as much as he needs us.'

He wanted to establish links with the firearms unit before he lost control of the incident room, but he did not reveal that thought to his officers. He provided a description of the Irishman while reminding them of the younger man with the ear-ring, saying that those descriptions would be circulated with a warning that the men would be armed. If found, neither man must be approached and armed officers must be directed to the scene so that the suspects could be detained for questioning about the murder of D/C Holdsworth. He concluded his address to the conference by saying that, as from Tuesday morning, the incident room would be discontinued and re-established in Rainesbury as part of the murder enquiry. There were groans of disappointment so Mark said, 'It would be nice if we could wrap up our side of things before we go!'

Larkin said, 'Derek's death might have provided us with the impetus for exactly that, sir.'

'Perhaps,' said Mark Pemberton, thinking of those awful screams. 'Next, I'll ask D/I Larkin to talk to you about your actions for today but don't leave just yet. I have a meeting with the Chief at eleven, it's a very important one so far as our specific task is concerned, so hang about until I return. I was hoping some of us could have this afternoon off, and tomorrow too, but – well, I'm afraid that's gone for a burton. It's a working weekend, I'm afraid, a very busy and harrowing one. Now, I don't know about you, but I could do with a strong black coffee.'

Around the same time, the body of Derek Holdsworth was being removed from the scene of his death. Detective Chief Inspector French, the Scenes of Crime officers, the force photographer, the force video unit, a forensic pathologist and the doctor had all completed their specialized examinations, and the body had been formally identified. When French was sure that all the necessary and highly important procedures at the scene had been concluded, he authorized removal to the mortuary for the next stage, the post-mortem examination. Task Force officers then moved in to make a fingertip search of the car-park and the surrounding vegetation, gardens and streets – if a bullet had been used, as seemed likely from first sight of the corpse, then its discarded shell must be somewhere around.

If so, it would be found. The bullet itself was still lodged in the brain of the dead officer, for no exit hole had been made. That suggested that a pistol or handgun had been used; a rifle would have sent a bullet straight through the skull and brain. That the bullet remained was good news, for a ballistic examination was guaranteed to reveal helpful information.

Scenes of Crime now turned their attention to Holdsworth's police car for it did seem as if an attempt had been made to force the driver's door. A tiny portion of paintwork along the top had been damaged. It had all the hallmarks of the kind of entry which was so easily effected with a screwdriver and a wire coat-hanger and so a minute examination of the car began, supported by stills photography and a video recording.

House-to-house enquiries were already in progress in the neighbouring streets, uniformed officers having been drafted in to undertake that task, and Lagan's bedroom in Mermaid Villa was being subjected to a very specialized and careful examination. At Agar's request, Doug Weston, the landlord of the Smugglers' Arms, was to be questioned at length to ascertain whether he knew the Irishman and his colleague – Agar recalled that Pemberton, upon earlier quizzing the landlord, had felt the fellow was concealing something. Likewise, those boarding houses where Lagan was known to have stayed would be closely examined and their proprietors questioned.

As the routine of the murder investigation got under way, the media were informed by the force press officer who issued a short verbal news release which said, 'During the early hours of this morning, a detective constable aged thirty-two, who was on duty in Rainesbury, was found dead. Preliminary examination suggests that a firearm was used and that he died from gunshot wounds. The death is suspicious and an incident room has been established at Rainesbury police station. Forty officers have been drafted on to the enquiry which is being led by Detective Chief Inspector Howard French. The name of the officer will be released when his relatives have been notified. No one is yet in custody for this crime and a post-mortem has been arranged. There will be a news conference at Rainesbury police station at 4 p.m. today.'

The fact that the age and rank of the dead officer had been given to the media would alleviate a lot of families' worries even though the name had not yet been released; from this briefest of information, most families would be able to rule out their own loved ones.

At eleven o'clock Mark once again presented himself at the Chief Constable's office, now in a calmer frame of mind, and he waited for permission to enter. After a few moments, he was allowed in. He entered to find a pretty blonde woman seated before the desk and she stood up as he entered. He was astonished to find that it was Rebecca Eden, the woman he had seen in the safe house when he had called on Mrs Dawson last Wednesday.

'Good morning, superintendent.' She smiled somewhat apprehensively.

21

'Mrs Eden?' The surprise was evident on Mark's face and he knew his shock was visible to her although she made no apology for any deception.

The Chief made the necessary introductions and invited Mark to be seated at the small conference table in the corner of the office. Moore's secretary brought in some coffee and biscuits and attended to each in turn. As the coffee was organized, Mark studied the woman opposite. The bulk of her long hair was piled high upon her head and held there with slides and ribbons to give it a rather untidy and casual appearance, while further long silky tresses hung down her back to be highlighted against her dress. She had discarded her 'abandoned wife' image and wore a neat black dress with a deep neckline which enhanced her slim figure and emphasized her small breasts. In her middle thirties, she had a long, intelligent face with good teeth and smiling blue eyes; her skin was pale without any hint of suntan or make-up. Although her head and face had the appearance of strength and character, her body looked fragile and slender. Mark anticipated that this was also a deception – she'd be tough, uncompromising and intelligent. She wouldn't be doing this job otherwise.

'Rebecca has been working very closely on the Potter file for several years, Mark. You need to hear what she has to say.'

Mark said nothing at this stage. MI5 involvement with the Irish problem was supposed to be a recent innovation, but he wasn't interested in politics. He just wanted to hear what had been happening in the background, for he felt that this woman was in possession of far more information than he was.

Sipping her coffee, she began by saying she had been one of Potter's prison visitors. Over a period of five or six years, and especially since Potter had come to the open prison some two years ago, Rebecca had visited her on a very regular and frequent basis. She had grown to know the killer while simultaneously gaining her trust and confidence. Over the years, she had become both a friend and confidante of Potter.

'I was – and am – an adviser to the Parole Board,' she added. 'My true role is not known to any of my colleagues, but it was my report, supported by two prison governors, which led to Louisa Potter's release.'

'In other words,' Mark's anger was simmering beneath the surface, 'the whole thing has been fixed? There's been collusion between your service, the Prison Service, the Special Branch, the Home Office and the Parole Board. There must have been, for this woman to be freed. She'd never be let out under normal circumstances. Does Potter know who you are really working for?'

'Yes, she does now. I must admit that at first she thought I was a widow wanting to do some useful public service by visiting prisoners, but as time went by, she came to regard me as a friend.

I am her friend, that's one of the reasons I have come to the safe house, to be with her when she's freed. It took a long time; even though I discovered she'd been mentally ill at the time, I had to overcome my deep revulsion over her crimes and, yes, there was some collusion between the agencies . . . But having said all that, she is being released and we must all maintain contact with her.'

'But why?' Mark demanded. 'Why are you here? Is it because it's your job, some operation your service is engaged in? You were in the Smugglers' Arms last Sunday, weren't you? You passed on the information to us, about the threat to her?'

'Yes, that was me. I'd been observing those men. If we learn of such threats, particularly those which are genuine, we pass the information to the local constabulary, or to the military, whichever is appropriate. That's common practice. Dealing with such threats is their province, not ours.'

'So just what is going on?' Mark demanded.

'Give Rebecca a fair chance to explain, Mark.' Moore poured more coffee for each of them and invited them to take another biscuit. Mark declined; Rebecca Eden accepted.

'It goes back a long time,' said Mrs Eden. 'To a time long before I joined the Security Service in fact. It began with a man called Joseph Patrick Balleen, and I understand from Mr Moore that you know of him, superintendent?'

Mark nodded. 'Yes, I do. I've discovered a good deal.'

'He was working for the IRA. Young, idealistic, clever, charming, a lilywhite. It was his job to raise funds in the UK and he did so by robbery, a well-tried tactic. Rob your enemies, let them pay for their mistakes, that's the theory. He was successful too. I believe you had become aware of that? His duty was to steal the money and safeguard it in the UK, keeping it available for future use. I believe he was allowed to keep a small percentage of his ill-gotten gains, five per cent or so, which made him appear to have lots of cash. As he stored the money, he was under the tight supervision of his controllers; clearly, they did not trust him totally even if they were using him for their own ends. They made sure the necessary precautions were taken. He kept the cash in deposit accounts in English building societies; there, the monies would gain interest, another way of making Britain pay for its sins. At that time, it was easy to open a cash account in a false name and this is what he did. Balleen was sent letters to accommodation addresses and they bore one or other of his false names; he could always show the envelopes if he needed to persuade a building society clerk that he was who he said he was. Our sources in Eire, and our covert contacts within the IRA itself, have provided us with that information.

'Then, as you know, superintendent, Mr Balleen vanished. At the time, his girlfriend in the UK was Louisa Mary Potter, and I have been told by Mr Moore of your enquiries into that relationship. We feel he was using her as part of his cover. He got involved with various activities in Rainesbury, he took Potter out, she introduced him to useful people and although she was older, she really was charmed by him. He opened a joint bank account as part of his cover – she thought it was because he had plans to continue or develop their relationship, even marry her, but in fact he needed someone over twenty-one to act as a guarantor. She did love him, we're sure. He took her to expensive restaurants, bought her cars and gave her a way of life she'd never experienced. He didn't touch the IRA monies for that – he wouldn't dare. He used his own commission and cash from car dealing and there's no doubt he enjoyed himself. But Louisa became greedy . . . she knew he'd go back to Ireland one day. She thought it was because of his strong family associations, but in reality, it was because he was under the control of his masters. If he stayed too long in one place, there was always a risk of identification and capture, especially as he was committing serious crimes. He knew he'd be moved on, he knew that one day he would be withdrawn from Rainesbury and placed somewhere else, either here or in the Emerald Isle. We think she knew this might happen and we think he must have said that he could not continue their relationship, perhaps giving a false reason. We are not sure whether she knew of all his IRA activities, although it's pretty certain she was aware of his sympathies towards their cause and his family's links. She did know about his robberies, perhaps not at first, but we think she did eventually realize what he was doing. She read the papers, she knew he was handling large amounts and that men came to inspect some passbooks he kept in safe storage; we think she began to wonder what was happening to the cash because he was so secretive. If we add to this her idea that he intended to return to Ireland, it might explain why she decided she was going to have some of that money . . .'

'By manipulating the joint account?' Mark asked.

'Yes. She was the key figure, the over-twenty-one signatory, so she could withdraw it once he'd gone home. But he was too clever for her. We do not know what went on between them, but I get the impression that he was aware of her moods and underlying evil nature, so he kept a minimum of cash in that joint bank account, just enough to service the banker's orders. He'd put all his stolen money into umpteen building society accounts under all manner of names, and he deposited the passbooks, for safe keeping, in the ASP Safe Deposit Centre – under orders from his masters. Although there was only one irreplaceable key to the safe deposit box, the account there was in joint names, again as part of his cover while in the UK. That key and a signature gave access – he kept the precious key, he made sure she never got her hands on it and so the money, in umpteen cash books, was secure. If he lost that key, he was dead . . . the IRA would see to that.'

'Did the IRA know all this?' Moore now asked the question.

'Yes, that's how we know. We have some excellent sources within the IRA.' She smiled. 'Now, initially he put the key, for safe keeping, into the vaults of the Country and Coast Bank in Rainesbury; that account was also in their joint names, and he told Louisa what he'd done. He said that if anything happened to him, the key was there and it would allow her access to the safe deposit box. It was his way to maintain her silence about the robberies; she'd come to realize he was a crook, although we're not totally sure whether she realized why he was stealing the cash. She'd often said she ought to have a share because of her loyalty to him, but he put her off by saying the money was traceable and so it had to be stored away until the heat had died down. But, of course, he hid the key elsewhere. He did not trust her; we think he did trust her in the early stages of the relationship, but as time progressed, he became aware of her true nature. He realized she was determined to get her hands on the money; as security agencies on both sides of the Irish Sea were watching money transfers while the Provisionals were being set up, he was told to store the money in the UK until it was safe to transfer it. It meant he was custodian of hundreds of thousands of pounds, even if he was being scrutinized by his commanders, and she was anxious to get her hands on it. He began to deceive her – he had to, to be faithful to his masters. We know he kept them informed. If she'd got her hands on that money, he'd have been shot.'

'The poor devil probably died anyway,' Mark said. 'Or that's what I think happened. Do you know if she killed him?'

'That is something that not even I know,' went on Rebecca Eden. 'We think she did. He just disappeared without trace and his body has never been found. Neither the IRA nor his family have heard anything of him. But he had not left the key in the Rainesbury bank vault; he'd hidden it. We think he intended telling his masters where it was, but he vanished before he had the opportunity. When Louisa went to look for the key in the suitcase, it had gone, the case was empty. He'd left a note – and in her anger, we think, she killed him. That is our belief, gentlemen, based on informed sources. She knew he would never hand over the key, and that the passbooks were still in the Rainesbury safe deposit box. So what had Balleen done with the precious key? We are convinced she killed those children because she had somehow worked out that one of them possessed the key; if they did, they never knew. Balleen had hidden it – he could have given it to one of those children, he was always telling them how to keep secrets, but, superintendent, that key has never been found. Without it, there is no access to those funds. No way, not ever. They will remain locked away for eternity. It's not surprising, therefore, that the IRA want that key. They know that not even their explosive skills can blow a hole in the Safe Deposit Centre, otherwise they'd have had a crack at it or the manager before now.

'They have never forgotten about the money. They want it; in fact, they now need it desperately. They are very short of funds, particularly as the Soviet Union's support has dried up, there no longer being a Soviet Union. The IRA intends to get the money, which it believes is rightfully theirs, so they have launched an attempt to obtain that key.'

'But why do it now?' Mark asked. 'Why, after all this time and just as Potter is being paroled, have they suddenly decided to try and recover the money?'

'Because we planted the idea in their heads.' She smiled that secret smile again. 'We've always known of their desire to get their hands on it – with compound interest, it has grown into millions of pounds, we are assured, and so we felt the time was right. As a result, we have established our operation which has persuaded them that the money is now within reach. We leaked to them that Potter was coming out of prison and that she knows where to find the key. They want the key – and we want them. We want to trap their top men, and with four million pounds at stake, their top men have been drafted in to supervise its recovery. At this juncture, that sort of money is a most useful asset to them; it's our bait for the trap.'

'I could do with four million too,' dreamed Mark.

'The IRA is very short of funds. They've had a few knocks recently, what with arms dumps being discovered, explosives stores located, deaths of key members, the collapse of Communism and the resultant reduction in financial support. When it became known to the IRA leaders that Potter, the only person with knowledge of the whereabouts of the money, would soon be released, they saw their opportunity. They think they got the information through their own intelligence units. The IRA knows she will attempt to get the money. They don't want the key, they want the passbooks. They will follow her and attempt to reclaim them by whatever means are necessary, even torture.'

'Just as she attempted to do through the children all those years ago,' commented Mark. 'But if she never found the key in spite of the bloodshed, how will she find it now? I mean, Mrs Eden, would Balleen hide something as precious as that key?'

'We think he did. If he carried it with him, he could lose it; if he got arrested due to his robberies both he and his home could be searched and the police might find it and trace its source; if he got attacked and mugged in the street, he might have it stolen; if he went home to Ireland, he might lose it or have it stolen. It had become an enormous worry to him and so we believe he decided to place it somewhere safe, somewhere secret where he had access to it whenever it became necessary. Now I believe that Louisa, during her time in prison, has worked out where Balleen concealed the key, but she's not saying . . . she wouldn't even tell me, her best friend . . .'

'Best friend!' sneered Mark. 'Some friend you turned out to be. You've set her up as a target for the IRA! She's being released from prison because it will draw the rats out of the woodwork, and all your people, plus half the British Army, will be waiting to deal with the IRA who track her down.'

'That's how things work, Mr Pemberton. But one thing you should know – after I told her all about Balleen's activities, she volunteered for this,' Rebecca Eden said. 'She said that if I, as her friend and prison visitor, could persuade the prison governor, the authorities and the Parole Board to release her, she would act as a target for the IRA. She knew what was at stake. She knows she could lose her life, but she's come to realize just what Balleen was doing against this country, what evils the IRA were – and still are – perpetrating and so Balleen's ideals have lost her support. She has become appalled by years of IRA atrocities and she knows how Balleen used her for IRA purposes. He didn't love her, he used her. Now she's willing to draw them into our net, it's her way of making reparation for her wrongs, and she'll put her own life at risk so we can identify and take out the UK leaders . . .'

'Is that what she told you?' Mark was incredulous. 'You don't believe all that noble sentiment, do you? She's evil, Mrs Eden, she's conned you all; she's bluffed her way out of prison! If she's come out for any reason at all, it's because she wants to get her hands on that money and then vanish . . . Bloody hell, she's cunning, she really is.'

'I'm not sure she could actually get her hands on the money,' said Mrs Eden. 'It will be in various names, all men, and it would require forgery on a large scale to gain access.'

'That's not difficult with criminal connections and four million pounds to pay for the finest possible forgery service!' said Mark. 'Besides, it might be hers quite legally – she has been joint custodian for all this time.'

'Yes, well, that might be your opinion and we are aware of that possibility. But ownership of the cash is not our problem. We know her record while she was in prison, superintendent,' was all that Mrs Eden said. 'Our association with the prison authorities goes back a long way . . .'

'But you don't know *her* . . . So where is the key? Is she hiding the truth of its whereabouts? Did those little girls really die for nothing?'

'Perhaps, unknowingly, one of them did have the key,' said Mrs Eden. 'I must admit I was uncertain whether he would really entrust such an important key to a child.'

'Where else could Balleen have put it?' Mark puzzled. 'Potter had access to the suitcase in the bank and he didn't trust her, that's obvious. He had to conceal it from *her*, so he daren't leave it in his room at the digs. Who could he trust? He'd already trained those little girls to keep his secrets. It wouldn't surprise me if he had given it as a special secret to one of those children. He could trust them, he'd previously put them to the test. And they all died because of it.'

The Chief Constable butted in. 'Mark, you can see what's going to happen. Potter is going to be attacked by the IRA when she has the passbooks in her possession. If she hides them, she'll be pressured or tortured to give them up. Whoever gets those passbooks gets the money, legally or otherwise.'

'Can't we freeze those building society funds?'

'There is no proof the accounts contain stolen money; besides, we have no such powers. On top of that, we don't know the names on the accounts, do we?'

'So, the key alone is no use?' Mark commented.

'No, she must present it and go through the other security procedures before the passbooks will be released. But this is what's planned – we, that is MI5, ourselves and the SAS, secure those passbooks before the IRA gets them . . .'

Rebecca Eden continued, 'We were going to organize a leak to the press, superintendent, once Potter had got herself established in the safe house. Our plans, over the coming weeks, were to ring the *Sun* or the *News of the World* and tell them that the woman Hicks in your safe house was really Louisa Mary Potter. The outcry and publicity would have drawn the IRA to her. We'd then have been able to keep tabs on them. We were going to announce her parole in the normal way, saying she'd gone to a secret address, and that would have added fuel to the information we'd already fed to the IRA. Later press reports revealing her address would have sealed it nicely and would have ensured our control over events. But the sad death of your detective has escalated things because the killer of Mr Holdsworth is almost certainly the assassin who's been hired by the IRA to deal with Louisa. The killer is not the Irishman who stays with him as a minder. Your ballistics people might identify the bullet and with a murder hunt on his tail, he'll want to get the job over as soon as he can, and get the hell out of England.'

'How do you know the IRA will activate their plans the moment she's released?'

'Because we've already told them where to find her.'

'My God ... Sir, this is too big for one sergeant and a few unarmed officers waiting at a safe house ...'

'Calm down, Mark, you are not alone in this. MI5 have got Rainesbury sewn up, with just a little help from the SAS. Your men will be fully engaged in keeping an eye on the safe house, as you've already planned. The IRA will not go there, in spite of publicity – they'll think it has been set up as a trap, which it has. So they'll keep clear ...'

'They might respond, sir, simply to make us think we've anticipated their movements while tackling Potter elsewhere ...'

'A token, Mark, a token shot or two. We'll cope – crack army marksmen to be around the safe house, Sergeant Ashton will be provided with details so he can arrange a rendezvous.'

'Sir, but doesn't Potter stand a very grave risk of being shot?'

'She knows the risks,' said Mrs Eden.

'She knows we won't let her die, Mrs Eden,' Mark fumed. 'She's after the loot, just like she was all those years ago ... Anyway, it seems I'm superfluous now. It makes me wonder what I'm doing among all this ...' Mark sounded bitter.

'You are the officer in charge of reopening enquiries into the case of three missing children, Mark. That's what you are doing ...'

'That was a cover, sir. I was put in to create a diversion, nothing more, to stir up things in Rainesbury, to make it look as if we expected something to happen ...'

'Superintendent,' said Mrs Eden, 'we are dealing with a bunch of dangerous people who claim they are at war, not a band of criminals who are wanting to get their hands on some stolen loot. Rest assured that we have taken all necessary steps to ensure protection of everyone involved.'

'And I don't know what those steps are?'

'We operate on a need-to-know basis,' said Mrs Eden.

'Sir, having heard all this, I think I ought to tell my teams that Miss Hicks is really Louisa Mary Potter.'

Rebecca Eden looked at Moore who, after a moment's consideration, gave his approval. 'All right, do that,' he said.

'So just what is my role now?' Mark asked his Chief Constable.

'Exactly the same as it was right at the beginning, Mark. To protect Louisa Mary Potter at the safe house in Swandale.

Instruct your Sergeant Ashton to call this number.' The Chief scribbled a telephone number on a piece of paper. 'He should do it immediately upon your return. He must ask for Major Donaldson of the SAS. They will work together to protect the safe house and the people in it, Mrs Eden included. Mrs Eden may be in the house, remember. This is being done now because of Holdsworth's death; through that, Potter is being released earlier than planned. Potter is coming out today, Mark. Rebecca will collect her at the prison at two thirty this afternoon, consequently she will be at Swandale from today. There will not be a public announcement until Monday, so she will have a short time to establish herself. The IRA, however, will be aware of her early release.'

'Bloody hell, sir, so what do you expect of me?'

'Nothing more, Mark. Everything's in hand. We'll contact you if we need you. Once the safe house operation has been finalized, you can go and rearrange your incident room in readiness for Tuesday's move to Rainesbury.'

Mark said nothing. He got up and walked out, not even bothering to shake the outstretched hand of Rebecca Eden.

22

Mark Pemberton felt humiliation rather than anger and he was in a low mood when he returned to the incident room. His teams had waited patiently and they lapsed into silence as he entered, sensing that the meeting had gone far from smoothly. On this occasion his anger and disappointment were not manifested in a sudden burst of rage. Instead, he looked unseeingly at them, a sea of expectant pink faces awaiting something, anything, from him: but he had so little to deliver. He smiled weakly, sorrowfully almost, then went into his room intending to summon Paul Larkin for a private conversation about his meeting with Rebecca Eden, but he immediately changed his mind and decided to address them all.

He went out and stood behind his table and they waited.

'Anything to report?' he asked blandly.

Larkin spoke. 'The car's been found abandoned, sir, Lagan's Volvo. Found in a street near Middlesbrough docks, so Rainesbury tell us. Their Scenes of Crime have gone to check it over and collect it. They've checked with the docks. There's no reports of Lagan getting a ship so he might have gone to ground. Cleveland Police will look out for him. D/C/I French asked that you be informed.'

'Lagan will come again,' said Mark, knowing his quarry would react to the news which would soon break. 'Has anyone done the rounds of car hirers? Warned them? Asked for their co-operation?' It was hard to appreciate that he was not in charge of the murder enquiry; somebody else would be seeing to that sort of routine commitment.

'Cleveland are doing that, sir. The Rainesbury incident room's fixed it.'

'It's their show, not ours, eh?' Mark acknowledged. 'Any news of the PM yet?'

'Yes, sir, it's been completed. Death was instantaneous from a single bullet wound in the brain. It's from a .38, sir, the bullet's been recovered and is on its way by car to Nottingham for ballistics tests. Task Force found the empty shell too. The examination's being treated as urgent.'

'Good. Anything else from Rainesbury?'

'They're trying to decide whether to issue a description of the Irishman to the press or to keep it under wraps for the time being, in view of our enquiries. They won't refer to the second suspect, they want to lull him into a false sense of security and make the Irishman think we're after him. At the same time, they don't want to botch up our side of things,' said Larkin. 'Can you give D/C/I French a ring about it?'

'I'll call him,' promised Mark. 'Details of Lagan will have been circulated to police forces but I don't think we want the newspapers shouting that we're on to him; his bosses could substitute someone else that we don't know. Better the devil. . . and all that. I'll suggest that to French.'

Stressing the secrecy of his forthcoming words, he then provided his teams with a brief résumé of what had transpired at the meeting with Mrs Eden, emphasizing the supporting role to be played by Sergeant Ashton and his firearms team and stressing the dangers facing both them and Louisa Mary Potter.

'The woman at the safe house will be Louisa Mary Potter herself,' Mark now admitted to them. 'She will be using the name of Kathleen Hicks. I remind you that this is secret. I want no leaks to the press or gossip to your families and friends about this woman being protected by us. I want her kept alive, personally; I want her to stand trial for more murders, even if it takes me until my retirement to see it through.'

Having imparted his information, Mark looked at his watch. It was twelve forty-five.

'I'm going to the canteen for lunch,' he said wearily. 'See you this afternoon.'

When he returned after his gammon without chips but with salad, Lorraine Cashmore was waiting.

'Sir.' She smiled sympathetically. 'You look shattered.'

'I feel useless!' He managed a tired smile. 'It's not a happy time, is it? Losing Derek's hit me deeper than I thought. I feel responsible. I *am* responsible. But, well, I'm sure Mr French will find his killer without our help; it's all made us somewhat superfluous. So how's it going? Are we winding up our end of things neatly, ready for the transfer?'

'None of us feels keen to move, sir . . .'

'We've still a big job to do, Lorraine, guarding that house, making sure our Louisa Mary isn't shot. We'll all be involved in that. I'll get Mr Larkin to sort out who does what and when.'

'What I came for, sir, was to say that I've been looking through more of those statements, finishing off the task I'd set myself before we close down.'

'And you've found something else?'

'It's not a lot, sir – I've been checking statements made by the families of the dead and missing girls. It's just that, after talking to Sister Bernadette, I thought I'd see if he treated those other girls like he treated her.'

'In what way, Lorraine?'

'Giving them presents. He gave Bernadette, or Jeanette as she then was, a rosary the day before she moved to York. All the Catholic girls got things like statues or rosaries.'

'I remember Helen Stabler got a statue of St Patrick, it's still in her room.'

'Yes, and Suzanne Hayes got a model of a leprechaun, Michele Brown a piece of stone in a jar that was supposed to have come from the Blarney Stone and Tracy Halliday a tiny book with pages like postage stamps said to have been printed for the little people. All magic things in the eyes of small children. Rachel got a statue of Our Lady of Knock, where the Virgin is supposed to have appeared.'

'Is there some significance in this, Lorraine?' If there was, Mark had missed it.

'Well, maybe not, but in view of what we know about Balleen, I thought it strange that he gave so many presents all at once, to all those children.'

'He wasn't molesting them, Lorraine, he wasn't a dirty old man giving them sweets in return for favours, we know that.'

'I know. I wondered whether he gave other children presents, whether he treated other children like those six, so I checked. HOLMES helped a lot. Well, sir, he didn't. There are statements in the file from other Brownies and their families, and from members of the church clubs and other groups. He mixed with those youngsters too, quite a lot of them, but he never gave them presents. It was just those six – well, seven, counting Sister Bernadette.'

'And she is the only one alive?' Mark put in. 'Is that significant, Lorraine?'

'I'm not sure, sir, but it does seem odd that a man like that – a terrorist, rogue, robber – would give presents to the six children that were later killed by his girlfriend.'

'Can you suggest why, Lorraine?'

She sighed. 'I've tried. My instincts tell me that it was not normal, that there must have been some reason for this . . .'

'What about having another word with Sister Bernadette?'

'I think she knows more than she realizes, sir.'

'I agree. She's the only living person who received one of his pressies, isn't she? Therefore she's unique – and valuable. Find out, if you can, exactly what he said when he gave her the present, and see if all the other girls were there when the presents were distributed. Find out what he said to them all, if possible.'

'Yes, sir.'

'Right, the job's yours. Take a car.'

'Thank you, sir, I'll do my best,' and Mark was pleased that Lorraine had set her heart on solving the riddle of her own making. Next, he went into his office. With the winding down of his incident room, there was a lot of paperwork to clear up, and a report to write about the circumstances that had led to the death of Detective Constable Holdsworth. Now that things were fairly quiet, he decided to settle down and clear up a few of those necessary chores.

At 2.30 p.m. that Saturday, Rebecca Eden waited outside the main entrance to Askham Grange Open Prison which is just off the York to Leeds road not far from Tadcaster. She was in a pale blue Volkswagen Golf and kept her eyes on the main door.

At a discreet distance there was another car, a grey BMW with a man at the wheel, a member of MI5. Rebecca was pleased that the system was working and that Louisa was being afforded close protection. There were no other cars around and no one lurking about the exterior, no press and no public.

It suggested there had been no unauthorized leak and that the IRA considered it a possible trap, thus keeping away. Besides, at this point, she'd have nothing to interest them. A few minutes after half-past, a sturdy grey-haired woman wearing rimless glasses and carrying a large suitcase left the main door; the governor was there to bid farewell, and as the door stood open for a brief moment, Rebecca saw the little knot of prisoners standing and waving inside. Louisa had had a pleasant and somewhat moving farewell.

Rebecca left her car and went to meet her. Louisa turned and waved to the governor, to the staff at the windows and to the inmates grouped inside the door, and then, with tears running down her face, turned and walked to her freedom. Rebecca took her case and indicated the waiting Golf. Within seconds, the car was speeding in the direction of York and heading towards the bypass and the A19. The protective BMW followed at a discreet distance.

Louisa Mary Potter, the most notorious child killer of this century, was finally out of prison.

In a small scruffy house in a back street of Rainesbury, an iron-grey-haired man called Sean Mulligan and a younger man called Leo Wilde sat over a miserable electric fire.

They were drinking tea and eating sandwiches brought for them by a third man. He was called Keith Wilson and was speaking.

'By dumping the car in Middlesbrough, it'll look as if you've gone there. I cleaned it first then rang the hire people to say it had been nicked . . . So settle down, eat that sandwich, then I'll take a dekko outside to see what I can learn.'

'What about the caravan?' asked Wilde.

'You'll be safer here,' Wilson advised him. 'People might have seen you knocking about the caravan site!'

'If only you hadn't done that copper . . .' Mulligan said for the hundredth time. 'You were a bit bloody quick . . .'

'I'm paid to be quick, I'm paid to sense danger and to react. I had no choice, Sean, he saw me – and he was watching you, living in the same bloody digs! That's how close they've got. He was one of those who'd been in the Smugglers', asking questions. They're on to something, I had to finish him off, there was no choice.'

'What's done is done,' said Wilson. 'What you need to do now is look ahead. She's due out on Monday, isn't she?'

'Yes, but we don't know what name she'll be using, do we? Or what she looks like now.'

'But she must come back to Rainesbury, that's where the money is. She's sure to come back. When she goes to the safe deposit place to pick up the passbooks, we'll get her.'

'How can we look out for her if we don't know what she looks like?' demanded Wilde.

'We've contacts.' Mulligan was confident. 'We're to get more gen soon, and a picture, aren't we, Keith?'

'Sure, it's all in hand. Now, you fellers lie low here, there's everything you need, television, food, a pack of cards, beer . . . I'll be out and about, your ears, eyes and shopping assistant for the next few days. There's no panic, she's not due out until Monday, so we can wait here until we're ready.'

'What if they do a house-to-house down this street?'

'You're two miles from that boarding house,' Wilson told them. 'It's hardly likely they'll quiz folks in this part of town. I'll know in advance if they are coming anyway, I'll warn you. Remember, this is a safe house, secure from nosy neighbours and the like.'

'I still wish you hadn't shot that lad,' said Mulligan to Wilde. 'You know what the English police are like when one of their own gets killed.'

'He's not the first and he'll not be the last,' said Wilde. 'That's what they get paid for and it's what I get paid for.'

Wilson called for them to stop arguing and said he'd pop out to buy an evening paper to see what progress there'd been with the murder hunt. Wilde asked him to get a bottle of whisky while he was out.

By five o'clock that Saturday, Dr Adam Firth, the Principal Scientific Officer specializing in ballistics at the Forensic Science Laboratory in Nottingham, had examined the bullet and its spent cartridge casing.

He confirmed that it was .38 calibre and that it had been fired by a Walther P38 automatic, the striations on the case matching a control bullet in his care. All .38 bullets fired from Walther P.38 automatic weapons bore identical striations, although each handgun had its own additional and individual characteristics. The bullet which had been subjected to his expert examination was not the only bullet to have been fired from that particular weapon – an English soldier on guard duty at a barracks near Lichfield had also been killed by a bullet fired by the same gun in 1990. It was known, through military intelligence, that the killer had been a professional assassin or mercenary called Wilde who was hired by the IRA. The same man, or to be more precise, the same gun, had killed Detective Constable Holdsworth.

Dr Firth rang the incident room and informed D/C/I French of his findings. A formal report together with a witness statement would be forwarded as soon as possible and the exhibits would be returned to the police for use as evidence in court.

French decided he needed to talk to Staffordshire Police and military security about that soldier's death.

When French rang Pemberton with this news, Mark felt a ripple of horror run down his spine.

'Now you know what we're up against, Howard,' he warned.

'When are you coming to join us?' asked French.

'Monday afternoon or Tuesday, it depends when we get packed up here. Why?'

'I could do with a run-down of the background of this crime,' admitted French. 'Can I come and talk to you?'

'You're the busy one now, Howard, and I could do with an outing. I'll come to Rainesbury tomorrow.' Mark thought he'd prefer to get out of the office as the others were packing up. The thought of a final bout of operational duty cheered him up.

'Would twelve be all right? We could manage a sandwich and a pint somewhere,' suggested French.

'You're on,' said Mark.

Mark went home intending to treat himself to a juicy steak and some red wine for dinner but as he walked into the house, the telephone was ringing. He groaned, expecting to find he'd been called out, but it was Rebecca Eden.

'I'm sorry to ring you at home, superintendent,' she said, not explaining how she had obtained his ex-directory number, 'but I'd like to have a word with you.'

'What? Now?' he asked sharply.

'No, tomorrow, in Rainesbury. Would two thirty be all right? At the southern end of Churchill Bridge?'

23

When Mark entered his incident room on Sunday morning, he found that most of the files had been packed into cardboard boxes and although there was a modicum of activity, the place did look like an office which was about to close. A morning conference seemed futile. Paul Larkin was on the telephone to Rainesbury to see if there had been any developments overnight while the number of officers actually present was depleted due to the shift system now being operated to protect the safe house. As he checked his in-tray to see if there had been any messages, he noticed Lorraine heading his way. He waved her into his office.

''Morning, Lorraine.' He was pleased to see her.

'Good morning, sir.' She was very formal. 'I thought I'd tell you about my visit to Sister Bernadette yesterday afternoon.'

'I was going to ask about it. Sit down,' and he offered her a chair. Through his open door, he caught Barbara's eye and indicated that two coffees would be acceptable. Barbara, efficient as ever, produced them within seconds.

'It was a useful visit,' Lorraine told him. She explained how the Secret Seven, as Bernadette had known the club, wore small badges bearing the figure 7 when they met in the clubhouse; the badges, pinned on, were taken from birthday cards. She had again described the secret sign of the clenched fist and reminded him that a condition of the club was that they always had a secret to share. She instanced a case where Rachel had found a full packet of twenty cigarettes in the street, so she'd brought that to the club and they'd all smoked one, making themselves ill. They'd hidden the rest so that no parents knew about it – that had been a very closely guarded secret. Another involved a well-known vicar of Rainesford whom Tracy had seen in the woods with Miss Clemence who did church flowers: they had kissed each other. That was a juicy secret. Joseph would often provide secrets for the club. Once he came to tell them he'd sold a car to a policeman in Rainesbury but the car overheated and broke down after about ten miles . . . he asked them to keep that a secret.

'It's all petty stuff, isn't it, Lorraine?' Mark said as the policewoman expanded the story. 'Hardly the stuff of murder?'

'It was serious to them at the time. Joseph did tell them he was leaving for Ireland, sir,' she went on. 'And that was one of the club secrets. He went to their clubhouse one Friday, Bernadette isn't sure when it was, and they wouldn't allow him in, so they came out and he talked to them outside. He said he would soon be leaving England for a few days to go home, but he'd return to see them. And he gave them all a present. It was the day before Bernadette's family moved to York. Potter never knew about it.

'Bernadette got a rosary. As he gave it to her, he stressed that his going back to Ireland was a secret; he was off to see his mum, but would return. He asked them not to tell anyone, and when he gave them their presents, he asked them each to promise to keep their present very safe until he got back. He'd want to see the presents when he got back, he told them, and he wanted to be sure they'd kept his secret.'

'And then what?'

'He never came back, sir, they never saw him again. And they all kept their presents just as he'd asked, Sister Bernadette has still got her rosary beads. One day when Potter popped in to see the kids, she learned about the presents to the six but no one told her about Jeanette's gift – Jeanette had just gone in time, she was never visited by Potter and so she lived. And young Jeanette never told anyone about that secret until now, funnily enough. Even when Mr Kenworthy interviewed her, she didn't tell him that bit. It was all one big secret to her, you see; she was only a tot. And she did display enormous loyalty to Joseph.'

'Joseph seems to have made a drama out of things, doesn't he?'

'I did wonder, sir,' she put to Pemberton, 'whether he was sneaking off without the knowledge of his controllers, without the IRA knowing . . . popping off quietly to see his mum and dad for some family reason. Divided loyalties perhaps?'

'He thought he'd soon have to return for ever. But whatever his real reason for going, he never got there even though he bought his ferry ticket,' Pemberton said. 'Thanks for getting all that, Lorraine. Enter the facts into the system; HOLMES is still up and running so see if you can glean any more snippets for us.'

'Yes, sir.' He watched the young woman leave his office and then spotted Detective Sergeant Agar.

'Jim?' he called.

As Agar entered the office, Pemberton's telephone rang. It was D/C/I French.

'Sir,' said French, 'I thought you'd like to know the outcome of the ballistics tests,' and he explained about the results and his discussions with Staffordshire Police and the military authorities about the Lichfield soldier's death and the role of Leo Wilde. Mark listened, allowing Agar to hear the conversation by holding the handset away from his ear.

'Does this confirm that the Irishman was not alone?' Pemberton asked French.

'Yes. Military sources believe that Mulligan or whatever he calls himself is in charge of the IRA's north of England campaign but he will not murder anyone, he must not be captured because he is the brains behind their present operations, the leader who remains aloof from the sharp end. His real name is Martin O'Docherty. The gunman is a paid assassin, an ex-paratrooper and mercenary called Leo Wilde; he's known to take on contract jobs for those who wish to have their enemies bumped off. He'll work for anyone who pays; if he got caught, there'd be no proven link with the IRA.'

'So for Derek's murder, we're seeking Wilde, not Lagan or O'Docherty or whatever name he's using.'

'Yes, sir,' said French. 'I've told the Chief, but thought you'd better know. If we could get evidence of their co-operation, we might consider a conspiracy charge.'

'Easier said than done, but thanks,' said Pemberton. 'See you shortly for lunch, Howard.'

When he put down the phone, Mark turned to Agar who was still waiting and asked, 'How are you feeling, Jim?'

'I came in, sir, I couldn't bear sitting about at home doing nothing. I want to nail that bastard who got Derek.'

'Good. Well, let's see what's outstanding, shall we? And by Tuesday, we'll all be working with Mr French, so you'll get your opportunity.'

Mark left shortly afterwards for the hour's drive to Rainesbury, thinking he'd have liked to take Lorraine with him, but his better judgement said there was no professional reason for that. So he drove alone and arrived at French's incident room in time for his noon appointment. D/C/I French brought in his shorthand typist to take notes of this important discussion and reinforced it with a desktop tape recorder.

Then Mark and the detective chief inspector went through everything that Mark had discovered during his abortive investigation, Mark telling him about Mr Kenworthy and his knowledge and the work done by his own teams. By one o'clock most of the aspects had been dealt with and Mark felt the meeting had been useful.

It had allowed him to expand his own thoughts, particularly about the peculiar nature of Joseph Patrick Balleen, and to have them assessed by another very experienced officer. He and D/C/I Howard French sealed their new working relationship with a pint and a sandwich at the King's Head, then Mark went to keep his appointment with Rebecca Eden.

When he arrived at the rendezvous point, he saw she was not alone. She was accompanied by a stoutish woman with greying hair and rimless spectacles, a woman dressed in what appeared to be old-fashioned clothes – a long, mottled grey and black overcoat with wide sleeves, thick grey stockings and black flat shoes. The woman was nervous, looking about her in what Mark believed was a state of considerable anxiety.

'Superintendent.' Rebecca was dressed in a warm coat with a scarf tied loosely around her mass of blonde hair and had jeans and thick shoes on. 'I'm glad you could make it. Now let me introduce Kathleen Hicks.'

So this was Louisa Mary Potter. Why in God's name had this woman brought her here?

Without speaking, Potter was extending her hand, somewhat shamefully, he felt, and for a few seconds he dithered about the morality of shaking hands with her. But, for the sake of appearances and because she'd been introduced as Kathleen Hicks, he swallowed his prejudice and shook her hand.

'Mark Pemberton.' He used his Christian name and she smiled, her deep brown eyes radiating friendliness from her pale face. His immediate impression of her was one of trust.

'I'm sorry to . . . well, I mean . . . it's not easy,' she said.

Rebecca took control. 'Can you follow us, Mr Pemberton? In your own car?'

He nodded and the women returned to their blue Golf; he followed them out of town. They drove for about five miles, then along a dirt track which led to a small reservoir close to a peat bog. Mrs Eden parked and both emerged from the vehicle, waiting for Mark. He joined them.

'What are we doing here, Rebecca?' he asked, surveying the moorland about the reservoir.

'You know who I am?' Kathleen Hicks asked him.

'Yes, I do,' Mark nodded. He was astonished at what followed.

'The three missing girls, they're here, in that peat bog. I wanted you to know. I was never going to tell anyone. Even lately, I thought about keeping this to myself because they'd never find the remains and any searching would open old wounds. I don't want old wounds opening, Mr Pemberton. But then I read that peat preserves human bodies and so I wondered, hoped, the bodies might still be here, might still be recognizable ... The parents, well, they might still be able to have funerals ...'

Mark looked at Rebecca and then at Louisa; Rebecca nodded almost imperceptibly and Mark asked, 'You killed them?'

'I'll give you a written statement when this is over, I promise. I just want everything cleared up, Mr Pemberton. Come with me, both of you.'

She led them to a large boulder and stood beneath it, her back against the rough surface as it towered above her head. From that point, she indicated a patch of peat before her, peat that had long ago provided fuel for moorland cottagers, but which had ceased to be cut around the end of World War II.

'Somewhere in there,' she said. 'I can't be too precise.'

'We'll start digging tomorrow,' Mark assured her. 'Look, Louisa, Kathleen, I must ask about Joseph Patrick as well, now that I've got you here ...'

'He's dead too. He's somewhere at the bottom of the sea. We went out in a rowing boat – a silly trip, looking back, because it was choppy, but he was going away and I wanted to be with him ... He was in a happy mood, jumping up and down in the boat, having fun, being silly really, laughing and showing off, I suppose ... Then he stumbled over one of the oars and fell overboard. He couldn't swim ... he had heavy clothes on. I tried to rescue him but he went under and just vanished. I waited for ages, rowing round and round. I thought he was joking, making me frightened, but I never saw him again. I went for walks on the beach afterwards, thinking his body might have been washed ashore somewhere, but I never heard anything.'

'Off this coast, was it?' he asked.

'Just off Rainesbury.'

'We can check the files for reports of unidentified bodies,' he said. 'You didn't report him missing?'

'No, I was terrified. I thought he might be teasing me at first but, well, as time went by and he didn't turn up, I was frightened; I thought no one would believe it was an accident.'

'So what did you do?' Mark asked.

'I went home, to my lodgings, and waited a day or two, just in case he came back, or was found. He was full of tricks, he might have been kidding me ... but he wasn't found dead or alive. Then I realized that if he was dead, all that money would be mine

. . . Rebecca's told you about it, I know. I had no idea how much there was, but if I couldn't have him, I wanted it, every penny. It was greed, Mr Pemberton. Madness and greed. I was sick, mentally at the time. I did undergo treatment in the prison hospital, for my mental state. You know that? Anyway, the cash was in a joint account and I knew he'd got a ticket home, so I told everyone he'd gone to Ireland – the bank, his employer, our landlady. It was easy convincing people, a damned sight easier than having to explain the accident. Everyone believed he'd gone. I sold some cars he had left and put the money into the bank account. Later, I cleared his room. I told Miss Clayton he'd asked me to move his things so she could let the room. Then I realized I couldn't get the passbooks without the key, you see, and I guessed one of the girls had got that . . .'

'Why tell me all this when you've just got out?'

'I wanted you, someone, someone in the police to know that I have reformed, superintendent. I am harmless now. I did a great evil, greater than anyone can really believe, and I am truly sorry. I did not kill Joseph, I wanted him too much, but I did kill all those girls. My priest told me to tell the police; when I became a Catholic he said that and it's taken me all this time to come to terms with that confession. Tonight, I shall go to Mass, after I've been to confession before a priest, and I will pray for those children and their parents. I wanted to get this off my conscience before I am caught by the IRA. They will be looking for me very soon, superintendent, once the newspapers release the news that I'm free. Now, Rebecca has a plan for you and me.'

'Can we talk somewhere else?' Mark suggested, eyeing the eerie windswept patch of peat bog. They drove to a deserted picnic area, parked and walked along a bridleway with the moorland air stinging their cheeks.

Rebecca said, 'You remember we talked about the money that Balleen concealed, superintendent?'

'Call me Mark,' he heard himself say, finding himself surprisingly at ease with the woman he'd always regarded as utterly evil. 'Yes, I believe there are building society passbooks in a safe deposit centre here in Rainesbury?'

'Accredited Security and Protection,' said Louisa Potter. 'Is it still called that?'

'It is,' said Mark.

'Only I can get access to the safe,' she said. 'But I need the key that Joseph was issued with. A combination of my signature and that key will give me access to the contents.'

'We guessed that,' he said. 'So where is the key?'

'I'm not sure.' She shook her head. 'I need time to look in places we visited. In prison, I had all the time in the world to work out where Joseph might have concealed it, but I need time to search. That's why I asked for six months in your safe house.'

'Your reopening of the missing child files was a bonus,' said Rebecca. 'We hoped it would produce the answer. Louisa felt sure those little girls did hold the clue . . . We wanted you to spare the time to talk to Louisa in the hope that, by pooling your knowledge, you might find the answer. Louisa is sure it is somewhere in this town, her bank doesn't have it . . .'

Mark shook his head. 'I've been puzzling over that myself and so have my staff. But why did Balleen hide it?'

'He wanted to go home without his controller's permission, just for a short visit. His mother was ill. He decided to risk it but daren't take the key in case he lost it. So he hid it just before he died.'

'It's not at the bottom of the sea, is it?' Mark asked.

'No, he hid it just before he died. I'm sure.'

'With the girls? The secret seven, or six as it became,' corrected Mark, explaining about the nun. 'You were bloody evil, taping them. Your voice isn't on the tapes?'

'I switched the recorder off when I was speaking, I thought my voice might be recognized. I taped them so I could hear what they said, afterwards, just in case I missed anything at the time . . .' She shuddered at the recollection. 'I must have been mad . . . I killed them trying to force them to reveal the whereabouts of the key, but none did. I wanted that money, I was evil, greedy . . .' She shuddered again. 'God, I was depraved, superintendent . . . I deserved everything I got, and more. But that key is somewhere, it has to be. Joseph hid it, I know. He went on about driving the evil out of Northern Ireland – he saw us, the British, as the evil. Like St Patrick driving all the snakes out of Ireland, he often said. I think he saw himself as some kind of modern St Patrick driving today's snakes out, snakes and evil being synonymous . . .'

'Asps,' said Mark. 'Bloody asps . . . they're snakes, aren't they?

My God, it's been staring me in the face . . . an asp is a snake. The logo of ASP Safe Deposit Centre is a snake . . .'

'The handle of the key was like a curled-up snake,' she told them. 'They used that logo on their headed paper too.'

'And I know the kind of mind that Joseph had and I know where there is a St Patrick now,' he said. 'In a bedroom that has not been altered since its small girl occupant was murdered, Louisa, by you . . . It's there now, and if I know anything about such statues, it will be hollow . . . and Joseph got her to swear to keep it until he returned.'

'If we get the key,' said Rebecca, 'we can go straight into our plan, the sooner the better.'

'Fine,' said Mark. 'I'll go and see if it's there.'

Mark's immediate dilemma was whether he should arrest Louisa for murder. But, other than this short confession, there was no evidence that she had killed the other three girls. Supporting evidence would be required before any prosecution could proceed and there would have to be post-mortems on the bodies if they were found. Besides, she was not going to run away, not with all the supervision she was having to endure. He decided not to make that arrest. Besides, there was more information to come from her, he was sure, and so he told Rebecca to follow him in her car, but suggested they wait outside the Stablers' house.

It wouldn't be wise for Hugh and Eileen Stabler to know that Louisa Mary Potter, their lodger, was in town, but it would be good for him to say that there had been a development in the search for Helen's body.

He'd have to tell the Hayes too, in Australia, and Bill and Jean Wiles who lived in Rainesbury. They must all be told before digging commenced. But first, there was a small girl's bedroom to examine.

Hugh and Eileen Stabler were enjoying a quiet afternoon at home over the fire, their shop being closed all day on Sunday, and they welcomed him. He declined a cup of tea, saying he had friends waiting outside.

He then announced that, as a result of information received from Potter herself, a contingent of Task Force officers would shortly commence a search of moorland near Thorburn Reservoir. Eileen's eyes grew moist but Mark cautioned her not to be too hopeful of a result; twenty-five years was a long time. They might find nothing. Then he asked to see the bedroom, asking if he could inspect the statue of St Patrick, and he gave brief reasons, without providing a full explanation. The Stablers agreed and led him to Helen's time-sealed bedroom.

'We prayed at Mass this morning,' said Eileen. 'We prayed that your efforts would produce results, especially as that poor detective had died . . . it's all so tragic . . .'

He lifted the statue from its resting place, turned it over and found that there was a hole in the base.

It was hollow and plugged with a wedge of cotton wool.

'Have you ever looked inside?' he asked them.

'No,' they said. 'We never gave it a thought . . .'

He tugged the grubby mass of cotton wool from its place; the statue was tightly packed with it. If the key was inside, it would not rattle or move among this packing.

And then it fell out.

A brass-coloured safe key with a handle in the shape of a coiled snake embossed with the letters ASP Safe Deposit Centre.

'Not a word to anyone about this,' he said. 'I'll tell you later. But, on your lives, do not breathe a word.'

And Mark left the premises bearing the key to a fortune worth some four million pounds as he went outside to discuss Rebecca's plans.

24

At ten o'clock on Monday morning, after Rebecca had made her plans following consultation with the SAS and her superiors, and after Mark had disturbed his Chief Constable's Sunday evening television viewing, Mark found himself waiting in the plush office of the manager of the ASP Safe Deposit Centre. He had been there since seven that morning by agreement and he had a large brown suitcase with him. He was wired with a transmitter in the form of a throat microphone and a receiver which looked like a deaf aid. He was also armed with a police issue revolver.

In a small terrace house not far away, Louisa Mary Potter waited with Rebecca Eden. Each was also wired with a throat microphone and a receiver which looked like a deaf aid. Both were in a high state of nervous tension as they awaited the order to move. On the floor was a large empty brown suitcase while the settee bore a selection of that morning's papers. All carried the front-page news, albeit not the lead story, that the Rainesbury murderess, Louisa Mary Potter, had been released on parole. The reports said she would be released at nine o'clock this morning and that she would be living in the south of England under an assumed name. There was a quote from an anonymous Home Office spokesman who had said, 'We are satisfied that Miss Potter has reformed and that she is no longer a danger to children. She has been in prison for some twenty-five years; she has paid for her crimes.'

There was the inevitable reprinting of the story of the Rainesbury Murders and interviews with members of the public who said the children's killer should have been hanged or kept in prison for the rest of her natural life. Louisa, for her part, said nothing. She had read the reports just as she had read countless similar reports ever since she had gone to prison. Rebecca was aware of the acute sadness on her pale face; this woman was truly attempting to make retribution.

As Mark waited with a coffee in his hands, he knew that about now teams of Task Force officers would already be digging within that peat bog, and it was inevitable that their activities would attract the notice of the press and that they would conclude that the work was due to the release of Potter. Their speculation would be accurate; Mark had left a suitable statement with the force press officer which was to be released if such enquiries were made. The parents of the three missing girls had all been told, as had the parents of those whose bodies had been recovered twenty-five years ago.

The IRA, Rebecca had assured him, would read about Louisa's release and they would know that the story about her living in the south was false. They would know it had been done to mislead them, which meant they knew she would be elsewhere – they would know she would come to Rainesbury.

The snippets of information 'leaked' to them through the intelligence services had led the IRA to believe that her first job would be to get her hands on the money. They had been told of her all-consuming greed, that she intended to get the money and disappear. And so, out there in the town, in the streets and houses adjacent to the bank and in the bank itself, there were armed officers from the police, the Security Service and a contingent of SAS personnel, all waiting and watching.

The IRA had no idea that others knew of the cache; they believed that Louisa's release was absolutely normal and that they alone were privy to her great secret. But, as such a huge amount of cash was involved, they were never going to trust a lone assassin or even a single member of their organization to retrieve the money. And so they had summoned five of their most important and senior officers to oversee the recovery of the money which they felt was rightfully theirs because it had been stolen for them. They were also watching.

And so everyone was waiting for the operation to begin.

It was a further half-hour before the word was given. Those with ear-pieces heard the code word, 'Acorn', and Rebecca said, 'Good luck, Louisa, you know what to do?'

Louisa came to Rebecca and hugged her tight, thanked her for all her support and advice, picked up the suitcase and walked out. She undertook a circuitous walk through the back streets and then approached the impressive front door of ASP with its huge snake logo looking down upon her.

As she walked along, looking like a stout granny with her old grey coat and flat shoes, everything seemed normal. There was a large British Telecom van parked near some men digging a hole in the road, a fish van with a man knocking on doors, a filthy Ford Transit with mud all over its bodywork and windows, a bread van delivering to a shop, a brewery wagon delivering to a pub, a post office van, several private cars, a couple of taxis, a mini-bus bearing the legend 'Rainesbury Care for the Aged', a cyclist mending a puncture, three window cleaners busy on shop fronts . . . a normal street in a normal town on a quiet Monday morning. But for Louisa, this was no ordinary Monday morning; it was her first Monday of freedom.

She entered the pleasant reception area with its soft grey carpets and discreet lighting, and asked to see Mr Scarth, the manager. He was expecting her; she gave the name Kathleen Hicks and when the receptionist had checked, she was shown into Mr Scarth's office. Pemberton was there, himself very nervous. He smiled at her; he was facing a very brave woman.

'Good morning, Louisa,' he said. 'This is Mr Scarth. He has been told everything. Are you ready?'

'Let's get it over,' she said, her eyes moist.

Scarth fulfilled his own security regulations, checking her signature and other details, then said, 'Follow me.'

He led them towards the underground vaults and, after he had executed his own sophisticated security procedures which opened several enormous doors, they entered a long, brightly lit passage, took an elevator down several flights and then walked several hundred yards along a cold, white corridor.

'We are now several hundred feet beneath the cliffs,' he told them. 'Apart from the land mass, we are protected by many feet of reinforced concrete; this vault can withstand any attempt at unauthorized entry.'

'Even by the IRA?'

'Even by the IRA or the world's best explosives operators and safe-breakers. Now, Miss Potter,' said Scarth, halting outside a door, 'your box is in this room. We can stay outside, unless you wish us to enter? We have no right to inspect your deposit, as I'm sure the superintendent knows.'

'Please, this is no longer for me, come in,' she invited.

Inside were tiers of what looked like red filing cabinets each with some twenty-five drawers of varying sizes. Each drawer had its own unique lock. Hers was number 650. Scarth guided her to it as Mark handed over the key. She fitted it into the lock; the drawer opened easily and they saw it was full of old building society passbooks. She handed one to Mark. It was with the Halifax in the name of P. G. Brown; it contained £3,000 and the last entry was in 1967. With Louisa, they emptied the box and placed all the passbooks in Mark's suitcase; he counted one hundred and eight. From time to time, he looked inside; every one he examined contained £3,000, the maximum deposit at that time, and all were in different names without the years of accrued interest being entered.

If every one held £3,000, it made a total of £324,000, so Kenworthy's estimate had not been far out. Today, these books represented something approaching four million pounds.

With the security box empty and Mark's suitcase full, they left the vaults and returned to the manager's office where he asked, 'Miss Potter, will you wish to continue the lease of this box?'

'No, thank you,' she said. 'I won't need it again. I have already stopped the banker's order, with effect from today.'

'Well, if we can help in the future, do contact us.'

'Now,' Mark addressed them both, 'I must leave as arranged, Mr Scarth, via the back door, please. My post office van is waiting. Louisa, fill your suitcase, lock it and give me twenty minutes, then leave. OK?'

'Yes,' she said.

'Goodbye.' Mark shook her hand. 'You are a very brave woman.'

'Goodbye.' She smiled gently. 'And thank you. I'm not brave, I'm terrified. But I have done what I intended. I hope my debt to society is almost complete.'

And Mark left the office. Fifteen minutes later he was in the police station at Rainesbury. The suitcase with its precious contents was in Chief Superintendent Ramsden's office safe. There were five minutes to go before Louisa Mary Potter walked out of the Safe Deposit Centre through the front door.

When the receiver in her ear gave the code word 'Seagull', Louisa picked up her suitcase, now heavy with packets of blank photocopy paper to give it the necessary weight, and walked out of the Safe Deposit Centre. Mark heard her nervous voice saying, 'I'm out now, I'm turning left to walk towards Crown Wharf . . .'

Another voice chipped in. 'Have target in sight. She is walking steadily on the footpath . . . Suitcase in right hand . . . Hello, action. A motor-cyclist has halted behind her . . . fifty yards maybe . . . Not one of ours . . .'

Another voice. 'Got her . . . yes . . . Moving well . . . Strangers in a car, entrance to Blythe Street, four men . . . Engine running . . . They've been waiting a while . . . Watched her go in . . .'

Another voice. 'Sniper sighted, upper window, block of flats . . . Hardman Flats . . . Move in, B group . . . Keep out of sight of front . . . C group, prepare to move . . . He's aiming . . . God!'

Louisa Mary Potter fell to the ground as two crisp shots crackled in the morning air. The motor-cyclist revved his machine which catapulted forwards, and as the suitcase fell into the road, he slid to a halt, seized it with considerable skill and placed it on the petrol tank between his arms as he accelerated away along the rising sweep of Coronation Road.

'Go, go, go,' shouted a voice over the radio sets.

'A very professional operation,' the Chief Constable said to Mark Pemberton next morning. 'Good work all round, I'd say. We got the lot with no more shots being fired, even the courier and the gunman in the flats were arrested. It proved the value of surprise, of containing a large area simultaneously, and it showed we can beat the IRA at their own game. We got five of their leaders – I think we can put them away for a long time. We should be able to prove conspiracy to murder, it's got a stronger penalty than mere murder. It's a major blow for them – and they've lost the money.'

'Our men have found those bodies, sir,' said Mark. 'They started digging at six yesterday morning and I got word just before coming here. They've found all three, all in a good state of preservation. Positive identification will be possible, I'm told; the parents will be able to have proper funerals.'

'Good. So what are we telling the press, Mark?'

'I've authorized a statement which will say that as a result of information received, a contingent of Task Force officers searched an area of peat bog close to Thorburn Reservoir. As a result, the bodies of three children have been found, having apparently been buried for more than twenty-five years. We are satisfied that they are the bodies of Suzanne Hayes, Helen Stabler and Clare Wiles who were reported missing in 1967. The cause of death in each case has not been ascertained and a post-mortem examination has been arranged.'

'That's fine. What about the sniper attack on Potter? What's the official line on that?'

'We've said that a middle-aged woman called Dorothy Brown of Middlesbrough was attacked by a youth while visiting the town and robbed of a suitcase containing photocopier paper. He escaped on a motor-cycle and was later arrested. We've said we cannot understand his motive. We did not mention the use of firearms and, of course, we did not refer to the other arrests. No one heard the shots, anyway.'

'And Louisa Potter?'

'The bullet-proof vest saved her life, sir. She's got one hell of a bruise on her back, but she is alive and has refused hospital treatment. She was a brave woman, sir, she knew the risks and it could have gone wrong; he could have shot her in the head.'

'The IRA wanted her dead, not merely injured,' said Rebecca. 'The body is a far better target at a distance, there's more of it.

Soldiers are trained to fire at the body in those circumstances. They believed she had killed one of theirs, Balleen, in order to get all that cash, so they wanted revenge – and the cash – otherwise I doubt if they would have used such tactics simply to steal a suitcase from her. A dead witness doesn't talk; otherwise, a mugging would have done the trick.'

'So,' said the Chief Constable, 'now that the fuss has died down, we have a problem. Mark, are we going to charge Louisa Mary Potter with the murder of those other three children?'

'I doubt it, sir. It will be difficult, if not impossible, to find any evidence of murder after all this time. First impressions by the pathologist are that, from the remains he's got, it will be impossible to determine the cause of death. Other than Potter's admission, we would have very little real evidence to present to a court. She has explained Balleen's disappearance too and we cannot prove or disprove her story, nor do we have any reports of unidentified bodies being washed ashore. I reckon the DPP would recommend no action – you know what the courts are like nowadays. You can admit anything and they won't believe you unless there's supporting evidence.'

'Right, thanks,' said Moore. 'When the pathologist's findings are complete, I'll send a file to the DPP and I will recommend that in the furtherance of natural justice, there is no justification in instituting further proceedings against Louisa Mary Potter. Quite simply, there's no point, is there, superintendent? It would be a waste of time. Even if she had been tried for the deaths of all six, she'd be free now, but because of her admission, we can at least write off three missing children as found and the three outstanding mysteries cleared up. That'll be good for our statistics!'

Mark remembered his angry statements of only a week ago. 'I agree with that,' he said. 'She has reformed, I'm sure. I just hope she is allowed to get on with her life now.'

'So where is she today?' asked Moore.

'She's at my house,' said Rebecca Eden. 'I'll be driving her south later today. She'll live somewhere in Kent under an assumed name. I have a job planned for her. If the DPP should decide to institute further proceedings, then she will attend court.'

'And you, Mark?' asked Moore. 'What are your plans? I'm told you are not needed at the Rainesbury incident room.'

'No, sir, the sniper we arrested was Leo Wilde, the one who'd shot Derek Holdsworth. He still had the automatic in his possession. We can prove links with the Lichfield soldier's death too, so it was a good arrest. We got Lagan or Mulligan or O'Docherty as he calls himself; he was keeping an eye on the others in case they ran off with those passbooks. They and the others are all being interrogated now, but we did nail some important IRA commanders. And when Louisa leaves, we can stand down the guard on the safe house.'

'And where are those passbooks?' asked the Chief.

'They're back in ASP Safe Deposit Centre, sir, under lock and key in the name of the force. They will remain pending a decision on ownership of the money. All sorts of people are expected to register a claim – the robbed banks, building societies, post offices among them, and of course the insurance companies who paid out compensation all those years ago.'

'But to recover stolen money, or goods which are the proceeds of stolen money, Mark,' the Chief said, 'you must prove it was the actual money which was in fact stolen, and to do that, you must convict the thief.'

'Yes, sir.'

'Balleen can never be prosecuted and so we can never prove that any of that money was stolen. It could be the result of his business dealings.'

'That's true, sir. Which means that Louisa Mary Potter was an innocent recipient, which in turn means the money could belong to her, being a joint account holder, although there is the problem of overcoming the range of false names. Or, of course, Balleen might have willed it to someone, perhaps his family or Potter. But I know of no law which says I couldn't open an account in any name I wished. Businessmen do it all the time. Whatever name I choose, the money is still mine. The point is that, in the absence of a will, Louisa Potter has a claim of right to all that money.'

'So, Mark, knowing that, do you still believe that she has reformed?' asked the Chief Constable.

'Only God knows the answer to that,' answered Detective Superintendent Pemberton. 'And He's not going to tell us.'